Yamini Polnati is a 22 year old girl from South India. She was born and brought up in Gollaprolu, Andhra Pradesh. She did her schooling in Madhuri Vidyalaya. She pursued her graduation in Aditya group of Educational Institutions, Kakinada. She is currently working in Infosys, Hyderabad.

Being a reader, she was always inspired by the writing ideas. The thought- 'Why am I a reader? Why can't I be a writer?' made her come up with such thing. It took her nine months to pen down the story. Apart from writing, playing Snooker is her favorite hobby. She is a member of Infosys Snooker team, Hyderabad.

For more updates, join her on
Facebook (facebook.com/Yamini.Polnati95)
Twitter @YaminiPolnati
Instagram @yamini.polnati95

YOU ARE MY SUNSHINE

...after all the storms

YAMINI POLNATI

Pengo
Publications India

Pengo Publications India
New Delhi 110078
Info.pengopublications@gmail.com

First published by Pengo Publications India

ISBN: 9788193225318

Typesett and layout by Ajay Verma
Printed and bound in India.

ACKNOWLEDGEMENTS

I would like to take this page to thank everyone who helped me in their best possible ways in the completion of this book.

Firstly, To God for putting me on this Earth.

To my Mom, Prabhavathi Polnati. Besides being a mom, she is a great human being. She wouldn't let any poor animal go hungry which passes our home, she never says no when any oldie knocks our door and she is the one who stood beside me in the worst of my times.

To my dad, Seetha babu Polnati, who deemed spending his income on our education to carve our future is more important than his luxuries and with whom I would never stop arguing.

To my sister, Sharada Polnati, when I admitted that I want to write a book in future, her reaction was priceless. "Don't wait for future, start working for it now" That's what she said. I thank you for giving me more than I need.

To Neha Singh, the best roommate, the cute Telugu speaking Noida girl, who has been a peer reviewer of my writings. Thanks for being so patient.

To Guru Prakash Iyengar, who is a dearest friend of mine, who strongly believed in my passion as much as I did and who made 'encouraging me' as a part of his homework.

To Ambuj chathurvedi, one of the best persons I met in Infosys, from whom I get the best suggestions.

To Vimidha, she has always been a darling to me.

To Prawin, my best buddy, my day never passes without even a single fight with him. Yet, he has been very sweet to me all the time.

To the wonderful people in my life- Pradyumna, Sid, Padmaja, Harish-my snooker partner, Sai Kiran-PVR photography, Shiva, Steve, Sneha, Vinay, Sonika, Neelesh, Ramya, Koushik, Chiranjev

Singh, Anil, Indraneel Varma, M.M. Lukose who believed that I was capable enough to make this thing happen.

And to the people who hate me, who belittled me, who deterred me, here is my answer. Without you, this would never have come true.

Finally, to myself, for taking up a thing which needs a lot of patience (which I actually lack in), dedication, and neck pain and for not giving up at times when I actually felt like giving up.

"Love" -It's not as easy as it sounds, well,
it's not that tough either!

It's smooth and then it's harsh.

It's kind and then it's rude.

Sometimes, it's a sleety wind that cheers you and then it's the creepy cyclone that scares you.

Sometimes, it's a lullaby that cuddles you and then it's the brattling sound that muddles you.

For some, it's the reason to smile and for others,
it's the reason behind those weary eyes.

For some, it may be a blissful moment to cherish for a lifetime and for others, it may be a horrifying memory, which they do not wish to remember.

For some, it may be a reason for their destruction but for others, it may be a reason for their survival.

After all, it's "Love"; it is never perfect and if it is,
then it's not love.

One needs to experience it themselves,
to really know how it feels to be in Love.

Only the ones who fall in love, can rise in love.
This is to all the ones, who dare to fall in love.

–Yamini Polnati

PROLOGUE

It was a crisp mistful day. The location was absolutely breathtaking.

Feeling the sand beneath our feet, listening to the splashy waves and letting the cool breeze escape through our hair, we entered the wooden cottage that had been booked for us. Rubbing the palms on our full sleeved woolen hoodies, getting ourselves warmed up beside the fireplace inside our room, we sat on the cozy bed.

We were at Crystal Cove Beach Resort, Canada. It was a family outing – with my husband's colleagues and their families.

"Ashritha! Let's have breakfast, everyone has already reached," Kate said, standing at the entrance of our room. I nodded as I smiled looking into her blue eyes. Kate was my husband's colleague, a married woman who is four years elder to me. She carried little weight than her ideal version which made her look older. Though we do not meet regularly, yet just in four to five meetings, I found her sweet and cordial. We walked through the wooden bridge and reached the dining hall.

In the next five minutes, we were served with toasts, poachers, pancakes, muesli, pasta and different kind of fruits, which are rarely found in India. Helping myself with toasts and pancakes, I moped. I missed India. I missed homemade food. I missed the South-Indian Dosa and coconut chutney.

"Food is yummy, no?" Kate said raising her brows while holding a knife and a fork.

"Yeah, it is" I faked an approval, nodding my head.

Within the next forty minutes, the dining hall was filled with laughter and empty plates.

"We'll relax for some time and then head to the beach," Kate said as we reached our rooms. I just nodded in agreement and then she left for her room.

I don't remember when I dozed off under the chunky blanket insufflating the cool breeze.

***

"The weather is quite dull today," Kate said dejectedly. We were sitting on the shore. It was around two in the afternoon but serene clouds were hiding the sun.

"Yeah" I confirmed staring at the blue sky.

"I want to get tanned, but I can't see the Sun anywhere" she sulked.

We Indians spend a lot of money to de-tan our dark skin and these people want to get tanned.

What a crazy world!

"Did you bring your marriage album?" Kate asked, making her eyes bigger.

"Yeah, I got it," I said unzipping my backpack.

"Wow, I'm so excited!" she rubbed her palms. Her face flushed with excitement.

"Here it is!" I placed the rectangular shaped heavy album in her hands.

"Careful," I warned when I noticed her fumbling.

"Don't worry, I'm alright" She smiled.

'It's the album I am worried about. The photographer charged three lakhs for both the video and the photos.' It was what I wanted to say but remained silent as I thought of her reaction. She would faint if she gets to know that Indians spend lakhs on marriage photographs.

"You look gorgeous in this picture," she exclaimed as she tossed the first page.

'What do you mean? You think I am not beautiful in real!' I wanted to ask. I smiled. I noticed her face executing different expressions with each flipping page.

"Ashritha, India is a developing country, right? Then how come you people have so much of gold, why doesn't Indian government use that in developing the country?" she enquired.

I burst into laughter. For Indians, country's economic development doesn't matter as much as the heavy necklaces around their necks do. I chose to ignore her question and thankfully she chose to ignore my laughter.

"Yours is a love marriage or an arranged one?" She posed a straight question.

Her one question made my heart fetch out all the memories that comprise happiness, pain, love and hatred. They flashed in front of my eyes one after another.

"Are you listening?" She jiggled my shoulder.

"Love," I confessed.

"Wow, really? Who proposed whom? How did it start? When did this start?" She fired all these questions in one go.

"That's a long story," I said looking away.

"That's okay because we've got nothing to do, we are free till evening. Please tell me, I want to know," she said.

I was amazed looking at her excitement. She looked like a tomato with her rosy cheeks. I inhaled deeply, as I decided to put my story in front of her.

"Okay," I nodded.

1.

"I can't walk anymore Paa," I bent down gasping, with hands on my knees. I was completely drenched in sweat. I had come for a morning walk with my grandpa to RK beach. We live in Vishakhapatnam, the City of destiny, one of the most beautiful coastal cities in India.

"Ok Ashi, you sit here. I will walk till the pole and come back," my grandpa said as my gaze followed his finger. I squinted to have a clear view of the pole in the smog. It was half a kilometer away. I nodded and he resumed his walk.

His daily routine started with a morning walk along the shore. As it was a Sunday, I thought of accompanying him. I saw him toddling at a distance and was surprised at how he managed to stay fit even in his old age when I could barely walk for half a kilometer.

Wrapping my toes in the warm sand, I settled down and immediately sipped water from the bottle. The morning breeze soothed my heartbeat from the core while the soughing waves soothed my ears. Slowly, the sun rose breaking the dawn, piercing the clouds and painting the sky with several shades of pink. From a distance, the sky and the sea seemed like they were embracing each other. The shimmering rays danced on the surface of the waves, which were heaving smoothly in a glorious motion. The chirping flock of seagull flew over the sea and then over my head. The entire picture was exhilarating.

"It has been more than a couple of months since I saw the sunrise! I am such a lazy girl" I scolded myself. As I inhaled the briny air, the foamy tides played with my feet leaving my pant cuffs wet. In a few moments, my face was relieved from the sweat beads as the warmth stole away the moisture. I sat there, watching people in night-suits with headsets and wearing sports shoes jogging along the shore.

I shifted my gaze towards a little girl near me who accompanied her mother. She was building a sand castle unwary of the fact that her cute frock has been turned into a mop cloth and how much amount of surf and effort it would take to remove the dirt.

I wanted to capture the entire scenic beauty on my phone. I took out my mobile from the pocket and started clicking few selfies from behind so that I could capture the sea. Like every other girl, I started zooming in every picture just to check the status of my acne scars.

In the first picture, I saw a guy looking towards the camera. I first ignored it, assuming it to be accidental. But in every picture, he stood there exactly at the same place looking into my camera.

"Can't he take pictures from his own phone?" I whispered as I swiped through the pictures. I lifted my head up from the phone to the place where that guy was standing.

There stood a guy in US polo white t-shirt exposing his well-built biceps, dark grey track pants and Puma sports shoes. The sweat beads on his forehead glinted in the sunlight. He had messy thick shiny hair and yeah, it won't be a sin to admit that he was quite handsome.

"Oh, he is here for jogging," I mumbled as I glanced at him.

"Well, he is not trying to pose for the photos, he is looking at you," my subconscious mind told me.

"But why is he staring at me like that? Does he know me? But I have never seen him before," I questioned and answered myself.

At first, I decided to shun his presence and started looking in the other direction. After few minutes I turned my head to check whether he had left or not. He had not moved a bit, he just lingered there, glaring at me, wiping his forehead with the sweatband. Suddenly he smiled.

His smile was very captivating and his eyes were even more intensifying. If there was another guy in his place, I would have broken his ribs just for glaring at me. But I had no idea what had happened to me then. It felt as if he had casted some magic spell on me. The more I tried ignoring him, the more I found myself glancing at him. Futile to say, I was attracted to him.

"Ashi, come let's go...I'm done," my grandpa's voice broke my thoughts.

'Oh, thank god! A better way to escape,' I thought and stood up patting my back to get off the sand that had stuck to my pants. I collected my water bottle, phone, bike keys and walked towards my bike. I turned on the ignition and as I was about to drive off, I turned back to look at him. He stood there with his utterly enchanting eyes and that alluring smile.

I drove off taking myself away from there, but leaving my mind behind.

2.

"Ashi... Ashi!! Wake up! Its 8 already," my mom blustered pulling the window curtains back.

"What Mom? It's too early. Let me sleep for some more time," I shouted back, twisting my body.

"Oh God! Look at this girl," she ranted and pulled the quilt I was covered with. The sun's rays directly spiked through the window of my room and hit my face.

"God must be sleeping too," I snoozed pulling the quilt back.,

"You think he is lazy like you?" she gave an instant counter.

"Mom, Please!"

"Okay, your wish! Last night, you requested me to wake you up at seven' o clock saying that you have some assignments to complete, its eight now. If you don't have any problem, why should I?" her tone decreased as she walked out of my room.

"Shit! Shit!" I sat on my bed pushing the blanket away. I pulled out my phone, which was lying beneath the pillow, and the drowsiness on my face had vanished as soon as I saw the missed calls from Nisha.

Shit... I am dead!

Nisha was my classmate, bench mate and my bestie, from the very first day of our college. She is originally from Maharashtra but her family was settled in Vizag. "What the hell are you doing, Ashritha?" she started rebuking me as soon as she picked up the call.

"I'm so sorry, babe. It's just eight and I will be there by eight thirty. I promise." I did my best to cool her down.

"You always keep doing this. You witch!" she taunted some more and disconnected the call. Nisha is a lady with good looks and short temper. Being a North Indian, she is fair in complexion and her cute, curly hair drive people crazy. Nevertheless, there was not even a single day when she wouldn't get jealous of my silky bouncy hair.

I grabbed the towel and rushed into the washroom. I turned on the tap. Instead the water came from the shower leaving me completely drenched. Do you know, what is the biggest betrayal? When you confidently turn on the tap expecting water from it but instead water dumps on you by coming from the shower.

"Varun is dead today. How many times have I told him not to use my bathroom?" I kept trolling my younger brother during the entire douche. Though I had no plans of washing my hair, I had to do it cause of my brother's naïve deed. I blow-dried my hair, got into a white cotton kurta, blue leggings and matching white stone studs.

Due to lack of time, I couldn't spend more minutes in front of the mirror like every other day, praising my curves and cursing my pimples.

***

"Ah! Sorry Akka, please!" Varun cried in pain when I pinched him holding his ear.

"Will you forget to turn off the shower next time?" I tightened the grip some more.

"No, please," he exhorted cutely. I released my hand when I noticed his ear turning pink.

"Ashi leave him, come and have your breakfast." Mom said serving *chutney* in dad's plate.

"No Mumma. I'm already late, Nisha will kill me," I said taking an apple from the fridge.

"It doesn't take much time to eat two idlis," my dad said without looking at me.

"No dad. I will have it in college, please!" I sulked.

"Leave your bike today, I need to go to the tailor," mom shouted as she walked into the kitchen.

"But I have to go right now," I shouted back.

"Dad will drop you," she advised coming back to the hall with a water bottle.

"I am already late Mumma," I pouted.

"Just five minutes, he has finished eating," she said pointing towards dad. Left with no choice, I agreed to her deal.

"Dad, please make it fast." I beseeched my dad who was busy in arranging his drawing sheets. He is a project design engineer in Vishaka steel plant, one of the biggest steel producing plants in India.

"Yeah Ashi, done." my dad said standing up from the sofa. Munching the apple, I occupied front seat in our Honda Amaze and we drove off.

"Have a nice day both of you," Mom shouted from behind waving her hand.

"Didn't you know yesterday that you have assignments to finish?" Dad lectured me when we stopped at the signal. I remained silent, staring out of the window.

"You played yesterday without taking a break," he continued. Varun and I had spent the whole Sunday by playing *Vice city*, which he got from his friend. I moped.

"Umm, don't worry, we will reach on time," he tried comforting me. Dads are like that only. They scold you, they belittle you and then they comfort you. I just smiled in response. I took my bag from the back seat as soon as I saw the board "GITAM UNIVERSITY" which had turned into a second home for me since past one and a half years. I got down from the car and bade bye to my dad.

"Call me in the evening. I will come to pick you up," my dad stopped and said.

"No Dad, it's fine. Nisha will drop me," I assured him. He nodded and his car sped off.

***

I walked briskly towards the classroom when everybody on my way looked at me weirdly assuming that I was heading for nature's call. Still, I chose to ignore that and hurried towards my classroom.

"CSE- second year"

"Ho, you came finally!" Nisha scorned.

"Uff, you can taunt me later, where are the other guys?" I asked removing the backpack from my shoulders.

"They are on the way, we will start writing," She said spreading her A4 sheets on the desk.

"Hey Guys!" Aditya, Vineet, Madhu said in unison as they entered the class. We were a batch of five who loved one another's company.

"Come, it's already late. Start writing," Nisha advised.

"You people always keep procrastinating things. I always have to keep reminding you. No one bothered to pick up my call yesterday," Madhu chaffed. She has been a studious girl from the day one. The thickness of her eyeglasses would explain that. Though she had finished her assignments, she came up early just to accompany us. We did not bother to answer her though.

"What the hell? Give it back," Vineet who was busy chatting with his girlfriend, raged when Madhu grabbed the mobile from his hand.

"Yeah, Prof. Anand will show you hell, if you don't complete your assignments by nine," she tried reaching his pitch.

He seemed convinced. He took out his record and started writing hastily. Madhu sighed and unlocked his phone when a message arrived.

"What is my baby boo doing?" It was from Geetha, Vineet's girlfriend. He rose from the bench and tried to snatch his mobile. He failed, she ran away reading the texts.

"Your Cutie pie is waiting for her bumblebee's reply :("

"Baby boo! Bumble bee! Are you fourteen? And you never told us that Bumble bee is your pet name," Aditya burst into laughter.

We joined him. Vineet moped. Madhu returned his mobile, as she couldn't see him with a sullen face. Vineet and Madhu were best friends from their plus two batch. We continued our scribbling. For the next twenty minutes, no one spoke. It was exactly nine, when we high fived, for having finished the assignments.

"Good morning folks!" Prof. Anand, our computer science lecturer greeted us, entering the classroom.

"Good morning sir," we shouted in unison. Palpably, we five shouted more energetically because of having finished the assignments.

"Okay, so everyone is ready with their assignments?" He asked sitting on the table. Some heads were moving side-to-side nervously (shaking) and some heads were moving up and down elatedly (nodding). We were included in the set of nodding heads though.

"Well, I know yesterday was a Sunday and most of you might not have finished the assignments, I will give you one more day, submit them tomorrow," he said opening the C++ textbook. Our faces turned pale. I sacrificed my sleep, my breakfast and rushed to complete this. Vineet, Adi and I turned to look at Nisha.

"What?" she grimaced. We stared at her without blinking.

"At least we finished today, we can sleep in peace tonight," she retorted.

"Yeah, you are right," we nodded approvingly.

"What do we use to state integers?" our lecturer questioned the entire class.

"Int sir, int!" Sameer our class topper shouted.

"Hmm very good," he praised him and started writing a binary tree program on which I couldn't concentrate. I looked at Aditya who was searching for sneakers on Flipkart. There is a guy in every group who does online shopping twenty-four- seven. In our group, it is undoubtedly Aditya. Aditya's father is a reputed advocate in Vizag. Reputation and wealth are siblings. Greater reputation comes with greater wealth. Filthy rich family's one and only son. Yet, Aditya is a cool, down to earth person. He raised his eyebrows when he caught me staring at him. I smiled and shook my head.

Then I looked at Vineet. He was typing… blushing, blushing… typing. He had got into a relationship with our junior Geetha, just a few days back. I dropped my idea of disturbing him, as I didn't want to make his cutie pie wait.

Then I saw Madhu seriously copying the binary program into her notes adjusting her spectacles, the trademark of any studious person. I sometimes wonder how such a studious girl accidentally became a member of our group.

"Okay, at least she is paying attention to the class," I thought dropping my idea of disturbing her. And then a smile flashed in my mind, the smile of the beach guy (the name I had given him) and automatically my lips turned into a curve. *His smile.* That was something different, something good which grabbed my attention.

"Am I thinking about a guy?" I couldn't believe myself. That never happened with me. It's not like I am lesbian or something. But I usually never pay attention to guys.

"Who is the guy in your mind Ashi?" Nisha whispered to me staring at Prof. Anand.

"Wow, babe. You are a mind reader," I thought. "Guy? No way!" I lied. "And by the way, why do you gawk at him like that?" I questioned her back, referring to our lecturer.

"You ask me why! Just look at him. He is so handsome," said Nisha looking at him seductively.

Yeah! He is.

"And you witch, don't switch the topic," she demanded and then I narrated the story. She listened to the entire story excitedly. "Wow! I should have been there. Do you have those pictures?" she whispered.

"Yeah." I unlocked my mobile and gave it to her.

"Woah! He is hot, look at those biceps," she said zooming in. "But I think I have seen him somewhere," she tapped her chin.

"Where?" I shouted suddenly, accentuating every pupil in the class.

"Ashritha and Nisha what's going on there?" our lecturer grumbled.

"Nothing sir." we apologized standing at our places.

"Did you guys complete the assignments?" he asked bluntly.

“Yes sir.” we nodded firmly.

“See, you should thank me!” Nisha whispered.

“Can anyone of you complete this program?” he asked looking at both of us.

“Oh my God! We are so dead,” Nisha moped.

“I can.” I raised my hand and walked towards the board. He handed the marker and gestured me to write.

“Hmm, good! Seems like nothing was happening there,” he said as I finished writing.

“Yes sir.” I faked an obsequious look.

“Go and sit,” he smiled.

“Ashritha, how did you really do that?” Nisha whispered as we sat down.

“That’s just a piece of cake to me, now you should thank me!” I simpered.

“Well! I should,” she nodded.

“First tell me, where did you see him?” I recited.

“I don’t remember,” she whispered back. For the rest of the period, we conversed through notes.

40 minutes had passed.

The class ended successfully. Aditya’s order for Reebok sneakers was placed successfully. Vineet’s message was delivered successfully. Madhu copied her notes successfully. Nisha filled her eyes with Prof. Anand’s charm successfully but I wasn’t successful in making Nisha recall where she had seen him. I sighed dolefully.

We headed to the canteen.

***

I toddled carefully towards the table holding the plate of snow white *idlis* and brimming cup of hot Boost milk. “How do you eat that daily?” Vineet asked Aditya, with a scowl on his face. Aditya took the *upma*. I had never seen him eating anything other than *upma* in the entire college life. Maybe he was the only customer of *upma* in our canteen.

"Shut up! It isn't that bad!" Aditya answered as he shoved his spoon into the *upma*. Nisha took juice and when I enquired why she wasn't having anything, she said, "I'm on diet."

"There begins her drama again!" Aditya teased her.

"You are not fat, Nisha. Stop doing all these things and eat!" I said pushing my plate towards her. She denied pushing it back. "Did you at least eat anything at home?" I pumped her.

"Nope, just this juice will do," she said and sipped her juice.

"Are you nuts? You should eat and not starve yourself. You will get sick if you skip meals," I shrieked.

"*Satya vachan!*" Aditya said nodding his head, imitating Farhan Akhtar from *Zindagi na milegi dobara*.

"No no, I'm on a strict diet," she said firmly.

"Fine. Go to hell then," I said and continued my munching. Then Sanjay came there, occupying the seat between Nisha and me. Sanjay was our friendly senior and most importantly Nisha's boyfriend. Naughty in thoughts, kind at heart. He fell in love with her in our first year and proposed her on our fresher's day. As she had same feelings for him, it didn't take much time for her to accept his proposal. There began their love story.

"You have amazing silky hair Ashritha," Sanjay said to me, showing off to Nisha.

"Sanjay you keep saying this, every day. Let me eat first," I replied gobbling.

"Oh, C'mon Ashritha! I mean it. Just look at your friend's hair, it's like Maggie, isn't it?" he said and broke into laughter.

"Haha yeah," Aditya laughed chomping the peanuts in *upma*. They both high fived and then Nisha punched Sanjay in his stomach. He teased her some more and they laughed together.

"Baby, are you crazy? Go and get breakfast," Sanjay chided her when he found that she wasn't eating anything. She stood up from her chair silently and brought a sandwich for herself. I looked at her with my mouth open.

"What happened?" Sanjay asked confused.

"Till now, everyone here had tried to make her eat something but she didn't. But now, you just said a word and she didn't even deny," I explained throwing my hands up.

"C'mon Ashritha. She is my girl," Sanjay winked at Nisha. I always loved their pair; they tease each other like friends and care for each other like a real married couple. That is what is important in a relationship.

I finished my breakfast and went to dispose my plate. I was returning slowly, staring at the ground, pondering whether I should eat *biryani* or meals for lunch. Then I found a pair of Nike white sneakers blocking my way. I looked at mine, Inc. 5 wedges. "Not bad," I thought.

I moved left, they moved left. I moved right, they moved right. Frustrated, I lifted my head up to look at the face of that shoe's owner. No sooner, I saw the face, my eyebrows rose and lips turned into curve.

Holy shit! It's him!!

I resisted my smile. "But how? Why?" I started thinking of every possibility.

"Hey Akash" Sanjay came there and shook hands with him.

"Ashritha, he is Akash, IT department, my parallel year," Sanjay introduced him.

"Akash, Nice name!" I muffled.

"Hello Ashritha," he said and extended his hand expecting a shake-hand. At the beach, I didn't get a close view. He was really handsome. His face was extremely clear and perfectly tanned. His thick eyelashes and lightly trimmed beard made him look manlier. His thick hair was messy but in a beautiful way. Myself being 5'5" tall, I reached his chin. (I really don't know why I compared my height with his).

We shook our hands softly and then Sanjay introduced him to my gang. But he didn't take his eyes off me and to my bad luck, Nisha noticed him staring at me. "You look pretty Ashritha," he said softly looking at me.

"Ahem! Ahem!" Nisha coughed impishly.

"Well okay. see you guys later," said Sanjay and both of them left. After walking a distance, Akash suddenly turned back and smiled looking at me.

"Oh. You look pretty! What's going on babe?" Nisha gave a smug smile.

"What? Am I not pretty? He just admitted the fact right!" I said adjusting my hair.

"You are pretty and that's obvious, but what about the glances he has been stealing?" she asked with her arms crossed. Then, I looked at her hair.

"How could Sanjay compare so perfectly?" I admired Sanjay. It exactly felt like noodles hanging from her scalp to her shoulder.

"Hello ma'am, speak up," she recited.

"He didn't," I lied.

"Of course he did. I saw him staring at you, and I noticed some sort of change in your body language when he was around," she said staring at me, narrowing her eyes.

"What? No way!" I denied.

"Oh please!" She is a stickler.

Can you please stop being a chewing gum?

I decided to reveal the suspense, as I knew that she can never stop being a chewing gum. "Come here," I said wrapping my arm around her shoulder.

"Ashritha, why do I feel that I have seen Akash somewhere?" she said walking beside me.

"Dumbo, that's because you did see him. I really don't understand how Sanjay is dealing with you," I said, annoyed.

"When?"

"Maybe in college earlier and in the pictures, in my phone today," I said removing my hand and walked ahead without looking at her.

"You mean Akash is the beach guy?" she shouted from behind.

I blushed. "Yes," I shouted without turning back. I knew her reaction and I could imagine it.

3.

"Ashritha and Nisha, you both are in the set of Dais committee organizers. Every day at exactly three you should assemble here," Harini, our senior, appointed us. Nisha and I nodded our heads. We were sitting in the meeting hall.

There is a cultural fest CARNIVAL which is conducted every year. In the first year, we were just participants, but now they appointed us as organizing members which we reckoned as prestigious positions.

"But I don't want to miss the classes, Nisha." I sulked.

"Uff!! Three to five are just labs. You can practice coding at home too," she sighed. I nodded solemnly.

"Few more seniors will join you," Harini said glaring at us adjusting her spectacles. We nodded. No sooner, I saw a familiar guy entering the hall, my lower jaw fell open. Yes! It was him, it was Akash.

"Yeah, Akash and Kiran, they are your seniors," she introduced. I looked at Nisha in astonishment, she was equally surprised.

"Hello Ashritha, good to see you again," Akash said and shook hands with me. I smiled and tried hard not to blush.

"Hey Hello," Kiran shook hands with me and Nisha.

"Now I understand the reason behind our selection as organizers," Nisha whispered in my ear. I eyed asking to shut her mouth.

"Well, I will quickly give you a brief introduction about the things which you need to do," Kiran said rubbing his hands. He seemed like an extremely frisky guy. We nodded approvingly. Akash remained silent. He just sat there, stealing glances at which Nisha has started teasing me about.

"Listen guys, being Dais committee organizers, we have to take care of a lot of things- Chief guests, the host, anchors, Dais decoration, everything," Kiran narrated drawing parallel and horizontal lines in the notes.

"First of all, you have to get names of participants of the events including junior and senior classes," Kiran said drawing circles on his book. "And later we will request few lecturers and arrange auditions for all the cultural events," he drew squares this time.

"What is he trying to draw Ashritha?" Nisha whispered in my ear.

"Even I am wondering the same," I whispered back.

"Any problem?" Kiran enquired. We shook our heads and tried listening to him. Even though, I couldn't pay attention to what Kiran was trying to say, at least I bluffed like I did, but Akash didn't even bother to do that. He just sat silently staring at me constantly and smiling occasionally.

"Actually, there are few more seniors who have to join, but unfortunately they didn't come to college, so we will pause for today," Kiran said, closing his book. We stood up and when we were about to turn back, Kiran called us. "We will exchange numbers and that would be quite helpful," he said standing from his chair.

"Yeah, quite helpful," Nisha murmured in a sarcastic tone. We agreed and moved forward. After sharing my number with Kiran, I turned towards Akash. He was already waiting with his keypad open. I shared my number, which he saved it as Ashritha and added a smile emoticon.

"Okay, we will catch up tomorrow at sharp three," Kiran instructed.

Before exiting the meeting hall, I don't know what exactly happened to me. I stopped on my tracks, turned back and found two captivating eyeballs smiling at me which sent a magical shiver in my body.

4.

It was 2:30 and our English ma'am was still teaching. I paid the least attention in her class. "It's been 5 minutes and you have checked your watch at least 10 times, how long are you are going to do that?" Nisha questioned without looking at me.

"Till my watch shows three," I shot back.

"Then set your time at three, problem solved!" she winked.

"Haha, very funny," I sneered. The expression on my face scared my front bench pal who suddenly turned back to borrow a pen.

"I know," Nisha scorned. "Oh yes! We have to go to the meeting hall at three, right?" Nisha said suddenly sitting straight.

"Yeah, that's what. This class is so boring," I moped.

"Yeah, and the meeting hall makes you excited! Isn't it?" she whispered in my ear.

"Oh please!" I tried acting normal. She was right indeed. The thought that I was going to meet Akash made me excited.

She spoke again, "Yesterday you said, you don't want to skip the classes and now you are eager to go to the meeting. There is something fishy."

"No Nisha, there is nothing," I tried making her believe. She didn't though.

"What? Don't tell me that you both don't like each other. I am not going to believe that," she said and looked at me for my answer.

Yes, we do. I experience a different feeling when he is around, when he stares at me and when he smiles.

I still remember the feeling that I experienced when I received a text from him, the previous night,

"Hey, Akash this side." I got a text from Akash at around eight, when I was watching TV.

"Hi Akash, Btw I saved your number," I replied him.

"Hmm, so had dinner?" He enquired.

"Yes."

"And you?" I asked him back.

Yes! I am concerned about him.

"Yeah, finished just now, I felt like talking to you, so I texted you. I hope I didn't disturb you" was his reply.

'Disturb? You think so? I would have texted you if you hadn't. I have been waiting since evening.' I wanted to write but didn't. Yes, I was waiting for him to text me. Whenever I saw his profile picture in WhatsApp, I spoke to myself "When are you going to text me?"

Actually, at one point I wrote a "Hi" and erased it because I am a girl. Girls are not supposed to message first. They should make boys text them first. It's the tradition (which Nisha taught me).

"Hopefully, you did not" I added a smiley to that.

"Great! Actually, I returned home just now from a function, so couldn't text you in the evening," he replied.

"Aww baby, that's okay" when backspace deleted it, "Oh okay" got delivered.

"Humm, yeah. So tell me, what are your hobbies?" I got an instant reply from him.

"What are you going to do with my hobbies?" I added a winking emoticon to not to sound rude.

"Well! To get closer we have to know each other, right?" He questioned me back. When I was thinking what to reply him, I got another text.

"Can I call you? Please" It read.

"Okay," I accepted. My phone buzzed in a jiffy displaying his name which eventually created a smile on my face.

"Hi Ashritha." My name sounded new to me.

"Hi." I responded, maintaining a casual tone.

"So what's up?" he tried starting the conversation.

"Nothing much, I was just watching TV," I said latching my door silently.

"Hmm, tell me about yourself," he asked as he sighed deeply.

Is this some sort of interview?

"Me? Ask me something, I will tell you," I said sitting cross-legged on my bed.

"Umm, what should I ask?" he said. I imagined him, thinking with the index finger on his chin (the thinker's pose). "Okay, why don't you tell me about your family?" He finally came up with a basic question.

"Mmm, my dad works as a project design engineer in Vishaka steel plant. Mom used to work as a teacher but she gave up her job when she realized handling two children is far better than handling half a century kids and then I got a younger brother who is in eighth standard now. My grandpa and granny live with us," I said and inhaled.

"Umm cool," he said.

I didn't ask about his family, but still, he chose to express. "My dad is a bank manager. Mom is a home maker. I have an elder sister. She has done MBA recently, and mom is making her watch cookery shows as she will be getting married soon but the problem is, she experiments every dish on us," he laughed lightly. I was listening to him, playing with the pillow in my lap.

"You look really pretty," he complimented all of a sudden. I didn't understand what to answer. "You there?" he inquired. I laughed. "I complimented you and you are laughing?" He was confused.

"Well! Actually, I'm really bad at responding to compliments." I laughed again. This time, he joined my laughter.

"Ashritha, I want to ask you something. If you don't want to answer it, you can simply ignore," he said elaborating.

"Yeah sure," I confirmed.

"Are you in any relationship?" He came up with a routine question which every guy usually comes up with. Though my answer was a no, I wanted to tease him.

"Yes, I am," I said softly.

"Oh!" he sounded low, I could sense that. "Who is he?" he asked.

"He is my neighbor, just the next immediate house," I said leaning against the wall. I tried hard not to laugh.

"Hmm" that was his response. I felt bad. I wished I was right next to him to see his expression.

"Okay, what is his name?" he asked again.

"Joy" I blurted out. Joy is my neighbor's dog, a German shepherd.

"Joy, what kind of a name is it? Okay, what does he do?" he asked failing to find the logic.

"Well, he protects house from robbers," I laughed.

"You mean a Watchman? I didn't get you." I broke into a huge laughter. "Why are you laughing?" he questioned.

I paused to speak. "Joy is my neighbor's dog," I said and continued my laughter.

"Oh Ashritha, you scared me for a life time," he sighed. I could hear his breath. I was still laughing.

"Ashritha, you are not sleeping?" Mom shouted from the living room when she heard whispers from my room.

"Yes Mumma! Sleeping now," I shouted back covering the speaker with my hand.

"You didn't like anyone yet?" he asked me, not ending the topic.

"Like in the sense, yeah, I like many people," I tried teasing again.

"Not that Ashritha, I mean love," he asked straight.

"For me, Love hasn't happened yet," I concluded.

"Hmm, good." He was back with his happy tone. We spoke for some more time and I dozed off with a smile on my face.

"Hey, where are you? Wake up, it's three," said Nisha, breaking my thoughts. I panicked for a moment. "Pack your bag, we will directly leave for home from there," she instructed, packing her bag. I nodded and did the same. "Fast Ashi, don't you remember the guy Kiran, with the ever serious face. I just hate him," Nisha moped.

"So what?" I was confused.

"I don't know; I just don't like him," she confessed.

"Well, why do you have to like him?" I shot back.

"I don't know," said Nisha.

'She keeps blabbering all the time,' I thought.

***

"You people came?" Kiran asked looking at us entering the hall. We collapsed in the chairs, panting. The meeting hall was about five hundred meters away from our classroom. We were completely tired out with the walk.

"Water?" Akash offered his water bottle. Before I could take it, Nisha grabbed it and started drinking. I thanked God when she left few drops of water for me.

"If you are done, we will start," Kiran said glaring at us.

"This man is not even letting us drink water," I murmured. Nisha was right. He was always serious. I hated his hegemony. We nodded insipidly. He pulled out a notebook and a pen from his bag and started scribbling.

"Listen, Ashritha and Akash you both will have to go to both junior and senior sessions and get the names of the participants. I want the entire list by the end of the day," he instructed us.

"But, Nisha?" I intervened.

"We will prepare the list regarding the timings to be allotted to each event," he said and looked at Nisha.

'Nisha has a boyfriend,' I wanted to say when I felt Kiran was showing some interest in her. I knew my allusion was wrong; he was just bothered about the event.

'He? Thinking about girls?! Just forget it,' I scolded myself.

"Come Ashritha," Akash stood up and extended his hand. I looked at him nervously and joined my hand. He smiled. I smiled too. The other seniors were already waiting outside. We headed towards the junior's block. My hands shivered in nervousness. Akash noticed it. "Listen Ashritha, you have nothing to do, just stand in the center of the class and read out this paper," he said offering me a paper on which a note was already handwritten.

I smiled gratefully. He smiled gracefully.

"Well! Good afternoon everyone. As all of you are aware of the fest "Carnival" which is to be conducted the coming week, I want every one of you to participate in any event of your choice. We have games, singing, and dance competitions. Whoever is interested, you can give your names to your class representative," I said and took a pause. "If you have doubts regarding anything or if you need any help from our end, you can ask us, we would be happy to help you," I added.

"Okay, I want to dance in Rumba style, will you be my dance partner?" A guy from the last bench shouted. The entire class burst into huge laughter as if they were watching Kapil Sharma show. I felt embarrassed.

"Who is that rogue?" Akash raged in anger.

"Who the hell are you?" the same guy shouted again. Akash rushed towards him and held his collar. Luckily, the lecturer stepped out of the classroom a few minutes back.

"What were you asking? Ask me now," he was fuming in anger. I stood there trembling, having no idea how to stop the issue. The entire class was watching the scene with keen interest.

"Tell me now, what did you say?" Hemanth, Akash's friend who accompanied me and Akash walked near him rolling his sleeves up.

"You want me to repeat that again?" the junior mocked.

"Akash please leave," I walked near him gaining courage. He didn't leave his collar.

"Don't you know how to behave with your seniors?" another guy from our group asked him.

"I will teach him a lesson today," Akash said pulling him out of the bench.

"What is going on there?" the lecturer asked coming back, hearing the dispute.

"Akash please, for my sake," I pleaded him. "Please." I said sternly and held his hand. He looked into my eyes, he could sense the fear in my eyes. He released his grip from the collar.

"Who is the CR of this class?" Akash shouted. Then a guy in the first bench stood up. "You collect the names of the people who are interested and give it to Kiran, your senior, in the meeting hall and teach this bastard how to behave with seniors," Akash instructed and the guy bobbed his head. We came out and I heaved a sigh of relief.

"No, I can't do this please," I said shaking my head.

"Please Ashritha, don't say that, you asked me to stop that's why I remained silent or else I would have broken his ribs," Akash said clenching his teeth and fists.

"No, it's not about that. I'm just nervous," I tried cooling him down.

"No Ashritha, you are not. Trust me," he said looking at me. I looked into his eyes.

I do. I smiled and nodded.

"Yes! That's my girl." I noticed him biting his tongue as he stammered. "I meant that's good," he said and turned back. In the next one hour we announced in all the classes, I stopped looking at the paper. I announced and discussed with smile and confidence.

We high-fived once our task was finished and moved to the meeting hall.

"Good, I got all the names," Kiran appreciated us.

'Oh, this man appreciates too!' I wondered. I looked at my watch, it was seven already, I had no idea how the time flew. We spent the time cracking jokes, gossiping and stealing glances frequently.

"I think we should leave, it's already late," Nisha suggested looking at all of us. Though I didn't wish to go from there, I nodded. Akash's face sulked on hearing that but he didn't stop us.

"Okay, we will assemble tomorrow; we have to arrange screening for the selections," Kiran instructed as he walked out. I bade bye to Akash and walked out of the meeting hall.

5.

I don't know why it felt difficult for me to open my eyes. It felt like someone was ramming on my head with a hammer constantly. It felt like the world around me was spinning. It felt like boiling hot fluid was flowing through my nerves yet at the same time I was shivering with terrible cold. When I opened my mouth to call out for mom, the voice didn't come out. I couldn't speak. My throat burned. My whole body was aching.

"Ashritha, from how long I have been calling you? Wake up!" Mom came into my room in a rush.

In the process of waking me up, she held my hand.

"Ho God! Your body is burning," she shrieked worriedly. She ran into her room and in a moment appeared in front of me with a thermometer. "102!!" she yelled removing the thermometer from my armpit. I couldn't move. Dad came there tensed hearing my mom's squeals.

"What happened?" he asked. I looked at him. He was ready, almost about to leave for work. Mom did not answer instead she showed the thermometer. "She was fine last night, but what is this fever all of a sudden?" dad said, buttoning his handcuffs. Dads always try to find logics. "I will call the doctor, you just take care of her," dad said dialing the doctor's number, his dearest friend.

"He is in the clinic now, he will be coming in an hour or two," he said coming back into my room.

"I will take care of her," mom said and sat near my legs.

"Mumma! College!" I whispered. That was the first thing I spoke in the entire day.

"Are you out of your mind? You have hundred and two degrees' fever and you want to go to college? No college for the entire week," she concluded. Failing to speak, I moped. I lay on the bed whooping. Mom caressed me, massaging my hands and legs. I was still stuck in the bed.

"Drink this," mom said offering me a glass of milk.

"No Mumma, my tongue is really bitter," I denied.

"You will become weak. Please drink," mom requested, making me lean against the wall. Not wanting to feel the bitterness, I gulped down the entire glass in one go, forcefully. Though my mom insisted me to sleep, I couldn't. My eyes burned. Breathing was tough. Still, I was yearning to talk to Akash. Though I was sick and barely able to move in my bed, there was one thing running in my mind. It felt like I was wanting something or maybe someone and then I realized that I wanted Akash. I missed him. It was one such feeling which I had never experienced before.

"Mumma, where is my phone?" I asked my mom when I couldn't find it on my bed.

"I saw Varun playing with it this morning, but why do you need it now? Just sleep," she insisted again.

"I need to call Nisha," I lied.

"You can call her in the evening. Just sleep. The doctor shall arrive in some time," she said covering me with the blanket.

"How are you?" Doctor Uncle asked waking me up. It was around three. I just got a nap and then he disturbed me. I cursed him for that.

'Yeah, I'm perfect. I was dying to see you, so got sick purposely and that's why my dad called you,' I wanted to rant, but couldn't. "Better" I answered faking a smile.

"What did you have for breakfast and lunch?" he inquired sitting on the chair.

"Only milk. The rice which I had fed her during lunch, she puked it," Mom opened her complaint box as the doctor opened his aid box. He nodded examining my heart beat with his stethoscope. He stank of medicines.

"Any problem other than fever?" he asked again.

"Body pain, throat pain," I spoke low.

"Okay, nothing to worry. It's a normal fever. I will give you some tablets. You will recover in two days," he uttered. My mom's breaths got easier.

"No, I don't want tablets. Just give me an injection," I requested. Since childhood I hated eating tablets. The smell itself would make me sick again. I preferred injections, which gave me instant relief.

He laughed at my impatience and took out a new needle and syringe, and started filling it with liquid. "You sleep now and take leave for two days," he advised. I wanted to break his glasses.

"But college..." I interrupted.

"Even in the morning, she said she wants to go to college," mom intervened again. I gave an annoying look. "What?" she ranted. I chose to remain silent. I knew I can't win her in an argument. On this Earth, only mothers have the super natural power of making their children's mouth shut with just a single look. They don't do it every time but whenever they do, it works!! It can be so effective that even the most stubborn kid in the store crying for a chocolate would wipe his tears and turn silent.

"If she gets better by evening, she can go," he said lastly. I smiled pleasantly hearing that. He walked out of the room. Before I could get up and search for my mobile, the dizziness of the medicine invaded me and I slept under the warm blanket.

It was then when I woke up pushing the blanket away as I could feel the sweat forming on my body. I wasn't feeling cold anymore. My whole body felt light. The head ache was reduced considerably. "Mumma!" Well, I was able to scream too! She came running.

"You woke up. How are you feeling now?" she asked placing her hand on my forehead.

"Yeah, Mumma. I'm fine," I said sitting up.

"Wait, I will check the temperature," she said placing the thermometer under my armpit. "Hmm, ninety-eight," she sighed.

"What time is it?" I asked glaring out from the window. It was dark.

"It's seven. Go and sit in the living room, I will serve dinner in 10 minutes," mom said as she walked out.

"I slept for four hours? God!" I mumbled. I hurried into the living room where my brother was ogling seriously at my mobile.

"Please Akka," he beseeched when I snatched my mobile from his hand. "Aaah!" the *temple run* guy screamed as he fell from the cliff. I walked into my room ignoring his requests and locked myself in the room. Few missed calls from Nisha and lot of messages from Akash. I called up Akash immediately as his worried messages started worrying me.

"Ashritha. How are you feeling now?" he asked as soon as he picked up the call.

"Yeah, Akash. I'm fine," I whispered.

"You sound low, are you alright, seriously?" he shouted. *He must be somewhere outside.*

"Yeah, and I'm so sorry I couldn't respond to your messages. My phone wasn't with me and I woke up just now," I explained. "But how did you get to know that I am sick?" I questioned him.

"I requested Nisha to call you and inquire, then your brother said that you are sick," he answered. "Okay tell me, are you fine now?" he was almost shouting. I could hear the buzzing vehicle horns clearly than his voice.

"Where are you Akash? There's a lot of disturbance," I shouted back.

"I will call you in ten minutes, bye," he said and disconnected the call without waiting for my answer.

"What's wrong with him?" I was fuming in anger.

I am ill and I thought he would be worried and now he is brushing me aside?

"I'm not going to talk to him" I made a decision. Exactly in ten minutes, my phone buzzed. "I'm not going to pick the call." In the next moment, I found myself swiping the screen towards green.

"Ashritha. Can you come up, I mean your terrace?" these were the first words he asked after picking up the call. My heart started beating fast.

"Where are you Akash?" I asked him.

"Please, come fast," he said, disconnecting the call, leaving me confused and nervous.

"Where are you going Ashi?" Mom asked suspiciously when she saw me toddling towards the stairs.

"Terrace Mumma," I tried sounding normal.

"Terrace? Now? You will catch fever again," she said.

"No Mumma. Just five minutes, I want fresh air," I lied.

"Okay, come back in five minutes," she agreed and I ran up through the stairs.

"Yeah, I'm on the terrace, where are you?" I was gasping.

"Come near the edge and look towards your left." He instructed. Exactly at the street's end, I found Akash sitting on his bike. He waved his hand as I saw him there. No one spoke for few minutes. We were just looking at each other.

"What are you doing here?" I asked.

"Well! I came to say 'Hi' to your boyfriend Joy," he winked laughing. I laughed with him. "You are sick, I badly wanted to see you, so I thought I would just come." He answered on call. The sick feeling which I had been carrying since that morning has left me as soon as I saw him smiling.

I wanted to admit that even I was hankering to see him, but being a girl I couldn't. That moment I understood that I wasn't the only one who had the feeling of missing him. Even he had the same feeling for me. It was clearly a two-way thing.

"I'm happy to see you, but not like this. I want to see the active Ashritha," he said. In the blinking street lights, I could see him widening his eyes when he said active Ashritha. I smiled and nodded.

"Akka. Mom is calling you," Varun came there.

"Yeah, Nisha. I will see you tomorrow." I faked and signaled Akash to leave.

Mom fed me rice with hot tomato rasam that tasted divine on my sore throat. "Go and sleep. Take rest for tomorrow also. You will get better," mom advised wiping my mouth with her wet hand.

"No Mumma. I am perfectly fine. I will go to college as the fest date is arriving," I explained to her as if that was an international issue.

"You never listen. Okay, but if you feel uneasy, come back home," she finally agreed.

"Thanks, Mumma," I said and ran to my room jumping.

"Thank you so much for coming." I texted Akash lying on my bed.

"But you didn't invite me to your home." came his reply.

"Actually I wanted to, but the time isn't appropriate." I replied stating the reason.

"Chill babe, I was just kidding, but you look so weak."

"I'm fine Akash. You will see the smiling active Ashritha tomorrow." I added extra smileys.

"That's my girl." was his reply. That night, I couldn't sleep. Not because of the physical illness, but because of the overwhelming joy. He could have just called me to inquire about my health, but instead he chose to come over to my place.

Doesn't that mean he is really concerned about me?

6.

"How are you feeling now? Did you take your tablets?" Akash asked me as soon as I entered the hall.

"Yeah, I'm alright," I smiled.

"How are you, Ashritha?" Kiran asked me.

'Oh, he talks about things other than the event as well?' I wondered. "Yeah I'm fine now," I said sitting on the chair.

"Have this," Akash said extending his hand. I looked at him. It was an ORS tetra pack.

"Aww… That's so sweet of you," I murmured taking it. He noticed my blush affected pink cheeks. He smiled. Kiran looked at me shockingly.

"Was I too loud?" I whispered to Nisha.

"You were," she whispered back.

"Thanks" I mumbled embarrassingly without making any eye contact.

"Okay, listen! Today our work is to get donations from sponsors," Kiran started.

"Oh God! This man!" Nisha moped.

"Nisha, he is far better than RDBMS Murthy." I whispered in Nisha's ear reminding her about the lab which we had skipped to attend the meeting.

"Yeah, you are right," she admitted nodding her head.

"Well, as part of the fest, we are planning to donate books and blankets for poor people, so we need to collect funds from outside as well. So, today we will go to different showrooms, explain them about our event in a convincing way and accept to advertise their brand in our event, on condition, if they accept to sponsor our event," Kiran explained moving his hands. "So, it's three thirty now. We will start," he said standing up from his chair.

"Nisha, we are dead. In this roasting temperature, we have to go out on a bike. We are going to turn into *kebabs,*" I moped.

"Ashritha, chill. Kiran had already told me about this plan, so I brought my car. You need not worry about the temperature," Akash smiled.

"Wow, thank you so much. You know, I'm really tired out," I said taking the backpack from the chair.

"I know. I requested my dad, for you," he said looking into my eyes. "I mean for all of us," he stammered again gazing at everyone. I loved him doing that. First, he speaks out his heart and then he stammers to cover up.

He smiled again making me blush.

***

It was seven when I concluded that all the businessmen in Vizag are stingy. We visited nearly ten different showrooms asking them for sponsorship. All we got was four-thousand five hundred rupees from three showrooms. The rest of the showroom people invited us, they listened to our part so interestingly and admiringly but when we said that we were expecting sponsorship from them, their faces turned pale and they rejected us.

"I just can't believe this," I said shaking my head.

"These bastards just want to make more and more money," Nisha raged.

"Oh God! I'm tired. I'm starving," I almost cried holding my stomach.

"My house is right here, just a kilometer away. We can go there," Akash suggested as we walked out of the pulsar show room.

"Is this a way to invite you to his home?" Nisha whispered.

"Okay," Kiran nodded.

"Yeah mom... on the way. We are four people. Okay mom. Bye." Akash spoke to his mom over call. My heart started beating fast as we reached his home. Nisha was normal. Even the over-enthusiastic guy Kiran was normal. I don't know why my mind started wandering in thoughts.

"Come in," Akash's mom invited us as she unbolted the door.

"Namaste Aunty," Nisha and I greeted her. She smiled pleasantly. Akash resembled his mom.

"So, they are your classmates?" she asked as we snuggled ourselves on the sofa.

"No mom, I think I don't need to introduce you," Akash chaffed, pointing at Kiran. "She is Nisha, my junior and she is Ashritha" He paused for a moment, looked at me in a way which made me smile and then he stammered "she is my junior too." I wanted to run right away near him and pinch his cheeks.

"Okay, show them your room. I will get something to eat," she said and walked into the kitchen.

"There is nothing new to see in your room. I would rather watch TV," Kiran stated as he bent down to reach the remote.

"Who invited you?" Akash shrugged.

"Ashritha, come," he gestured me to come. "And Nisha," he added.

"I am fine here, you people carry on," Akash smiled at her reply and Nisha winked at me.

"You are so evil," I muffled. We climbed the duplex steps and reached his room on the first floor.

"It's a little clumsy," Akash hurried with the bed sheets and books on the bed.

"Actually not little," I laughed moving my eyes around the room.

"Yeah, please sit," he said making a place on the bed for me to sit.

"Sorry, I didn't know that you will be coming to my home so soon," he said.

"So soon?" I asked confused. Well, I wasn't really confused. I understood what he meant.

"I mean nothing," he stammered again. "You want something to drink? Wait, I will get something," he said and ran downstairs.

I stood up smiling and explored his room. The room had a bed which was too small for two people and too big for one. A desktop in the corner with a rotating chair and racks with books stuffed in. I could clearly see the dust formed on the first book in each rack. Pictures of different sports players hung on the walls. It wasn't well maintained but I kind of liked it, though.

"Here, have this," he said, offering me a glass of orange juice and sat next to me. Our bodies almost touched each other's.

"Thanks," I said taking the glass from his hand nervously.

"I am so happy that you are in my room," he said softly.

"So am I," I chuckled. "Where is your sister?" I enquired sipping the juice.

"She must be out with her friends. She didn't know that you were coming home. If she had known, she might have stayed back," Akash answered playing with cork ball in his hand.

"She knows me? How?" I asked looking at him.

"Yeah, I told her about you many times," he smiled.

"About me? What did you say?" I asked eagerly.

"Nothing, just casually," he lied. I could sense that.

"You want to have some?" I asked extending my hand. He took the glass happily and sipped it. "Tell me, what did you tell her?" I stressed again.

"Just casually, like, Ashritha… a pretty girl, studious girl and…" he said and looked into my eyes.

"And?" I lifted my brows.

"That I really like you," he didn't blink. I looked away trying to break the sedulous eye contact.

"Shall we go down?" I asked as I finished the drink and stood up.

"Why? Don't you like it here?" he suddenly held my hand. I froze there. "Tell me!" He tightened his grip.

"Akash!" I mumbled. He grabbed my hand hard and then stood up facing me.

"Can I tell you something?" he whispered.

I smiled as I nodded.

"You look so beautiful," he said brushing my hair away from my face. We both froze looking into each other's eyes. I would rather say, we were lost into each other's eyes. There was a beautiful intimacy in the aura around us. I looked down smiling, breaking the eye contact.

"Akash, come snacks are ready!" his mom shouted from downstairs. He sighed and we went down.

"Why are you not eating anything?" Akash's mom asked pushing the plate with cut fruits towards me. She served us spinach pakora, bhujia sev, cut fruits that included water melon, banana, grapes and a round of orange juice.

I ate a handful of bhujia, pakora, and fruits as well. 'Oh God! My stomach will burst!' I wanted to rant as loud as possible. "No Aunty, I am already full." I answered pleasantly.

"Look, she is concerned only about you. She did not even ask me," Nisha complained.

"You finished the whole plate without asking and I wonder how many plates you are going to empty if she insists you," I mocked. She moped. "I think it's getting late; we should leave," I said glancing at everyone.

"Have dinner and go," Akash's mother insisted.

Oh God! Why every mother on this earth is so caring?

"Your mother-in-law-to-be is so caring. Be careful, that care might add extra pounds to your slim body," Nisha giggled. I couldn't hear the words, *pounds* and *slim*. The only thing that made me think was 'mother-in-law-to-be'. That thought was really different (of course in a positive way).

"No Aunty, It's already late. Next time please," I tried convincing her looking at my watch. She seemed convinced. When we were about to step out of his home, Akash's mom caught my hand.

"Visit again soon," she smiled. She had no idea, what impact her words and smile showed on me. I felt a motherly thing in her eyes, which I find in my Mumma's eyes.

"Sure Aunty," I assured her.

"Aunty is so sweet!" I texted Akash lying on my bed.

"Yep, she is and she really liked you," came his reply.

"Really?" I raised my eyebrows while typing.

"Yeah, I think you should visit more often."

I typed blushing, "If you say so!!!"

"Aww, so had dinner?" came his reply halting the process of turning me into a tomato.

"How do you expect me to have dinner?" I asked him.

"Why, what happened?" He enquired. "Can I call you?" His text interrupted my typing. I erased the text which I was typing and sent okay. "Why didn't you eat?" He asked me as I picked his call.

"Don't you remember how aunty stuffed fruits into my mouth?" I answered.

"She is like that, if she likes someone," he chuckled.

"So, did you eat?" I enquired about him.

"I did, just now. Actually I called up to ask you something?" he sighed. When people want to ask you something, can't they directly pose the question? They come up with- "Can I ask you something?" The statement is no way lesser than a mini heart attack.

"What?" I asked sitting on the bed.

"My cousins are here and they are planning to go for a movie. They are forcing me to join them. Can I go?" he asked me.

'Wait, is he asking for my permission?' I asked myself. "Is this what you wanted to ask?" I was bewildered.

"Yeah"

"Of course, you can. But why are you asking me?" I laughed lightly. I stopped laughing as soon as I heard him saying,

"Actually, I wanted to spend time with you over texts and calls. I thought that you would be feeling the same," he paused to listen to my answer. I remained silent. "I tried denying them, but they are not even trying to understand," he added.

"Akash, it's fine, please go," I appealed.

"Are you sure?" he asked again.

"Yes, I am. Please go… have fun. I will see you in college tomorrow," I confirmed.

"Can we have lunch together in college tomorrow?" he asked with excitement.

"Yeah sure," I smiled.

"Okay then… they are waiting," he said. I could hear the guys calling Akash's name.

"Bye Ashritha, Miss you!" he disconnected the call.

He just said he is missing me, right?

I don't know why I tossed and turned on the bed holding the bolster, blushing silently reminiscing each word he spoke on call.

7.

"Wow, you look great today! Anything special?" he admired moving his eyes on me from top to bottom. I wore a white and lavender color cotton suit and a pair of silver colored *Jhumkas*.

'It's for you,' I wanted to say. "No, nothing special… just casual," I dropped a light smile. I know that might have sounded stupid as I never preferred wearing *salwar* to college.

"Where are your friends?" he asked looking around.

"No, they didn't come. I came alone," I answered as we walked inside the canteen.

"Come sit," he said pointing at the chair.

"So, how was the movie?" I asked settling down.

"Who knows? I just slept," he shrugged. "Did you miss me?" he posed a straight question. I nodded without making an eye contact.

"You want some?" I asked trying to switch the topic when I noticed him glancing at me adoringly.

"Yeah, please," he said pushing his plate towards me. I asked my mom to prepare prawn fry for lunch knowing that Akash is fond of sea foods. "This is really good," he said munching.

"I am really glad that you came to my home," Akash said looking at me. I smiled. "Aren't you happy?" he questioned me.

"I am."

"I am not yet out of the moment when we were together in my room," he smiled looking at me, expecting a reply. I didn't understand what to answer.

He choked suddenly breaking my thoughts. "Wait a moment, I will get water," I hurried to the water filter and appeared with a glass of water in a moment. He stared at me for little long, strikingly.

"Thank you Ashritha," he said gulping the water.

I smiled in response.

"Akash, can I ask you something?" I asked him. *Yes, I wanted to give him a mini heart attack.*

"Yeah, tell me," he said as he placed both his hands on the table.

"Do you remember that you came to see me when I was sick?"

"Yeah," he nodded casually.

"How do you know my address?"

I caught him looking here and there with a mischievous smile on his face.

"C'mon answer," I recited as I smiled lightly.

"One of my classmates lives in your colony, he told me," he answered after a long pause.

I knew that he was lying but I didn't want to make him uncomfortable with my constant questioning.

I nodded.

"I don't want to leave," he sulked as we finished lunch.

"But we have to," I said standing up.

"Thanks for coming," he smiled as he stood up.

"Thanks to you too," I smiled. Though both of us didn't want to move an inch away, we parted away to our respective classrooms.

***

"You don't know the square of seventeen?" I taunted Varun. It was around eight and I was helping Varun in his mathematics homework. He shook his head pathetically. "Then, what are you doing in school without listening to the classes? I will ask dad to enroll you in tuition," I warned him making a serious face.

He caught me smiling, looking at the mobile when I read the message which I received from Akash. "*Aaj humko bade hi pyaar aarahe hai madam ji ke upar.*" He sent me a text in Hindi.

"Haha, you know Hindi?" I typed as I walked towards my room.

"Akka, please tell the answer and go," Varun beseeched.

"It's two eighty-nine," I answered him and bolted the door.

"No, just this line, that too I wanted to convey this message in a different way, so" came Akash's reply.

"Aww, that's really sweet of you!! But tell me what great thing did I do today that made you send this line," I asked referring the previous message. "You got me water when I choked, you shared your food with me and you took my box from my hand when you found me struggling with the plate when we went to dispose the plates. You have no attitude Ashritha. Your heart is crystal clear. I'm so lucky." I instantly smiled at the last line. I know what it meant.

"Lucky for what?" I asked him intentionally.

"For being my friend" he replied. I smiled at that. I imagined him stammering and biting his tongue. From the day one, we both knew that we were not just friends, but definitely something more than that.

"Oh, friend! Okay" I tried teasing him.

"No it's not like that" he texted back trying to convince.

"Oh. Then, how is it?" I asked again.

"Please Ashritha. Forget about that," he said trying to switch the topic.

After a lot of teasing and affectionate chat, we dozed off in our respective homes.

8.

Finally, it was the day, the cultural fest "Carnival". It was one such pleasant evening in the Amphitheatre with people dressed colorfully resembling bunch of flowers in a garden, their energetic faces, the cool breeze that gently stroked us, the setting peachy sun that was biding goodbye, the colorful lights, the balloons and the flowers added elegance to that evening.

"Harini, are you listening to me? Who is the host? Did the guest arrive? Why are the balloons uneven at the corner? Bouquets are with Tarun, right?" Kiran was performing his usual task- 'getting tensed for no reason'. Apart from his semi-formal suit, he still had the same anxiety on his face.

"Swetha is going to host, the guest is in the guest room, they are still decorating Kiran, and yeah, bouquets are with Tarun, you please stop shouting." Harini went near him hurriedly answering all his questions. I wondered how she was able to run in her sari while I was struggling to stand comfortably.

Well! The seven-day journey in organizing the event went on smoothly apart from the funds from the sponsors. The funds which we collected did not meet the minimum criteria of fund amount and the remaining; we collected from the benign students.

Where is Akash? My eyes started searching for him, but I couldn't find him anywhere.

Am I searching for him? Am I waiting for him?

Though it was pretty tough for me to grasp the change in myself, it was indeed true. Akash and I had got so close to each other. I always loved the feeling when he was around me and whenever he looked at me, the way he took care of me, the way his smile lit up a smile on my face. I enjoyed every small thing.

"Oh my God! You are like Wow!!" Akash came there complimenting me. I didn't respond. I was just gazing him from top to bottom. He looked really handsome in his white t-shirt, dark blue jeans, and a casual brown blazer. His white sneakers completed the whole look. "Hello, I am talking to you!" he waved his hand in front of my eyes.

"Thanks," I smiled breaking my gaze. I wore a cream colored sari with black and red border with a full sleeve designer blouse. My long ear hangings moved in synchronization with my neck.

"Ashi… Ashi… I have some great news to tell you," Nisha shouted from a distance. I was standing near the dais and Akash stood next to me. Her curly hair swayed as she came jumping towards me.

"What?" I shouted back.

"Come with me," she took me little away from the speakers, holding my hand.

"Tell me, what is it?" I asked adjusting my sari.

"Mom and dad will be out of town for two days," Nisha's face beamed with happiness.

"So?" I asked raising my eye brows.

"So, we will stay tonight in my home- you, Sanjay, Vineet, Adi," she explained counting her fingers.

"But Akash?" I asked breaking her sentence.

"Uff, can't you wait for me to complete? Sanjay said he is going to invite Akash too," she clarified.

"Is that really a good idea? I mean alone at your home? I need to ask mom," I spoke slowly.

"Leave that to me, I can convince her," she flaunted. "I am going to drink tonight; it's been so long Ashritha," Nisha gulped.

"You are so stupid," I laughed and turned back to leave.

"But Ashritha, I will be leaving early, I need to help mom in packing stuff. So you people come once the event is done," she suggested.

"Hmm… Okay!" I accepted and walked inside.

"So, are you okay with that?" I was shouting in Akash's ear.

"Yeah, Sanjay told me. That is perfect. We will go straight there after the function," he shouted back. He seemed pretty excited about that.

I smiled looking at his excitement.

"It was really a great event Ashritha, you people helped us a lot," Kiran appreciated us.

"I can't believe this! Nisha should have been here," I murmured. It was Eleven when the event was called off and the crowd dispersed. Only the organizers stayed back to discuss the payments regarding food and decoration stuff. I smiled, bringing myself out of the shock.

"Where is Nisha?" he inquired.

"She isn't well, so she left for home," I lied.

"Oh!What about Akash?" he asked again.

"Must be somewhere here," I said looking around.

Though Akash and I couldn't spend much time together during the day, I was glad that we would be getting to spend some peaceful time together in the night. During the event, I noticed Akash stealing glances at me from some corner and would throw a smile whenever I caught him staring. But I am not sure whether he knows that I stole glances at him too.

"Okay then, it's time to leave," Kiran said breaking my thoughts.

He walked away without waiting for my answer. He didn't even bother to ask if I wanted to go with him.

"Where are you Akash? Kiran left me here, alone," I shrieked on the phone when my phone buzzed.

"I am sorry! He is like that. Listen, can you please come near the basketball court?" He requested.

"Basketball court? Now? But Adi and Vineet have already left, I am here at the parking," I brought up every other reason pushing the real reason aside. I couldn't tell him that I can't walk in the sari for such a long distance.

"Please come. I am waiting," he disconnected the call. Left with no choice, I started walking towards the basketball court.

From almost 20 feet away, I found a group of boys in the basketball court. In the dim light of the pole, I couldn't spot anyone except Akash. With the atmosphere there, I could understand that something was not right. I stopped at a distance thinking whether to go or not. Akash waved me gesturing to come near him. As I walked slowly, I spotted another face. He was the junior guy, who goaded me when I went to announce in his class. "Is everything fine?" I asked in confusion.

"Absolutely, come here," Akash said and I walked near him.

"This bastard and his group were teasing girls in the auditorium. I think it is his part time job," he said clenching his teeth. Another guy from Akash's group was holding his collar. I started trembling.

"Akash, please let's go," I appealed.

"What are you looking at? Say sorry," Akash shouted.

"Sorry Madam," the guy was literally trembling as much as I was.

Madam? Do I look like an oldie?

It might be a world war, but the only things that freak out a girl are the pimples, hair fall and the boys who call them - fat, madam or aunty. "Akash, Let's go," I demanded.

"Akash, you carry on," his friends suggested.

"Come," I caught his hand. Yes, Akash's hand. He held mine too. I smiled inside.

9.

"Why did you stop here?" I asked Akash looking out of the window. He stopped the car on an empty road on the way to Nisha's home. He did not answer. Instead, he took my hand into his. A wave of warmth rushed inside me. "Akash," I whispered. He slowly rubbed my palm with his fingers looking into my eyes. I looked into his. Those captivating eyeballs had frozen me. Though I wanted to hold his hand, I didn't. He tightened his grip looking into my eyes. I liked it.

"Ashritha. I want to tell you something," he whispered.

"Not now Akash," I spoke to myself.

"Ashritha… I like you so much," he confessed. I smiled looking away.

"You don't like me?" he questioned shaking my hand.

I didn't answer. I smiled instead.

Pin drop silence in the car and then my phone rang displaying Nisha's name.

"Thank you, Nisha. This is the best thing you did in your entire life," I mumbled. "Yeah, Nisha. We have almost reached. We will be there in ten minutes. Aditya… Vineet… reached! Oh okay, we are coming," I cut the call. "Akash everybody has reached, they are waiting for us," I said adjusting my *pallu*. Though I wanted to spend some time with Akash, I wasn't feeling comfortable in the *saree*. I was literally frustrated as I was carrying it since the past seven hours. I salute to all the superwomen who wear *sarees* every day and run errands at home.

"Okay, we will go, but before that, answer my question?" he looked at me.

"I do," I nodded without looking at him.

I saw him, turning on the ignition with his gleamy smile.

***

"Nisha, I want to change immediately. Please give me some clothes," I shouted as soon as I got down from the car.

"You want to change inside or you want to change on the road itself," she scoffed. Sanjay came there laughing.

"Come inside," Sanjay invited Akash. I noticed Aditya lying in the bean bag and watching TV in the living room.

"Hello, Ashritha. What made you people travel ten minutes' destination for half an hour?" Aditya sniggered. Nisha house is just a ten minutes' ride from our college. It would take a maximum of fifteen minutes in peak hours.

"Traffic," I lied.

"Oh, really! I don't think so," he said smiling impishly.

"Oh, please!" I said and turned back. However, I was blushing inside.

"Here, take this," Nisha said pulling out a dress from the wardrobe. "Hey, tell me one thing. Did something happen in the car on the way?" she whispered as she came closer to me.

"Something! In what sense?" I asked in confusion.

"I mean, you know… Kiss or something?" she smirked.

"Whaaat? Are you crazy?" I said, pushing her away. "You are an evil person; we were just stuck in traffic," I ranted.

"Oh… Okay," she nodded sarcastically.

"I will change and come; you go and offer something to drink to Akash. He seems tired," I suggested.

"Oh baby, you are so caring. Akash should definitely hear this," she teased me walking out of the room. Your friends will never miss a chance when it comes to teasing you with your crush's name. I still remember how I used to pull Nisha's leg in the beginning of her relationship. Now, it's her turn to take the revenge.

I came out of the room with grey ankle length pajamas and a white tee. Actually, those were full-length pajamas for Nisha. But, myself, being taller than her by two inches, they ended near my ankle itself.

"Where is Akash?" I asked Nisha when I couldn't find him in the drawing room.

"He is on a call… balcony," she said pointing her finger towards Akash who was talking to his mom on the phone. He changed into boxers (must be Sanjay's).

"Guys please order the food, I am starving," Vineet said, taking out a water bottle from the fridge.

"But, what about the drinks?" Aditya frowned.

"Sanjay already brought them. They are in the freezer, and Vineet, the food is on the way," Nisha said.

"Please don't tell me that you people are serious about the boozing plan," I made a face.

"Obviously we are going to booze, how we are going to miss this chance?" Aditya was almost dancing in his bean bag.

"Oh, no! What should I do then?" I moped.

"Have pizza and go to sleep," Vineet teased me.

"Why? Why, only Pizza?" Akash came there finishing his call.

"Oh, you don't know. Ashritha doesn't booze, she is such a boring girl you know," Vineet said throwing up his hands in the air.

"C'mon, just because she doesn't booze, doesn't make her boring," Akash defended. I looked at him. I liked it.

"And these days, girls who don't booze are rare man! Not that I am complaining about the girls who booze," he added. I didn't take my eyes away. He raised his brows. I smiled. So did he.

"Right," Sanjay joined him. We finished four large pizzas sitting on the couch, rolling on the floor, laughing. It was around two o'clock when I walked onto the balcony when the dizziness of the whiskey had overtaken my friend's senses and they started buzzing.

"You are here? I thought you were in the room," I asked Akash when I found him on the balcony. He smiled. "You are not drinking?" I asked again.

"No," he smiled shaking head.

"Please don't tell me that you don't drink at all!" I laughed.

"Actually I do, but today I don't feel like," he conceded.

I nodded. "But Why?"

"May be because I don't want to miss a chance of spending time with you like this," he looked at me. I tried hard not to blush. I turned back to look at my pals. Aditya was snoring on the couch. Sanjay, Nisha, and Vineet were rolling on the floor. They were completely high. I looked at the sky. It seemed pleasant with the moon and those foggy, grey clouds. That would be a perfect time for a long walk. "Ashritha, wanna go out?" he raised his eye brows.

"Sure," I countered. In the next five minutes, he grabbed the keys, I got into the car and we were on the beach road. The city seemed peaceful. There was no traffic, unlike daytime. Deserted roads shone in the street lights. The emphatic sound of the tides enticed me.

"Can we go to the beach, please?" I made a plea.

"Now? I don't think people are allowed during nights," he said slowing down the car.

"I know, but please," I impelled.

"Okay we will try. We can't park the car near the beach, we will park it somewhere else and then go there on foot," he said looking for a parking area. We saw a cop at the entrance who was snoring in his chair leaning against the wall. "Shh…" Akash gestured bringing his finger on to his lips. I tiptoed behind him. I knew, it was risky but I didn't want to step back. We walked along the shore as we slowly sneaked inside and reached the rocks, which were quite far away from the cop.

We sat on rocks staring at the deep blue sky above us. Besides temple, I find beaches as the most peaceful places. Whenever I feel low, I just come and sit on the shore. The sound of these waves makes me forget my woes. The mesmerizing sound of the waves that greet the shore, the smell of the sand, the stroke of the slight wind has the power of lightening up a person's mood.

"It's so peaceful here, isn't it?" I said inhaling the cool breeze.

He nodded cordially .

"I heard that you are a topper," he asked.

"Well, not exactly, may be one of the top five students," I countered.

"Hmm," he nodded soberly.

"Actually, I want to do MBA in an IIM; I am just trying to make it. That's it. But, I am not a book bug" I laughed. He laughed with me.

"Ashritha, did you ever meet a person when you felt like '*He is the one*'?" he asked.

Yep, when I saw you on the beach.

"If I had found one, you think I will be sitting and blabbering here with you?" I countered. He laughed. "What about you?" I asked him expecting a "no".

"Well, I don't know" he looked away.

"What?! No crush kind of too?" I raised my eye brows.

"Ummm... Yeah. I had a huge crush on my English teacher in my plus two," he confessed. I burst into laughter.

"Crush on a teacher?" I found it funny.

"Yeah, she was really beautiful," he admired gazing the sea. I turned mute. I don't know what exactly happened; I just couldn't hear Akash praising some other lady.

What happened to you Ashritha? What's going on? Are you getting jealous? Why are you getting jealous? Because you like him? Is this feeling called 'love'?

"What happened?" Akash's question halted my thoughts.

"Nothing," I shook my head with a smile. He sat silently, glancing at me with a smile on his face. I could see his eyes glittering in the moon light.

"Ashritha, tell me your type of guy," he said turning towards me.

"My type?! I don't have any list," I said tucking strands of hair behind my ear.

"Everyone does. Okay, tell me what do you expect from your man," he said folding his legs.

"Ummm… Okay," I sighed. "I want a man who can reciprocate the love and care which I give him, who counts me precious, who wouldn't hesitate to kiss my sweaty forehead when I am exhausted in the kitchen, who wouldn't mind to wipe my mouth when I eat in a messy way, who brushes my hair away when my hands aren't clean, who loves the child inside me and wouldn't ask me to grow up. Who would walk ahead holding my hand while crossing the road, who would chase behind me when I walk away crying after a huge fight. Who would treat me as a child and wouldn't mind tying my shoe lace, who would comfort me with his hugs when I am jealous, who would encourage me, who would defend me, and most importantly who would never let me go, no matter what." I don't know what made me speak like that. I spoke without a pause. I spoke without prior thinking. May be all those words came out from my, so called "girl core". To be honest I never had such a sort of list but when Akash asked me, I was glad that he asked me, that he wanted to know what kind of guy I was looking for and I want 'him' to be the 'one'.

"That's really nice!" he sighed.

"And what about you?" I asked bringing my hand under the chin.

"You, I mean I would definitely wish for a girl like you," he stammered.

What does that mean? He means me or some other girl with my features.

Though I wanted to ask him, I didn't.

10.

We never passed a day without chatting and calling. Not that we were happy if we did chat or talk, it was like, we were sad when we didn't.

In no time, Akash occupied the first place in the chat list of my WhatsApp. Actually, not the first, he became the only one. I stopped replying to all my other friends. The mornings and nights made no sense without his texts. Slowly, we got dedicated to each other. I, myself couldn't believe the change in me. My books were replaced by the phone and the content was replaced by the lovely conversations. I never knew that skipping classes and spending time with people we like, can be so much fun. I never experienced till then what it is like to be lost into someone and what it is like to fill our mind with only one person's thoughts. The more I restrained my feelings for him, the more they got eventually raced up with each passing moment. From the day, when we spent one of the most memorable nights of our lives, things were really different between me and Akash.

We had spent the whole night at the beach talking to each other and asking each other's opinions on different things. When the tides played with our toes, our fingers played with each other. When the millions of stars shone in the foggy dusky clouds, our dark brown eyes spoke millions of things, forgetting the world around us. The memorable moments in our life are not special because of the place or time, it's because of the person with whom we experience those.

The police saw us at around four in the morning and when he chased, Akash held my hand and we ran towards the car and we drove off. I even forgot to lock the gate of Nisha's home for which she taunted me for three whole days. Whenever I think about that, it makes me smile.

Though Akash and I didn't officially propose each other, we both were aware that there is some strong and exceptional bond between us.

11.

"It's already late Mumma, please," I yelled at my mom who was feeding me *kheer* when I was packing my sling bag with the comb, wallet, and lipstick. *Kheer* is the mandatory sweet which we get to taste on every single occasion in our home.

Well! The occasion was my birthday. I turned nineteen. It was a Sunday and I promised Akash that I would meet him at eleven at CMR central. It was already 10:50 am. "Eat this first! Then go to grandma and grandpa take their blessings and then step out," my mom kind of warned me.

My granny was reading a book when I entered her room and I was least bothered to look at the title of the book. I went in and sat on my knees.

"Happy birthday, Ashritha. May God bless you," she said putting her right hand on my head.

"Thank you, Amma," I said kissing her on the cheek. She then took out her purse took out two five hundred notes and gave me. I took them shamelessly without denying. "How am I looking?" I asked her spreading my dress with both hands. I wore a black colored one piece with Yellow colour floral print on it that ended near my knees.

"It's too good. But you forgot to wear pants," she said adjusting her spectacles, when she noticed my bare shins.

"Arey... This is a one-piece Amma. There is no pant for this," I said shaking my head.

"Ho... but why don't you wear a sari?" she advised.

"Offo... sari! Okay, I am leaving," I said and got my sling bag on. My dad and grandpa went out for some work and I chose to meet them once I returned. I struggled to balance with one leg on the floor and with the other in air while adjusting the belt of my T-strap flat sandals. I was about to get into an auto when the driver stopped by my way gawking at my legs, my mom came rushing behind and put a dot of *kajal* behind my ear (It's a belief that kajal protects us from the evil eye). "Mumma, does this dress look odd?" I asked moping. Though I had no plans of changing it, even if it looked odd, I just wanted to confirm.

"No no. You look stunning...Have a wonderful day. It's your special day," she said brushing away the strands of my hair.

"It's your special day too because you are the one who brought me into this world on this day," I said giving a peck on her cheek and got into the auto. I kept waving her until the driver took a right turn from where I couldn't spot her anymore.

***

I walked swiftly as well as stealthily when I noticed people staring at my bare legs as soon as I entered the mall.

"Thank God! I didn't forget to get my legs waxed," I murmured. Then a little boy of around eight years old came running towards me. He had a rose in his hand. He pulled my hand and I sat on my knees. Handing me the rose, he said "Happy birthday!"

"Aww… thank you. But who gave you this?" I asked him. He grinned exposing his chocolate tainted teeth and ran towards his mother who was standing at a distance. I stood up and looked at her. She smiled and pointed upstairs. I looked up and found no one. I went to the first floor and then a girl of almost my age came to me and handed me a Cadbury silk and wished me. When I asked her, "Who gave you this?" she smiled and left. Out of over-enthusiasm, I texted Akash,

"Please tell me, where are you?"

"Food lounge, first table," came his reply. I hurried to the food lounge and felt dejected as I couldn't find him at the first table. I sat there silently replying my school friends who wished me over text. Then suddenly, someone from behind closed my eyes. I was startled for a moment. Assuming that it was Akash, I ran my fingers over those hands gently. I sensed long nails with nail paint on them.

'Oh God! When did Akash start painting his nails?' I panicked. 'Ew no. Why would he?' I scolded myself. When my touch failed to identify, I let my nose to take its turn.

I know this odor. Playboy-play it lovely.Got it!

"Nisha!!" I screamed in joy. She released my eyes and wrapped her arms around my neck from behind.

"Happy birthday baby," she said and kissed my cheek affectionately.

"Thank you Nisha," I said rubbing the lipstick mark which Nisha left on my cheek.

"Happy birthday!" Aditya, Madhu and Vineet shouted in unison from behind. I stood up and hugged them. There was a box in Aditya's hand, they unwrapped it and placed it in front of me. It was a blue berry cheese cake. 'Happy birthday Ashi' was written on it.

'These people never fail in making me feel special,' I thought. "The cake looks yum," I said rubbing my hands together.

"Then why delay? Cut it no!" Vineet said, his eyes glued to his mobile.

"Wait! Let the hero come," Nisha smirked. Everybody hooted teasing me. Then there came my hero in a sky-blue shirt, dark blue jeans with a pair of Woodland shoes.

"Happy birthday Ashritha," he said and extended his arms anticipating a hug.

"Thanks," I said and gave him a side-hug.

"So, please cut the cake. I'm starving" said Madhu. Aditya gave me the knife and Vineet lit the candles.

"Oh… thank god! At least now he left his mobile," I murmured. I cut the cake and everybody started singing the birthday song. The most irritating moment you encounter is when people sing a birthday song for you. You literally have no idea what to do there. I stood there dumbly gazing at everyone. I shoved the knife into the cake. I couldn't decide whom should I offer the first piece, to Nisha or Akash.

If I give it to Akash, Nisha would taunt me for the rest of my life. If I give it to Nisha, Akash would feel bad.

In the midst of the confusion, I cut the piece and swallowed the first piece myself. Everyone laughed. "You are an idiot!" Nisha said shaking her head.

"What? It's my birthday and moreover, it's blueberry cheese cake," I said licking my fingers. Akash laughed looking at me. Very soon, everyone fell on the table to grab the biggest possible size of the cake.

"You look stunning," Akash wrote a text. I blushed in response. We clicked few selfies and ate lunch there itself. Sanjay joined us for lunch. He gifted me a palm-sized rose-colored teddy, which I totally loved. Nisha gifted me a cute Mickey Mouse printed t-shirt. We finished our lunch and left for the movie at INOX.

12.

"Come Ashi, get down," Akash asked as he turned off the ignition. I got down adjusting my dress. We had come to Rishikonda beach. The best beach in Vizag and it's very close to our college. Nisha and Sanjay stayed back in central as Nisha wanted to buy some stuff and Madhu, Aditya and Vineet went to their respective houses. It was 6 when the movie was finished and Akash insisted to spend some private time with me, we thought the beach would be the perfect place.

I didn't want to miss the chance of taking few snaps. I handed my phone to Akash and asked him to click few pictures. I smiled, I grinned, I pouted. He clicked each picture patiently with a smile on his face. He suddenly came close to me and put his arm around my shoulder which made a chill run down my spine. Then he eyed me to look at the phone. He was taking a selfie of both of us.

"Uff… thank god!" I murmured. After the photo session, we walked along the shore. He held my hand which I secretly enjoyed. We walked till the rocks and settled down there. The cool, October breeze started blowing, throwing my dress up, which I had to hold to keep down. The sun began to set slowly increasing the intensity of the tides. Birds were making way to their nests. The light house was glowing and I could see the flickering lights of the ships which were sailing away in the sea which made the view adorable. The two most beautiful things you witness on a beach are sunrise and sunset, surprisingly, both are incomparably beautiful.

"Ashi, you just stay here. I will be right back," he said standing up.

"May be, he needs to pee," I thought. I smiled and nodded, he left. It started getting dark slowly. I just sat looking at the children playing happily with the waves.

"Ashritha," he called my name from behind. My mouth fell open when I turned back. I couldn't believe my eyes. He stood there with a bunch of heart-shaped balloons in his hand and a bouquet of red roses. I walked near him. He handed me the bouquet and balloons and then opened the cake box which was placed on one of the rocks. It was a heart shaped red velvet cake. Everything around me looked red. The balloons, roses, cake and even the sky turned red with the setting sun. It felt as if the nature around me was trying to convey something to me. I stood dumb cherishing every moment. He lit the candles and asked me to cut it, taking back the balloons from my hands. He held his hands above the candles as the heavy wind blew on them. I couldn't see the light of the candles though, as the tears invaded my eyes. The best feeling in the world is when the person you like tries his best to surprise you on your special day. I cut the cake and unlike morning I gave him the first piece. And then, he also put a piece in my mouth. He released the balloons and they flew high. "Close your eyes," he demanded.

"Why?" I asked confused.

"Please baby… Close your eyes," he said putting my hands over my eyes. I stood with my eyes closed, listening to the mellifluous waves. In a couple of minutes, he asked me to release my hands. I started jumping with joy as soon as I saw the four pawed surprise in his hand. It was definitely something more than a surprise.

Yes! It was a puppy. Not a toy, a real one. A golden Retriever, exactly the size of both my palms. It had a red color ribbon tied around its neck that made it look even more adorable. "How cute!" I exclaimed taking it in my hands. It looked at me, puzzled. Its eyes sparkled in the moon light. "Thank you Akash, I don't know how to thank you. I just can't believe this," I stammered as I started crying in happiness.

"Hey, Ashi...I understand please don't cry," he said patting my back. I remember I had told him once in our casual chats that I like Retrievers and I was looking for one. You feel exceptionally special when someone remembers every minute thing about you. That is the feeling which I was cherishing at that moment. "You need not say thanks and I know your love for dogs and you know how much I am scared of dogs. Actually, you should appreciate my courage for carrying it to you," he said looking at his hands. He looked cute.

"That's really sweet of you," I said smiling. It started scratching my hand which was an indication that it needed to pee. I let it down and it did the same. "Wow, Ashritha. You are an expert in understanding dog's signs," I appreciated myself. But I wanted to check whether it's a she or he. But I couldn't figure it out in the darkness.

"Ashritha, I have something to tell you," he said.

Oh, God! He is going to propose!!

I could sense the nervousness on his face. Well, I was equally nervous. My heart started racing. "Hmm," I said without eye contact.

"Do you know when I saw you for the first time?" he asked expecting an answer from me.

"Umm… beach, right?" I said reminding him when I first saw him.

"No, I saw you before that. You remember when you got into a fight in Poorna market in June?" he said reminding me about the incident which happened about five months back.

And I was like *what?*

"How do you know?" I stammered in confusion.

It was June and summer in Vizag was extremely torrid. Mom wanted to buy some stuff for puja and she asked me to accompany her. It was almost three at noon and I was feeling exhausted in the market.

"Mumma, I will sit there. You call me once you finish," I said pointing to a tea stall. She nodded. I went there and occupied a wooden bench. I noticed a stray dog who came near the place searching for water.I took out money from my pocket, bought a water packet and I was looking around for a bowl.

"You bloody bitch. Get off from here," a man suddenly came there and threw a ball sized stone at her and the dog started bleeding. She was crying in pain and she couldn't move.

"What the hell are you doing? How dare you, how can you be so insolent?" I stood up and howled at him. He looked at me, startled for my egregious behavior. "What kind of a man you are? Showing your guts to a dumb animal?" I was fuming in anger. Everyone stopped their jobs, having a nice time, watching the dispute. He grumbled. "Are you out of your senses?" I yelled at him.

"What did I do?" he questioned back.

"What did you do? If you can't help the dog, just be silent. How dare you to hurt her?" I said pointing to the dog. "It is a living being on the earth, same as you. I will file a complaint against you in BlueCross," I said and saw him escaping.

My mom came there hurriedly "What happened Ashi? Why are you shouting?" she asked cleaning the sweat on my face with her saree's pallu.

"Nothing Mumma.Just look at her!" I said pointing to the dog and I broke down. I ran towards the dog and it was shuddering. My mom took out the water bottle from her bag and cleaned the wound. Luckily, my mom always carried basic first aid things. We dressed the wound with a hanky and bought some milk and bread and she ate them silently. Before starting back, I gave some money to the tea stall owner and asked him to offer some milk whenever the dog visits the stall. He smiled and agreed.

He was talking about that incident. "I came there to meet a friend and then I was right next to you in the crowd but you didn't notice me," he said breaking my thoughts. I nodded my head in disbelief.

"That moment I witnessed your boldness and your kind heart. It takes a lot of courage to stand up for what is right and fight for it. I wanted to appreciate you that moment itself but I noticed that you were completely disturbed. After that incident, to my luck, I saw you on the beach. Even then, I thought I should talk to you but you left. The next morning, I went to the beach hoping that I can see you again, but I couldn't. I thought I lost you forever. But the same day, I saw you in college, that moment took my breath away. Your eyes pierced my soul. I couldn't believe my eyes. It felt like happiness came in the form of you. I wholeheartedly concede that, yes, I was attracted to your flawless beauty. No denial in that. Your eyes, your smile, your face, each and everything about you made me fall for you. I don't know why I feel sad the day when I don't see you. I have no idea how time just flies when I am around you. I experience different feelings when I am with you which I never experienced before with anyone. With each passing day, you gave me a new reason to love you. You held my hand, brought me to reality from fantasy. Ashritha! You are the kind of girl, any guy would ever wish for. I love you, Ashritha. I want you to be mine, forever" he said and held my hand. "And can you believe that I was never regular to college before I met you, even my mom was so surprised when she started noticing that I became so regular," he laughed. "Do you remember that day, you asked me how do I know your address? I followed you the first day when I saw you," he added.

I was totally taken back. The inner *me* was already dancing on *Sheila ki Jawani* track. He spoke again, "I promise I will keep you happy for the rest of my life. I am not saying these words to woo you or something; I really mean every word that I had said." I was literally on seventh heaven. I stood there, dumb, blushing. I wanted to hug him, propose him back but I couldn't do that. To be honest, I never wanted to get into a relationship before twenty-one. I had set my priorities. I had been a strong headed girl to get into IIM. But who would have thought that there comes a time in my life where a guy turns out to be my first priority. Yes! I loved him, I loved Akash. No doubt in that. But I wanted to be sure.

I looked around, the intensity of the tides increased, then I looked at my baby, it was digging burrows with its little paws. "How cute! But what should I name him?" I murmured. Akash shook my hand asking me to respond. "Akash. I do like you, so much, may be even more than that, but I need some time to think," I said looking away.

"Don't you trust me?" he asked disappointed.

"I do. But it's not about you, it's about me," I said holding his hand.

"Okay, Ashi. Think and tell me your decision." he said and kissed my palm. We left the place and he dropped me at my home.

“Thanks again, for the pup...Varun named it BRUNO :-)” I texted Akash after dinner. Everyone was so happy for Bruno. Varun had started feeding him continuously with biscuits and milk. Yes! It was him (Bruno). I checked it in the car itself.

“Bruno! Nice!” came his reply. Varun and I had a half an hour fight about the name. I insisted Rocky and he protested Bruno. Finally, he won because he owned the cutest cheeks.

“How was your day?” He sent a message again.

“Lovely! Definitely, it’s all because of you.” I replied and dozed off without waiting for his reply.

13.

"Akash, I'm so sorry," I apologized to Akash on text, one morning.

"For what?" He wrote back.

"I can't meet you this afternoon," I replied with a sad emoticon. We had planned to meet for lunch that day as it was a Sunday. The next moment my phone started ringing.

"Why baby, what happened?" he asked worriedly.

"You know my cousin, Deepthi right. She is pregnant and there is a baby shower function tomorrow. We suddenly got a call and we have to leave now," I explained him the entire scenario.

"Shit! At least you will come to college tomorrow, right?" he asked.

"No Akash. I will be coming day after tomorrow"

"What! Two days? No baby, I can't stay," he said like a little boy who would be going to stay away from his mother.

Yes! He is my acha bacha!

"And one more thing, Akash. That is a village, phone signals suck there, only BSNL sim works there and I don't have one," I added.

"I'm done baby. Two days… I just can't. I will miss you," he protested. He was completely dejected. "Please tell something to your parents and you stay back, let them go," he urged.

"I already did that. Mom didn't accept. I have to go, no other choice." I sighed.

"But, please at least talk to me on phone," he pleaded.

"Akash. Do you think I can stay happy without talking to you?" I questioned him back.

"No baby, but..." he paused.

"Just two days, Akash. I will definitely call you if I get any signal," I assured him.

"Please take care, Ashritha. I will miss you," he sounded low.

"Okay, you take care. Mumma is calling me, I have to leave, bye" I disconnected the call. He said he will miss me, but I didn't. But I knew that I had already started missing him. I tried convincing mom that I will stay back alone which she denied.

"Come, get into the car. We have to start now," she insisted locking the zip of her Baggit handbag. Dispirited, I occupied the front seat of the Mahindra XUV which dad brought from one of his friends as he was aware that our Honda city can't accommodate all the members of our family.

"Hello, Ashritha? How are you?" Deepthi Akka greeted me when she saw me entering the house.

"Hello, I'm good and congratulations," I wished and hugged her lightly. "Hey, can I touch your stomach?" I was excited seeing her balloon *kinda* stomach.

"Sure," she smiled.

"Wow, I can feel something," I said running my hand over her stomach. I was amazed when I felt some movement inside her womb.

"Where is Varun?" she inquired about my brother.

"He is sleeping in the car. Mom has to wake him up," I said removing my hand.

"Thanks for coming, Ashritha," she smiled and held my hand.

"Yeah you should definitely thank me, I left *my* Akash there and came for you," I murmured.

"You said something?" she asked failing to hear my murmurs.

"Nothing," I smiled and walked in.

"Come let's have lunch," Deepthi akka's mom, my *pedhamma* called us from the kitchen. It was exactly one. They already served us with coconut water, special regional sweets, and mangoes and then they started serving us the lunch.

"Did Akash have his lunch?" My heart was concerned. I looked at my phone, no signal. I wanted to slam it on the floor but didn't. I wanted to run away from there but couldn't. Apart from the stupid phone signals, Bheemili is an awesome village. When I was in school, my summer vacation destination would be Bheemili. The weather and the beach are the best things. But now, I was not able to stay in peace even for a single hour. People say things change when you are in love, like you start loving things which you hated once, like *rain* and start hating things which you loved once like *Bheemili* (a clear example). *Strange, but true.* Forcefully, we had lunch and then I dozed off thinking about Akash.

"Akka, I need to make a call, can I use your phone," I asked Deepthi who was busy in getting a Mehandi design.

"Yeah sure, it's there," she said pointing to the table.

"Whom do you want to call Ashritha?" my *pedhamma* asked in a way too loud voice.

"My friend Nisha, I need to inform about my leave tomorrow," I lied. She nodded and I came out. I dialed Akash's number. "Hey, Akash" I whispered when he picked the call.

"Ashritha, how are you?" he inquired tensely.

"What do you mean by how are you, I came here just a few hours back Akash," I whispered.

"I know but I am missing you," he said low.

"I miss you too" I murmured to myself. Yeah, it has been just a few hours but the feeling *I am away from him physically* was pricking my heart. In addition to that, the sucking signals. *Damn*!

"Please come back soon Ashritha. I'm dying here," he impelled.

"Yeah, we will return tomorrow evening… Listen. I have to go now," I whispered as I saw my mom coming towards me.

"It's not even two minutes. Please talk to me, Ashritha," he urged.

"Please… Akash, understand and do not call back on this number," I disconnected without listening to him.

"What are you doing here?" Mom asked me.

"I was just talking to…" she cut me off.

"Okay come. Everybody is waiting for you" she said pulling my hand.

"Mom, why would everybody wait for me?" I muttered. Moms just need a reason to make their children spend time with relatives which children openly hate. I never liked my relatives.

***

I sat there on the chair watching the rituals that were being performed. Women applying turmeric paste on Deepthi Akka's cheeks and making her wear glass bangles. In no time the bangles reached the elbow line. I asked my mom for the reason behind bangles worn to pregnant ladies.

"The child inside will start listening all the sounds. So the bangles help the ears function more effectively," she replied. Behind every custom an Indian follows, there is a definite scientific reason. Though the customs seemed really interesting, I just wished the function should end soon. I would just go back to my home and call Akash.

It was exactly five when all the relatives left. It was our turn. Then my *pedhamma* caught my mom's hand. "Sumati, why don't you stay back tonight and leave tomorrow," she came up with a really bad idea. Mom looked at me. I moped and I knew I would start crying if my mom said yes. She knew that as well so she politely denied saying,

"No Akka, she has college and even Varun's exams start next week."

My *pedhamma* seemed to be convinced and she nodded approvingly. I thanked God besides my mom. I sat in the front seat peeping through the closed window calculating time and distance. Well! Don't expect that I was solving some time and distance problems, I really suck at Maths! I was just pining to listen to Akash's voice. That afternoon when I called Akash from my sister's mobile, it said switched off for which I was pretty angry at him. I thought he would be waiting for my phone call but he switched off his mobile. "Ma. I'm thirsty, I want Coke," Varun asked mom rubbing his eyes,waking up from his nap

"Now? We will reach home in an hour. You can have it at home" Mom suggested.

"No, I want it now," he insisted.

"Okay dad, stop the car if you find any store or else he will start crying," I advised. He stopped the car near a grocery store. We got down. Other than Coke, Varun bought some chips, chocolates and many eatables which would suffice the following week snacks. As he finished gulping his drink, we moved towards the car. I turned my head side wards when I saw a familiar bike parked near the end of the lane. It was a black R15. I smiled in myself when I remembered that Akash has the same bike. Out of enthusiasm, I looked at the number plate which startled me for a moment. *Same number*.

How can two bikes have the same number? I looked around for the bike's owner. I could find none.

"Come Akka," Varun said pulling my hand. My mom waved her hand to cross the road. I slowly walked without looking at the road, my eyes were searching for the bike's owner. Then he came out of the store. A warmth gushed inside my lungs.I couldn't believe my eyes. It was Akash. *Is it a dream?* I wanted to run and hug him right away. He smiled and started walking towards me. I signaled him not to come. He stopped there and stood, glaring at me.

I opened the car door and sat in front. Though my heart commanded me to go and meet him, I couldn't. I noticed him from the rear view mirror following our car. Other than Akash there was some other guy behind him, he was Akash's classmate. Till then, my journey was boring, lengthy, but that moment when I saw Akash smiling in the mirror, I wished the journey to go endless. That moment I realized, that he missed me as much as I missed him, maybe he did more, that's why he came searching for me.

"Oh, his phone must have been dead, that's why it said switched off," I spoke to myself. It started getting dark and it became tough to spot his face clearly. He overtook our car while we were about to reach our lane. I jumped out of the car happily and I ran into my room while mom unlocked the main door.

I dialed his number, it said switched off.

He must be on his way.

I waited for some more time and then my phone buzzed when Akash called me. For the first few seconds, no one spoke. I was breathing heavily.

"Akash, why did you come there?" I asked him even though I was aware of his answer.

"Don't you know?" he asked back.

"Please tell me," I insisted.

"For you, I couldn't stay without you," he whispered. I did not respond.

"I tried hard to wait; counting minutes and hours, but it seemed difficult, so I just grabbed my keys and started. Distance doesn't matter when you want to meet someone special," he said. A tear rolled down my cheek. I found it extremely lovely. When someone misses you, when someone chooses to come for you rather than waiting for you to come, isn't it special?

It definitely is.

"Say something," he said. He spoke again, "Actually, I started in the morning itself. I couldn't find the address. We almost roamed every street searching for you, my phone was dead. I couldn't understand what to do. Dejected, we started our journey back but luckily I found you. That moment when I saw you, I can't explain how happy I was. I just wanted to come running and hug you so tight that my hug alone will brief you how much I missed you. My travel wasn't wasted; in fact, it's even more worth when I saw you smiling looking at me."

"Akash!" I called his name softly.

"Yeah baby," he responded.

"I really don't know what to say, but yeah! I did miss you a lot and I was so glad to see you there," I confessed.

"I missed you so much, Ashritha," he avowed.

"You must be really tired. Please have dinner," I suggested.

"Yeah, baby. I will text you once I get freshen up, I got to tell you one more thing," he said. "I bought a BSNL sim card, so next time whenever you go there, take this with you," he added.

My baby.

"Okay," I smiled. That night, I dozed off in my fantasy world called LOVE. A world where everything seems easy and beautiful. A world where you start believing in things which you never did before. A world where it feels other person's happiness is more important than yours. A world which makes you feel better amidst the hurly-burly of the life. A world where you see their flaws and fears but that doesn't affect your feelings for them instead you work together through all the phases. A world where the other person's existence in your life makes you complete.

14.

"Why are you making him wait for so long, Ashritha?" Nisha was yelling at me. We were sitting in the canteen.

Yes, it's been almost a month when he proposed me.

Bruno had grown up a little. It has become my mom's pampered kid, the entire time he would walk behind mom. Bruno occupied a special place in my life and his hair occupied my every dress. There were many changes in life. But things never changed between me and Akash. In fact, my feelings for him progressed. We met every day in college and sometimes outside too. Every time when he came to the point of my decision, I would switch the topic talking about things that made no sense. Even I felt bad about myself for making him wait when my answer was a yes.

Yes... I had some special feelings since the start. Many times, I found myself staring at his pictures, blushing. Whenever he talked to some other girls, I would get jealous. The possessive feeling that *he is mine,* engulfed me completely.

"Ashi speak out," she ranted with food stuffed in her mouth. I looked into her plate. She gently took a little piece of bread pakora and dipped it in the tomato ketchup numerous times until it turned into red colour substance which no one would never guess that it's a bread pakora.

Before I could respond, she spoke again licking her fingers "This is not fair, it's been almost one month."

"Can you please pass me the ketchup bottle?" she requested the guy sitting next to us and he did the same.

"Nisha, I have a doubt?"

"Tell me," said Nisha.

"The ketchup is the accompaniment to the pakora or the pakora is the accompaniment to the ketchup?" I asked her completely ignoring the things which she has been trying to put in my head.

"I think you should stop concentrating on my ketchup and start thinking about Akash," she mocked. She stopped neither eating nor taunting me.

"You know that I want to crack CAT, right?" I raised my concern.

"Yeah, so?" she looked at me.

"I don't know, I am just scared that these things will distract me," I conceded.

"Tell me one thing, you love Akash or not? Just a yes or no," she asked with a serious face.

"I do," I confessed.

"Do you think Akash is that kind of person who wouldn't support you?" she questioned again. I shook my head.

"Then those things don't matter, Akash and CAT are noway linked, you are getting it?" she asked looking at me. I nodded thoughtfully.

"Whatever, Ashi. Akash is a really nice guy, don't lose him. Sometimes not confessing at the right time, will make you lose a person for lifetime," she said and finished the entire bottle of Coke in one go.

She has a point, valid indeed.

"I will," I nodded briefly.

"*Chalo*... then see you tomorrow," she said and we dispersed.

***

I reached home and then Bruno came wagging his tail. "Aww, my baby," I kissed him as I took him into my hands. In no time, his tongue had explored every inch of my face.

"You are not eating well these days," Mom complained as she served a *roti* in my plate. People say… you don't feel hungry when you are in love. Well! I was in that phase. "Ashi, these days your brain isn't working well?" she said sitting next to me.

Did she get to know anything about me and Akash? My heart started beating fast.

"What happened?" I asked without making an eye contact.

"You forgot something. You don't remember?" she questioned back.

What did I forget? Did I forget to delete my chat? Did she read that?

"No Mumma, what's that?" I exhorted.

"Did Nisha bring the box which I gave her last time when she visited our home? Even in the morning, I reminded you," Mom asked bending forward.

"This is what you wanted to ask?" I raised my head.

"Yeah," she nodded eagerly.

"No, mumma. I forgot," I shook my head.

"Ask her to get that," she advised.

"Mom, it's just a box, what's the big deal?" I frowned.

"Big deal? It's my favorite box," she glared.

There can be a favorite dress, favorite sandals, but what's the business with the favorite box?

There is an imperishable bond between moms and utensils, which children can never understand. "Okay. Don't worry, I will ask and get it" I assured. She smiled and served an extra *roti* in happiness.

15.

It was seventeenth of November. I woke up with the usual morning drama, mom yelling at me for not waking up early and at Varun for not having breakfast. Anyhow, those things didn't bother me. The only thing that made me nervous was- it was Akash's birthday and I was going to gift him the best gift I could. Yes, I was going to confess my love for him.

I quickly rushed into the bathroom and started fetching for ideas. The bathroom is the best place to think and you come up with really nice ideas. In the combined process of thinking and bathing, an idea took birth. I decided to picture the entire plan. The initial plan was to go to lunch with Akash as he invited me personally and gift him the presents which I bought for him.

My phone started buzzing when I came out of the bathroom and I simply ignored that as it was a part of my plan. I felt it was important for me to look good on Akash's birthday. I wore a grey colored, long *kurta* with mirror work on it and orange color leggings with matching silver metallic ear rings that had orange beads. A little lip color and mascara finished the entire look.

"Ashi, anything special?" My mom asked at the dining table.

Yes, Mumma. It's Akash's birthday.

"No mom. Just casually," I lied. Love can make us do stupid things. Lying comes first in the list.

"Done!" Nisha high-fived me. I narrated the entire plan to Aditya, Vineet, Madhu, and Nisha. It was 10:30 am, our break-time. Akash and I meet regularly in every break. But according to my plan, I didn't go to meet him. I started smiling when I saw my phone ringing. I didn't pick the call though. Aditya, who was standing outside the class came running into the class and informed that Akash was heading towards our class. I hid under the table. My front bench friends Ramya and Teju covered me.

"Nisha, where is Ashritha? She isn't picking up my calls..." he asked Nisha worriedly.

"I have no idea Akash, even I have been trying her number. She didn't come to college," she answered so innocently that even I looked around to confirm whether I was really in the class.

'She deserves an Oscar for this,' I thought. I peeped through the gap and saw him ogling at his mobile worriedly. He wore a white and black checked shirt with his sleeves rolled up and black trousers.

"She called me at twelve to wish me. After that, no calls, no texts," he said lifting his head up.

"Yeah, she was awake whole night to wish you, she might have fallen asleep," Nisha lied again.

"But she promised she would go out for lunch with me"

Aww my baby!

"Okay, please ask her to call me if she calls you," he said finally and left. The same scene got replayed during the lunch and evening break too. He sent me a hell lot of texts inquiring my whereabouts. I thought of replying him back when I saw a text.

"Ashritha, I'm so worried...Where are you, baby? Are you alright? Please reply to me. I'm dying here." I felt pity for him, yet, I decided not to. It was exactly five when I sent a message to Akash.

"Akash, can you come to my class?"

"Oh God! You came? I will be there in two minutes," came his instant reply. Instead of waiting for him, I borrowed a scarf from Nisha and went to the parking and drove to the fixed spot.

"Yeah Nisha, tell me. Did Akash come?" I asked as I got a call from her.

"Yeah Ashritha, I said that you are waiting on the beach, he must be on the way," she said.

"Okay then, you guys come soon," I ended the call. I arranged everything and called Akash.

"Ashritha, where are you?" he was panting.

"You tell me, where are you?" I asked in turn.

"I reached, parked my bike," he said. I noticed him hurrying towards the shore and I hid in a stall.

"I am sorry Akash, I had to go home suddenly," I lied on the call.

"Ashritha, is this supposed to be funny? First you said you were in college, then beach and now home? I have been waiting for you for the whole day," he ranted.

"Really?" I tried hard not to laugh.

"Okay then, I am leaving," he said curtly.

"Akash listen, I forgot my bag there. Can you see it near the rocks?" I knew how stupid it sounded.

"Yeah," he said staring at the backpack.

"You can open it, I don't mind," I said smilingly. I packed a backpack with four gifts and four post cards stuck to each gift with a message on it.

Surprised why 'four'?

Well, it has been four months since I met Akash. I saw him walking near the bag holding his phone to his ear. As he unlocked the zip, he took a frame wrapped in colored paper. "What is this?" he asked in confusion and excitement.

"See it yourself," I scoffed. He gently unwrapped the frame and I noticed him smiling.

"These pictures! Wow, Ashritha, they are lovely," he exclaimed. It was a collage of my selfies in the beach when I saw him for the first time. Well! It wasn't me alone in the pictures; Akash too was captured in them, 'accidentally'.

"There is something written in the card stuck to it, can you please read it for me?" I asked as if I didn't know what was written.

"There isn't a single day when I wouldn't stop seeing these pictures. It makes me think, how magical the destiny can be! Isn't it surprising that we have pictures of us together even before we got to know each other? Don't you think that there is really some strong reason behind that? The day when I saw you for the first time, I can never forget the look in your eyes. That day I really had no idea that you would become so important to me. Thanks for coming into my life in the most unexpected way. Happy Birthday, Akash."

"Thank you so much, Ashritha," he fumbled for words.

"That's it? There are still things waiting for you inside the bag," I smiled.

He placed the frame on the sand and took out a rolled sheet of paper with a ribbon tied to it. He untied the ribbon and I found him staring at it in appreciation. It was a pencil sketch of his picture which I drew myself. It took a whole one month for me to get the perfection. He opened the card and read. "I am so obsessed with your charm that I couldn't stop myself from picturing you on a sheet of paper. I never tried drawing someone's picture till the date, but I wanted to draw yours and I finally did. Hope you will like it; please stick this in your room opposite to your bed (even if you don't like it)."

"I will and this is beautiful," he assured me on the call.

"Okay, C'mon," I said and he took out the third gift. It was a Nike biker's full coverage head band. "I love the way your hair catches my attention every time I look at you. You know that I like your hair so much. But I noticed that your hair started losing its shine because of the helmet. So please cover your hair with this band and then wear your helmet. I don't want you to get bald. Will you do it for me?" I could hear him laughing when he read the message on the card.

And last but not the least. He took out the greeting card which I had prepared myself. It was a blue card with red love symbols and few quilled flowers. He read out the quote on the card which I wrote with a glitter- "Before I met you, I never knew what it is like to be able to look at someone and smile for no reason. Thanks for being the reason behind my smile. Before I met you, I never knew what it is like to be able to stare at the wall and think about someone for hours. Thanks for being the thought in my mind. Before I met you, I never knew what it is like to love someone or to be loved by someone, thanks for being my love and thanks for making me your love"

"Ashritha, I want to see you now, right now," he insisted.

"I am right here, Akash" I stood in front of him. He was surprised to see me but he did not speak anything, neither did I. We were just lost in each other's eyes.

"Where were you the whole day? Why didn't you meet me?" He asked me.

"To see this surprise and happiness on your face," I smiled.

He held my hand and said, "Ashritha, when I proposed you, I knew that I loved you but today, when I didn't meet you the whole day I realized how empty I am without you. Even my special day seemed so bland without you. This moment I confess that you have become the most important part of my life and you will always be." He had tears in his eyes. He spoke again "Your surprises. They are lovely."

I held his hand, "Akash, the way you proposed me on my birthday, trust me, I never felt so special before. Whenever I look into your eyes, they entice me to such an extent that I just feel like spending the whole time looking myself in them. They make me realize that I am the only one in this world. They show me how much I really mean to you."

"When you came to check me when I was sick, when you came to Bheemili just to catch a glimpse of me, and when you fought with the junior for me; there are many such incidents which made me feel like no one can ever care for me as much as you do. I always wanted someone who would want me more than anything else and now I believe that you are the one and I know I am not wrong."

"Whenever my mom catches me smiling and she questions me, I want to concede, *it's is because of Akash*. Whenever, my friends talk about you, I want to say- *Yeah, he is mine*. I started discovering a whole new person in me, which I never witnessed before- a person who would get possessive about you, a person who would get jealous when you talk to someone closely, and a person who started imagining a future with you. I am a whole new person because of you.

Akash, we are in love with each other and we would always be together. In future, things might not be as easy as they are now, things might get tough, there may be ups and downs but one thing I want to tell you is- you are not alone and I am not alone, no matter what happens we are going to stick together through thick and thin, through light and dark, through joy and misery. I want to tell you that nothing can break us apart if we are strong enough to not give up on each other. You are that one person on whom I would never give up no matter what. I love you, Akash." A tear rolled down my cheek.

"Love you too Ashritha, I can never let you go," he said affectionately. We embraced each other completely ignoring that we were hugging in a public place. As I already mentioned, Love makes you do stupid things. It really does. A little drop touched my forehead, it had started raining, neither of us wanted to leave. We hugged even tighter. We didn't speak anything; there was a silence around us, the most beautiful silence which I had ever witnessed. No words can be more beautiful than that silence. Under the pouring rain, I was on my toes trying to reach his face, his left hand on my waist and his right on my face with his thumb caressing my cheek and lips.

I looked at him. I captured the apprehension and excitement on his face. Our lips quivered. And then he pressed his lips against mine. We were completely drenched in rain and love, at the same time. Despite the coldness, the tender touch of his lips kept me warm.

My first kiss, in the rain and on the beach!

Till then, I never liked rain, but from that moment, I started loving it. I just wished it should rain more, some more and then freeze forever.

Then they arrived Nisha, Aditya, Madhu, and Vineet. They couldn't see us kissing because of the rain. "Thank god!" I heaved a sigh of relief.

"Sorry, Ashritha. Because of this rain, we got late" Aditya said panting.

"Ho… it's a combined plan huh," Akash said staring at them. I blushed. He put his hand around my waist, pulled closer and hugged me.

"OHHO!" everyone clapped. We cut the cake they had brought to mark the beginning of our never ending relationship.

16.

"Love is in the air," I emphasized extending my hands.

"Acha!" Nisha scorned. Nisha and I were sitting in the canteen. "I find a lot of difference in you," she said lifting her brows.

"What kind of?" I retorted.

"Like you are happy, full of energy," she said sipping her juice. Well, she wasn't wrong though. I blushed instantly.

"Yes, because I am in love," I exclaimed again. When you are in love, things around you start looking beautiful. You find love everywhere. Every morning I woke up smiling and every night before I doze off, I would carry the same graceful smile and the reason behind that smile is Akash. I was cherishing a concoction of feelings. Feelings in which you feel hungry but you do not spare to eat, yet that doesn't make you sick. Feelings in which you feel sleepy, but you find nights as the best hours to converse. Our days started with a pleasant morning message and ended with husky sleepy voices with good nights and sometimes good mornings, too (As we would just talk till the break of dawn). My daily routine has changed completely. Sleepless conversations, endless chats, selfless love intruded into our lives.

Lying to mom, bunking classes in order to spend some quality time with Akash became routine, though these things seem little awful, the moments I shared with Akash remained priceless and gave me immense happiness. We all know that those things are wrong but everything seems fair in Love, everything seems right in Love.

Hugging in public, which I used to deem as a crime before getting into a relationship, turned out to be a mandatory thing between me and Akash which had to be done before parting away. Sitting alone, reading the long chats, smiling for no reason and blushing silently made people assume that I have gone mad but trust me- those are the real symptoms that you are in love. I learnt that love is a blend of copious feelings like happiness, caring, possessiveness, fights, arguments and sometimes pain too.

It wasn't like we never fought, we did. There were times when we argued and fought over silly things, but by the end, we compromised. Every argument we did and every fight we had, made us closer. Relationship with no fights has no life.

You are gauged as lucky when you have wonderful friends who understand you. In that case, I am something beyond lucky. I started spending my whole time with Akash. Even the time which I used to spend with my gang became a property of Akash. Yet, they never pointed out me. Maybe that's why people say friends are more understanding than boyfriend/ girlfriend.

In no time, we started appreciating each other's feelings and accepting each other's flaws. The only thing which I always despised about Akash is his smoking habit. No matter how many times I have pleaded him, warned him, threatened him I couldn't make him quit that lousy habit. But he had considerably reduced the count of cigarettes day by day. Whenever I caught him smoking, I would just say "I don't want you to be impotent" and he would simply throw it.

Being aware of the fact that, *every smoker wants to quit smoking*, I couldn't blame him much.

17.

"Please Mumma, just for two days," I beseeched my mom.

Sanjay, Nisha, Akash and I, had planned a double date to Araku for two days. Everybody was ready with their parent's approval. It was my turn to convince mom. I lied to mom that I was going with my gang. Though I felt very bad about that, I couldn't help it. "I don't know, go and ask your dad," she said in a firm tone.

"Please aunty, only two days, and I promise we will be safe," Nisha intervened. I had requested her to help me in convincing mom. She seemed convinced, at least that's what I thought.

"Okay but you have to return home before eight o' clock on Sunday night," she said showing me the index finger, dough spread all over her hand.

"Oh my God. Love you Mumma," I said pinching her cheeks. Nisha took the rolling pin from mom's hands and started making *roti.*

"But dad?" I said with a puzzled expression.

"I will talk to him," she said without looking at me roasting the *roti*.

"Thanks, Mumma. You are the best mom," I said and ran into my room to text Akash.

"Mission accomplished!" I texted Akash with thumbs-up symbols.

"Aww... Great baby! Love you so much." came his reply and then my cheeks turned red in the process of blushing.

"Love you too." I sent back

"Chalo then, I will pick you in morning at six o' clock, don't be late Ashi. Good night sd."

"Yeah, have dinner, love you loads." I clicked on the sent button and went to the dining hall. Mom and Nisha had started arranging the dining table. Nisha chose to stay back in our house so that we could start in the morning together. We ate in silence. I warned Nisha not to blabber in front of dad. Mom informed dad about our plan. I was expecting a storm but instead, he said: "Do you need money?" I was spellbound by his cool response.

"No Dad. Mumma has already given me," I said chewing silently.

"Umm okay. But, be careful," he said without looking at me. Nisha and I shook hands under the dining table.

***

"Hurry up Ashi, they are waiting already," Nisha was yelling at me.

"Yeah done," I said tying the lace of my Adidas sneakers. I wore a blue denim Capri, orange t-shirt, and a grey hoodie. I grabbed my bag which Nisha had packed last night and tiptoed outside. It was six in the morning; I didn't want to wake up mom so I left a sticky note on the fridge.

Akash and Sanjay were waiting at the end of our street in Akash's Volkswagen Vento.

"Sorry sorry sorry," I said occupying the front seat. Nisha and Sanjay sat behind. Within the next half an hour we were on the outskirts of Vizag, the cool breeze touched our faces that escaped through the open windows.

"*Kya karoon haye kuch kuch hotha hai*" was playing in the music system. Some songs don't fade with time, just like the memories.

"Akash, why don't you put on the seatbelt?" I asked Akash.

"Ahh… No Ashi, I don't need that. I am with you," he winked.

"*Acha*," I chuckled. Akash took my hand which was resting on my thigh and pulled it closer. He gently kissed my hand. He placed my hand on the gear rod and his hand on mine. He squeezed it gently making me feel butterflies in my stomach.

"I am hungry," Nisha shouted from behind. I pulled back my hand hurriedly breaking the romantic moment. Akash sighed. I laughed looking at his face.

"Aww, my baby," I pinched his cheeks.

"What happened?" Nisha asked confused.

"You won't understand" I chose to ignore her question.

We stopped at a road side *Dhaba*, had *chai* and breakfast. Our journey went on smoothly even on the rough roads because of the romantic songs that were played in the music system and with my hand on the gear rod and Akash's hand on mine, grasping it affectionately. As our car mounted the inclined roads of the hill, I sat peeping out of the window. Hanging my hand out of the window, I watched the sun playing hide and seek with the clouds, the birds flying in the foggy sky and the perfectly maintained vegetation around. After a one-hour long meandering ride, we reached the hotel.

We checked into our rooms which we had pre-booked and decided to meet after freshening up. As we arrived in our rooms, my heart started beating fast with the nervousness which ensued because of the thought that *I am going to share room with a guy*!

He is your Akash. My heart reminded me, after which I felt comfortable. We entered the room. It wasn't very spacious. But it was enough for two people. A cozy bed with a white bed sheet spread on it, a TV, and a small sofa with a coffee table just next to the window. The best thing I liked about the room was, one would get a spectacular view from the window.

I unpacked my bag, took out my toiletry bag and clothes and rushed into the washroom. I came back in cream color nylon cap sleeves top and knee length denim shorts. All four of us, reconciled at the parking at exactly eleven. The first visiting place we decided was Waterfalls. The roaring sound of the waterfalls beckoned us. I ardently peeped through the window with my face craning out of the window.

"Ashi careful," Akash warned me holding my hand when we were walking on the rocks. Araku is a hill with deep valleys. Just a slip from a rock will make you land in the valley. Dead.

"Ok baba," I barely cared as my enthusiasm went on increasing. It was my first time seeing real waterfalls until then I had just watched waterfalls in movies. Tons of gallons of water came running from the hills and slammed our heads.

Akash kept gazing at me when I was playing under the water. I held his hand and pulled him closer and drenching him completely even though he denied. He grabbed my waist suddenly and locked his eyes with mine. I witnessed a passion in his eyes. I could feel the warmth running inside me. He tightened his grip some more. "Akash," my voice shook as I squeezed his shoulder.

"I love you," Akash said with his eyes still locked with mine.

"Hello, love birds, we exist here," Nisha splashed water on our faces. And then began our game of splashing water on each other. As I tried escaping from Nisha, I ran and slipped on a rock and landed on my knees. I had a deep cut on my left knee from which blood started streaming. My ankle was sprained too.

"Ashi," Akash came near and sat on his knees.

"I told you to be careful," he said so worriedly and blew at my ankle. I tried curbing the pain and stood up to make Akash believe.

"It's nothing Akash. See, I can walk," I said trying to walk. But he wasn't convinced because it was visible from the blood that was flowing continuously. He took out a handkerchief from his pocket and wrapped it around my knee. And then we decided to leave.

While walking, Akash stopped me and said "Wait." He took my arm and he put it around his neck.

'Aww...I love this guy,' I thought. We somehow managed to reach the nearest stall where alive bamboo chicken and bamboo *biryani* was being cooked. We ate there and headed to Burra caves.

Though we live in Vizag. I had never been to Araku. The Burra caves were exactly the same like I saw in one of the Chiranjeevi's films. The guides came running towards us and then Sanjay kicked them off as he was familiar with the place.

As we entered through the steps, we were taken into a huge dark cave which was packed with tourists. The weather was too cold inside and I started trembling in my wet clothes. However, the dim lights inside kept me warm to some extent. I somehow managed to walk inside with Akash's hand on my shoulder. He made me climb up the narrow steps which led to a rock, on which we found the *Shivling*. I was mesmerized with the smell of rocks inside the cave and the sound of droplets which gently slipped from the rocks and touched the ground. Akash didn't leave my hand even for a moment. I loved the way he took care of me.

Being loved is a bliss. The intensity of your love thrives when your loved one is in pain or distress.

It was almost ten when we returned to the hotel with tired faces. We had our dinner on our way and got into our respective rooms. I sat under the shower for almost one hour as I had got completely tanned. I got into a pair of blue boxers and a white t-shirt and went into the room where Akash was watching TV lying on the bed. I slowly walked near the bed and adjusted myself.

"How's your leg? Show me," he said placing his hand on my naked leg. His touch, touch of his fingertips sent shivers inside me.

"It's fine Akash." I felt some tickling sensation and pushed his hand away. "You look so tired," I said running my fingers in his hair. I love his hair, thick and shiny.

"Yeah baby, very tired," he said and buried his face in my laps. My heartbeat raced, I began to move as his beard started tickling me. Still, I caressed his hair. He switched off the TV and slowly crept over me, pushing me on to the bed. No one spoke; there was a pin drop silence in the room. All we could listen was each other's heartbeat. We were just looking into each other's eyes. "Ashi, I love you," he said looking straight into my eyes.

I smiled, shifting my gaze down at his chest. His fingers ran over my face gently, pushing away the strands of my wet hair from face. He brought his lips on my ears, eventually switching on my estrogen. As I ran my fingers through his hair, he gently kissed my eyes, nose, and cheeks and then he came near my lips. I shut my eyes tight and then he touched my lips. The touch felt cold but the warmth of our bodies increased. I responded with more intensity but couldn't reach his. He vigorously ran his hand over my waist with his lips on my neck. I moaned as he tried bringing his lips on to mine. He swathed me in his arms so tight that I could listen to his racing heartbeat. I could feel his sweat on my body. I could feel his breath on my hair. As he tried flipping me on him, his leg collided with my injured knee. "Ouch!" I screamed in pain.

"Oops, Baby I am so sorry," Akash sat on the bed holding my knee.

"It's okay Akash," I held his hand.

"I am really sorry," he apologized again. I pulled his hand and made him lie next to me and then I looked into his eyes, those beautiful eyeballs and I confessed "I love you".

He came closer to me and embraced me tight. "Really? How much?" he asked playing with my hair.

"Umm… as much as my mom loves her Tupperware." He laughed loud and then I buried my face into his chest. It felt haven. I don't remember when I dozed off cuddling him like a little baby.

The hauling sensation in my leg woke me up. Being tired for the entire day, I had got into a deep sleep. It took few moments for my eyes to open and then I found Akash massaging my leg. I sat up with the support of my hands "Akash what are you..."

He cut me off in between. "It's almost done Ashi. You lie down" he said applying ointment on my wound and dressing it.

"You didn't sleep?" I asked him in surprise. I looked at my phone. It was two.

"No Ashi...I couldn't sleep," he said looking at me. I pulled him closer holding his collar and whispered "I love you Akash...love you for this."

His eyes twinkled in the brightness of bed light. "Love you too," he said and gently placed my leg on the bed and lay next to me. This gesture from him, gesture of his care left me totally surprised and happy. I placed my head on his chest listening to his heartbeat, fingers entangled which made me feel so safe that nothing bad can happen, we dozed off wrapped in a single blanket.

Fortunately, Akash's massage worked well, the wound and the pain were reduced considerably. We got ready and then headed to the coffee gardens. We explored through the Padmapuram garden discovering a variety of species of plants and even plucked few flowers secretly. The clay statues in the Tribal museum which resembled humans perfectly showcasing the regional traditional art and culture, confounded us. Later, Nisha and I dressed up in the regional attire and posed for few photographs in the coffee garden with crafted bamboo baskets on our back. We couldn't carry the moments with us so instead; we captured the photos which would reminisce the precious moments. We bought coffee powder to take it to home and I bought some handmade chocolates for Varun.

Around three in the afternoon, we returned to the hotel and everyone's face changed displaying the fact that we would be dispersing to our respective houses in few hours. So, we chose to stay back in the room and decided to start our journey back home around six.

Our room was engulfed with intense silence. The journey of the two most beautiful days had come to an end. Akash and I sat on the bed, facing each other with packed bags beside us. No one spoke. Finally, in order to break the silence, I spoke "Akash!" His head was hung low and I noticed him wiping his tears.

'Wait. What? Is he crying?' I was kind of shocked. When I placed my hand on his hand, I noticed a tear running down his cheek. I sat there doing nothing; moreover, I had no idea about the reason behind his tears. "Akash. Did I hurt you in any way?" I asked worriedly. He shook his head and continued sobbing. I couldn't see him crying. "Please tell me," this time tears filled my eyes too and my voice changed.

Finally, he spoke, "I don't want this day to end. I wish time shall stop, I want you to stay with me forever," he said holding my hand with one hand and wiping his tears with other.

I took his chin into my hands and whispered "Akash, we are not going anywhere, we are just going back to our home. Aren't you glad that we experienced beautiful moments here together?" He nodded. I continued, "And you are thinking about the present. Once imagine our future, waking up together with a pop kiss in the morning. Having breakfast, lunch, dinner together, going to bed together cuddling each other," his face lightened up hearing these words. "I am all yours and you are all mine. I will never stop caring for you, I will never stop loving you", I added. He finally smiled. He hugged me tight.

Then I said, "Akash Do you know every night before going to sleep, I imagine both of us getting engaged and getting married."

Then he said releasing me "What? You are still at the marriage? In my imagination, we are already having kids." I punched him on his ribs. We kissed and then started our journey back.

That day, I realized how pleasant it feels to be in love. A doubt whether he really loves me or not, had vanished completely that moment. There were no 'you and me', only 'us and we'. In everybody's life, there should be a person who appreciates your presence, who misses you in your absence and cries at the thought of losing you. That moment I believed that I had found my 'one'.

Sanjay drove on the way back and I had no idea when I dozed off on Akash's lap. He woke me up when we reached MVP colony. He managed to force a smile when I bid bye. They drove off, other than my backpack I carried a lot of memories with me.

18.

"Akash, I have reached, I'm right here at the entrance," I was yelling over the phone. He booked tickets for a movie in Vishaka Central and he was waiting outside the screen. As usual, being a girl I couldn't make it early, I reached late.

"I am waiting at the entrance too, I can't find you anywhere," he shouted back.

"I mean at the main entrance, taking the escalator," I answered back.

"Do you know, for how long I have been waiting here?" he shrieked.

"Bike didn't start," I lied. "He would kill me if I say the actual reason," I spoke to myself. Well, the actual reason was I couldn't decide what to wear. If you give one hour to a girl to dress up and get ready, she would spend fifty minutes on just thinking what to wear and she would finally wear the dress which she didn't even consider to wear in the past fifty minutes. He waved his hand when he found me and disconnected the call.

"That is why I told you that I would pick you," he said throwing his hands.

"Oops! The show started, I don't want to miss Mukesh's entry," I said pulling his hand referring to the person in the ad of tobacco awareness, generally played at the beginning of the show. He laughed and followed me. "He is cute na?" I said glaring at Paul Walker. We were watching "Fast and Furious 6".

"Yeah but not more than me," Akash chuckled.

"*Achaa*!" I said pinching his thigh.

"Yeah," he winked. It has been more than a year, Akash and I got into a relationship. We were more than a couple now. Entire college was aware of our relationship. His friends were mine and my friends were his. We would always try finding time to hang out together.

"Aah," he screamed in pain when I pulled one of his hair from the beard.

"Oops sorry," I apologized. He smiled. His eyes shone in the screen light.

I still remember the day when I sat next to Akash for the first time on my birthday. I was scared, I was cautious, kind of excited, shy, but now, everything had changed. I never knew that even the touch of finger tips of your loved ones would give you goose bumps. I never experienced that just a smooth rub on your cheek by your loved ones can make a chill run down through your spine. I never thought that just an eye contact with your love can make you forget the world around you.

No matter how costly the tickets might be, we would never watch the movie. we would just spend time looking into each other's eyes, holding each other's hand, tightening the grip with every passing minute. My other hand would be on his beard playing with it and my head resting on his shoulder and Akash playing with my silky loose hair and sometimes pinching my cheek, fondling my neck and kissing my palm affectionately.

We would just spend time talking until the fellow audience glared at us for the disturbance. We would just ignore that though. When you are in love, you don't give a damn about the people around you. You can spend your entire day staring at your loved ones, still you would fall less in time. You start talking about things that actually make no sense, still they listen to you patiently and interestingly as well.

"Come, let's go," he stood up breaking my thoughts. The movie was over, I stood up and we both walked out.

"I am hungry Akash, let's eat something," I said moping.

"Yeah baby, come let's go up," he said and held my hand. We took an escalator to reach the food lounge.

"Oh no! Sushma aunty," I uttered crouching down behind Akash.

"What? Who is Sushma aunty?" he asked looking around.

"There, the one at the Frankie stall in the blue sari," I said pointing her.

"So what?" he was still confused.

"She is my neighbor Akash, the BBC of our entire colony," I said and took him into the lift. "Thank God!" I sighed.

"So where do you want to eat now?" he asked.

"Anywhere, but let's move from here," I said and started my bike and Akash was on his bike. We reached the Dominos outlet in MVP colony and he ordered a farm house large pizza. We spent the waiting time in clicking selfies in Akash's mobile and I was scrolling through the pictures.

My eyes glued to the screen when I came across a picture of a girl. She was in a Denim mini skirt and deep V neck pink crop top exposing her cleavage.

"Who is she?" I asked sternly, showing the screen to Akash.

"Ho, she? She is my schoolmate, she is into modeling now," he sounded casual.

"So, how did you get pictures of her?" I said folding my hands.

"She sent those pictures to the school group," he shrugged. I scrolled down some more. There were pictures of her exposing her waist, thighs. She barely covered her body. Seeing those pictures, I couldn't control my anger. I slammed the phone on the table, took my keys and walked out, leaving Akash and the pizza behind. "Ashritha, what happened?" he came behind me near the parking.

I didn't answer, instead just stormed off on my bike.

Thirty-seven missed calls and fourteen texts- displayed my mobile screen when I reached my home. I ignored them.

"Done with the movie?" Mom asked me who was watching TV in the living room.

“Yeah mom,” I answered without looking at her.

“You should have invited your friends na,” she added. I had lied to mom that I was going out for a movie with my friends.

“They all left mumma,” I said and went into my room. My phone rang again, it was him. I didn’t pick the call. “Why would I?” I was fuming; I don’t know whether it is called jealousy or possessiveness, I just couldn’t imagine Akash staring at some other girl’s nude pictures. (Well! They weren’t completely nude, though.) “How could he? He knows that I look super-hot than her in those dresses. Eww, why am I comparing myself to her,” I spoke to myself. My phone buzzed again. This time I picked it up.

“What was that, Ashritha?” He shouted at me as soon as I picked up the call.

I should be the one who has to shout, right?

“How did you just leave suddenly without informing?” he yelled again. “Speak up!” this time he shouted loud and I started sobbing. “Baby, please don’t cry, just tell me what happened?” he pleaded softly.

“Nothing, I want to sleep,” I countered.

“Do you think I will let you sleep like this, crying?” I loved his answer.

“Those pictures,” I said, wailing.

“Those are nothing, Ashritha. Why are you so worried about those?”

“I just couldn’t imagine you looking at those pictures,” I wailed.

“Trust me, she sent those in our school group, Ashritha. I swear.” I pictured him pinching his neck.

“You should have deleted them, right?” I asked again.

“Those were automatically saved from WhatsApp. I will delete them right now.” He appealed. “Please stop crying baby.”

“Mm,” I said wiping my tears off.

“But promise me one thing,” he asked.

“Tell me,” I sat on my bed.

"That you will never leave like that suddenly. If there is some misunderstanding, we will sit and solve it or if there is something which you don't like just tell me, I will rectify it," he said without taking a breath.

"Sorry," I apologized.

"No baby, don't be sorry. I don't want any sort of misunderstandings because of some other person."

"I love you Akash," I confessed.

"Love you too baby. Love you more," he said and gave me a telephonic kiss. "Ok then have dinner and sleep, see you tomorrow in college," he said

"Okay but delete those pictures, okay?" I whispered as I saw Varun coming into the room.

"Haha, my baby is so jealous, huh?" he teased me.

"Of course, you are mine, only mine," I demanded.

"Okay baby, I'm all yours, have dinner and sleep." We disconnected the call with a lot of telephonic kisses. I smiled rolling on the bed holding my bolster.

"Ashi come, let's have dinner," mom shouted from the drawing room.

"No Mumma, I am not hungry. I ate already," I shouted back. I lied, though I didn't eat, I wasn't hungry. Happiness filled my stomach. It is strange how a person's words can melt our anger. It happens when you are in love or when you are with your best friend. The happiness in the compromise after a huge fight, doesn't match with anything.

I dozed off happily dreaming the most beautiful dreams.

19.

"Yeah, dad. I will be back soon...drive safe," I said closing the car door. Dad dropped me and Nisha outside the function hall and he drove off. It was Akash's elder sister, Anjali's wedding. Akash had invited me personally and warned me to come in traditional attire as it would be the best occasion to get closer to his family.

"I'm not able to carry this, Nisha," I said lifting the lehenga with both hands till ankle length to have a comfortable walk. I wore an orange and blue colored lehenga with stone work. I wore it in South Indian style exposing my flat waist slightly from left with simple gold necklace and *Jhumkas*. I put on mascara and a little lip gloss. I set my hair loose.

"Haha. I can see that in your walking style," she chuckled. She wore a simple Anarkali suit and straightened her hair. Then Akash came near the entrance to receive us. He wore a white shirt and ash colored suit with leather shoes. His hair was lightly gelled that perfectly matched with his dress. He gave me an admiring look as he noticed me walking and finally said "Ashi, you look stunning."

"You are not looking any lesser mister," I winked at him.

Then Sanjay came there, "Ashritha, is it really you? You look gorgeous."

"Oh, really? What about me?" Nisha intervened.

"You always look stunning, my babe" Sanjay pinched Nisha's cheek. I smiled in response. I observed Akash's chest swelling with pride.

"This is what I like about South Indian girls, they can carry a pair of shorts and a sari with equal grace," he added. I noticed Akash's pride slowly turning into possessiveness. Every girl loves it when her guy gets possessive about her. "Okay let's go inside," Akash intervened and we moved inside. "Mom! Ashritha here, Nisha and Sanjay," Akash said.

"Namaste aunty," I greeted her.

"It's nice to meet you again," she said putting her hand on my shoulder. She wore a dark green silk sari with pink border. The extra shining diamond necklace around her neck glittered in the lights. "You are looking great today," she pinched my cheeks as I smiled. He introduced me to his father as well and some of his cousins. Akash got over-possessive that night when he noticed one of his cousins staring at me without even blinking.

We went up to the dais to wish the couple.

"Hi Ashritha. You look good in real than in pictures," Akash's sister Anjali said.

"Thanks," I said and smiled. Akash's sister was aware of our relationship. We spoke few times over call but never met face-to-face. She resembled her dad whereas Akash resembled his mom. The groom looked just like any typical software employee, nevertheless, he looked decent. I gifted a beautiful painting of Lord Radha Krishna which she loved a lot.

"Thank you so much Ashritha. It's beautiful," she said elatedly. We posed for a photograph and then got down. Despite the heavy *lehenga*, I still managed to hold the plate and had some *pulao*, mushroom curry and a *gulab jamun* in the dinner buffet.

Post dinner, we sat on the sofa, and the marriage ceremony had started. Before getting into relationship, I was never interested in attending marriages. But from the moment, I had fallen in love with Akash, I never missed any. I would sit in the first row observing bride and groom and imagining me and Akash in their places. When you are in love, you start observing happy couples so keenly that you end up imagining yourselves in their places.

Akash stood on the stage stealing glances. He winked at me gesturing that 'you and me' would be in those places and little did he know that I was already flying in my own imagination world. Mom kept calling me continuously. I promised her that I would be back by 12 o'clock and it was 12:40 am. Sanjay chose to drop Nisha and Akash came to drop me.

Akash stopped the car almost at a distance of twenty feet away from my home. The roads were dark and deserted. Well! Those street lights which were blinking occasionally didn't count. He held my hand and whispered "You really look stunning."

"Yeah I know," I grinned. He pinched my cheeks, he always loved doing that. "Akash, we would be getting married in front of our relatives, friends like this. Aren't you excited about it?" I asked holding his hand.

"Excited? I am badly waiting for that day," he chuckled.

"But what if our parents don't accept?" I exhorted.

"They will. My parents will accept because I will tell them that your son can't be happy without Ashritha and then I will get a job, I will come to your parents, convince them by telling them how much I love you, that I will be taking very good care of their daughter and then I will make you mine and then there will be no looking back. We will be cherishing every moment of our lives, together. You and me, together forever." He finished and kissed my palm.

"Love you Akash," I confessed as he gently kissed my lips. A dog's bark startled Akash, breaking our kiss. He dropped me and he drove back. I didn't text him as he was busy with the marriage, I just rolled over the bed thinking about the night which would make us one with the three precious knots.

20.

It was the end of our third year and our seniors had hardly one more month in college and many multi-national companies started visiting our college for the campus interviews.

Akash had cracked Wipro interview with an initial basic package of 3.3 LPA. My happiness knew no bounds. The moment when he shared that news with me, I found myself in tears. I was extremely happy for his success. Maybe that is called Love when you deem your loved one's success as yours, when you want to see them winning. Love is one such selfless thing.

The only thing that made me extremely sad was days would not be the same. He would be leaving to Pune for training. I sometimes cried during nights at the thought of missing him and then I made myself strong by telling myself that we will be away for only a few months and time flies. After all, that is all I could do.

I knew that I would miss him in the college canteen, in the library and he will be leaving Vizag. More than me Akash was sad. He once told me that he can't go so far leaving me behind. Actually, I wanted to ask him to stay back, but how could I? His career was more important and it mattered to both of us. I made him strong that we will be in contact with Skype regularly.

***

Exams ended and slowly everybody started getting their call letters. Akash was mailed to report on 3rd July at Pune. Barely, two months left.

The thought, *Akash is going far away from me*, started jabbing my heart. I never missed a chance of spending time with him. We spent most of the time together. Every alternate day I lied to mom that I was attending some java classes and went out with him.

We would spend our time in movie theatres, talking about the days ahead, we walked through the sea shore holding hands, looking into each other's eyes which were moist and consoling each other that distance doesn't matter as our hearts would always be together. We got even more intimate during the last days. We couldn't sleep during nights. We would just sit holding the phone at our ears listening to each other's breaths and sometimes wails.

When you want the time to fly, it becomes a turtle. When you don't want the time to pass, it flies at a jet speed. Maybe, it's just our presumption.

Days passed and finally the day arrived when he had to leave for Pune.

21.

"Please say something, baby," Akash held my hand. It was around six in the evening. The sun began to set slowly. We came to Kailashagiri. A hill at Vizag from where you get a spectacular view of the city. It is famous for the huge statues of Lord Shiva and Parvathi. It is always packed with couples to such extent that, you find couples romancing even in the clump of bushes. We were lucky enough to find a cemented bench which was facing the RK beach.

"Are you alright?" he asked while we settled on the bench. I nodded without looking at him.

"No, you are not," he concluded. That was his last day in Vizag. *How was I supposed to be Okay?*

"I will miss you," I conceded without making an eye contact. I knew that my tears would become unstoppable if I look at him.

"Ashritha, do you think I will be happy without you?" he scoffed. He held my face in his hands when he noticed tears rolling down my cheek.

"Ashritha, do you love me?" he asked looking into my eyes.

"Don't you know?" I asked with tears in my eyes.

"Please baby, then don't cry. I can't see you crying," his voice changed.

"It's definitely not easy for me to leave the person whom I love the most and going far, you don't want me to go? Please say yes, I will stay here with you like always," he said bending down to look into my eyes. I shook my head.

"Say yes," he had tears too.

"No Akash, it's not like that, it's just…I will miss you," I stammered and buried my face into his chest.

"Just three months Ashritha, I promise. After training, I will come to Hyderabad, that would be little easy for both of us," he said tugging the strands of my hair behind my ear. I nodded sobbing.

"By then, you will be taking CAT exam for MBA and you will be getting into IIM and then I will shift to Bangalore with you. We will be together, see… just three months, right?" he said raising my head holding my chin. I wished it could be that easy as it sounded. I looked into his eyes.

"Won't you miss me?" I asked without breaking eye contact. He shifted his gaze away.

"I will," he sounded low. I noticed the sudden change in his face.

"Akash," I whispered.

"I am just trying to make you strong; you don't know how much I am scared to be away from you. I will miss the way you make me feel about me. I will miss the way you take care of me. I will miss holding hands with you like this," he said eyeing the hands we were holding. He had tears in his eyes. There was a sudden change in the weather. The sky was spread with the dark huge clouds. The howling gales took control of the trees as they swayed lamely.

"Akash, I want to kiss you," I demanded as I held his hand tight.

"Now?" he frowned.

"Yes," I ordered.

"Baby, there are people around us, seems like it would start raining too, " he said staring at the sky.

"Let's go to the beach," I was determined.

"Are you sure?" he asked again when the winds started blowing heavy.

"Yes," I affirmed. As we were getting down the hill on the bike, it started drizzling. The crowd at RK beach disappeared. We could barely spot any person there.

"Akash, you remember, this is where we met for the first time?" I asked as I stood holding my sandals in hands.

"First time for you, second time for me," he reminded pinching my cheeks.

"Yeah," I nodded. We strode along the shore holding hands. As the grip of our hands tightened, the intensity of rain increased.

"Akash, will you promise me one thing?" I asked as I stood facing him.

"Sure," he nodded.

"I never knew that I could get into a relationship with someone so deep. When I first saw you here, I knew that it was really something different. And now, I know that we are going to stay together, breathe together, and leave the world together. I can never imagine my life without you. You are so special that even words can't explain. I love you so much; I just wish that these three months without you will fly away quickly." I paused when it became tough to breathe. Besides the water drops on my face, Akash could spot the tears and he held my face in his hands. We were completely drenched in rain, and in pain.

"Please try to quit smoking. It's not a restriction, it's not for me, and it's not for you," I sobbed.

"It's for us," he completed. I lifted my head to look at him, he smiled.

"I will definitely try," he added. I buried my face in his chest, I sobbed at the thought that *I can't hold him like this from now on whenever I want to.*

"Please don't cry," he was crying. The sky was crying too. Our hearts took a vow that no matter what happens, they will not let the distance separate them.

22.

"I have reached, Akash. I'm at the parking," I disconnected the call, parked my bike and hurried towards the departures. His flight was at 9:15 PM.

As I took an escalator, I noticed few faces which ousted with excitement and happiness at the arrivals section waiting for their loved ones to come and at the departures, people with pale faces and teary eyes, biding their hardest goodbyes to their children and spouses. Airport is a place of mixed feelings. I found Akash's mom holding his chin and wiping her tears with her *pallu.* He waved me from a distance and I started walking towards him.

"Hello, aunty. Hello, uncle," I greeted his parents. They just smiled. Akash came near me. I smiled, or at least I managed to fake one. He was left with only ten minutes to check in. I took out a small box which was wrapped in a colorful paper. He opened it and he was surprised when he saw the gift. It was a square-shaped transparent crystal paperweight that had a carving of our picture. It was a selfie that we took on his sister's marriage.

"This is amazing. This goes first on my desk," he said excitedly and carefully kept it in his shoulder bag. Then I took out a greeting card and handed him, he opened it and read-

"I will miss you when the dawn breaks; I will miss you when the dusk falls. When the rain falls and when everything looks bright and beautiful, I will miss you. When the leaves shed and when everything seems dull and gloomy, I will miss you. I will miss you when I am happy, I will miss you when I am sad. I will miss our cuddles. I will miss our kisses. I will miss holding your hand when we walk together, I will miss looking into your eyes when we talk to each other. I will miss you every moment of a day which I am going to spend without you. But my love for you will never change as each day goes by, I love you till the day I leave this world."

He lifted his head to look at me. My eyes were already moist, I looked away to stop the tears but they didn't. He held my hand. "I love you Ashritha," he said and hugged me and my forehead touched his chin. Then, he kissed on my forehead. It was very gentle and affectionate.

His mom looked at us with her mouth open. I bade him good bye with my best wishes and I drove back home with emptiness in my heart.

23.

"What happened, Akash? Is everything alright?" I enquired when he sounded low. It was his third day in Pune away from me. No response.

"Akash! Are you there?" I spoke again. My hands trembled. "Akash please don't be upset, what happened just tell me," I pleaded.

"I miss you Ashritha, I miss home. Everything is new here," his voice sounded very low.

"Akash, just three months right, try making new friends, talk to them after that, get posting in Hyderabad or Bangalore," I tried to console him while I was crying on the other end. I put my hand on my mouth, heaved a sigh and then continued again, "You have to be strong Akash. Do you think I'm not missing you here?" I questioned back.

I couldn't control anymore and I started crying too. "Akash I'm missing you. I thought it would be okay, but it is worse than I have ever thought. I never knew you would become such an important person in my life. I am just physically here but my mind is not with me. It's been only three days but it's like ages," I said sobbing. He cried with me. I could hear him sobbing. We cried together. I never wanted someone who would make me smile all the time. I just wanted a guy who would cry with me in my tough times. I consoled him, caressed him and finally, he smiled. That day, I decided that I would start spending much time with Akash over calls and texts. That is all I could do, to make him forget that *he is away from home.*

I stopped going to my CAT classes on weekends and would stay in my room for the whole day with my phone, writing texts and waiting for his. The first two weeks without him were a real struggle to me. I tried coping up with things around me physically but my mind couldn't help with that. Though there was nothing I could do from my side, I just started enduring the toughest phase of my life.

24.

"Baby, I got my first salary. Yayy" I read a text from Akash when I woke up. Instantly, a smile crept over my face. It's been a month since Akash joined the job, but it felt like a year. He got habituated with his flat mates and colleagues. He narrated me about his office, colleagues and he showed me his flat over Skype call.

People say love increases when it comes to long distance relationships. We spoke about everything, no matter how many hours we spent talking, we never fell short of words to say.

We got so intimate in love.

"Congrats baby, I'm so happy for you," I wrote a reply and got off from the bed. From the day Akash left for the job, I never left my mobile even for a minute. I always waited for his texts and calls. The first thing in the morning I did as soon as I opened my eyes was checking my mobile expecting a text from him. My phone beeped.

"I'm so happy, so tell me what do you want?" was his message. He wanted to buy something for me with his first salary. Though I liked the importance for me in his life, I didn't want him to spend his first salary on me.

"Akash. I will tell you but promise me that you will do that for sure," I wrote back.

"Ashi, go and bath, it's getting late," Mom shouted from the kitchen.

"Yeah, Mumma. I will." I shouted back and didn't move. I was waiting for his reply.

"Yeah, baby tell me," he sent reply in a minute.

"Buy a sari for your mom, a shirt for your dad and with remaining money get goggles for yourself. You told me that it is being tough for you while riding bike," I typed smiling.

"I want to buy something for you Ashi," he sent a reply with a pouted emoticon. I laughed out imagining him with that expression.

"Akash, family comes first. You can buy me with your second salary," I sent and left for the bathroom. My mom caught me smiling at the dining table for the text Akash had sent me- "You are my family too. But the way you put my parents above you, I love you for this."

"Why are you smiling, Ashritha?" mom asked me, feeding Varun. Dad lifted his head to look at my smiling face.

"Nothing, Mumma. Just something I remembered," I lied.

"Ho, really? Tell me too." Mom asked me settling down in the chair.

I am dead.

"Yesterday, Our English madam caught Aditya who was having lunch during the class. Madam questioned him and entire class started laughing," I started narrating the scene which happened in our first year.

"Um... then?" Mom was listening to my story.

"Then he said, 'Madam during lunch break, Vineet eats my box, he does not even let me have a single spoon. Today my mom made chicken, so I'm afraid that I wouldn't get a chance to taste if he gets to know that my mom prepared chicken. So I am eating it now.' He admitted innocently. Everyone in the class broke into laughter." I finished the short story, biting a piece of omelet. Mom laughed.

'Well done Ashritha, brilliantly escaped,' I appreciated myself.

That wasn't the only incident. My mom had seen me many times when I was blushing during our chats, when I spent most of my time on calls, when we Skyped. Though she found that something was fishy, she never asked me.

***

My attendance was back to normal because the main reason behind my bunks was in Pune. Nisha turned dull as Sanjay left for Bangalore for his training. She is such a lively girl full of energy. Never, I had seen her like that. Still, I never gave up trying to bring a smile on her face with my lame jokes amid the fact that I was missing Akash. With each passing day, I started missing him more and more. He got busy in his training, assignments, and exams. He barely had time to talk to me.

I understood his situations and never bothered him. Whenever he had assessments and slip tests, I would set alarm for myself and then I would call him to wake him up- just to be sure whether he was studying or not.

During weekends, he would spend the whole time roaming around and partying. I just always warned him to drink in a limit. He started adapting to the new culture very quickly, which I couldn't digest that quickly.

But I never told him how I felt, missing those old days. After all, life is about changes. I just wished that he would finish his training successfully and get posted to Hyderabad.

25.

"Hey, Ashritha. Great news!!" he shouted in happiness and that excited me.

"Yeah, Akash tell me," I sat cross legged on my bed to hear that good news.

"I cleared my training," he whooped.

"Oh. That's really great, congrats baby," I said pleased. "So how much percentile did you get?" I asked him.

"Uff...What will you do with the percentile? I know that you study better than me, you need not belittle me asking about percentile," he shot back.

"Akash, I never said that. Why would I belittle you? Why are you thinking in a negative way?" I asked him wanting him to realize. I seriously had no intentions of such kind. I just wanted to extend the conversation.

"Listen, Ashritha. I'm in no mood to fight with you," he shot back.

"Fight? Do you think I'm fighting with you?" I asked softly.

"Ashritha, please!"

"Okay sorry, leave that. I am happy that you have cleared your training, at least today we can talk in peace," I smiled taking the pillow into my laps.

"No Ashritha! We are celebrating. We are going out," he answered in a rush.

"But Akash, it's been many days. We haven't been spending much time on calls. Please talk to me for some time," I urged.

"No Ashritha, I can't. Anyhow you have your friends, you will not miss me. I am leaving. Bye!" he mocked.

"Akash, that doesn't make any sense." All the response I got was the beep sound. Yes! He disconnected the call. He really did. For few minutes, I couldn't understand what was happening.

"Did I speak anything wrong?" I questioned myself. I failed in figuring out the reason for his rudeness. Without my knowledge tears rolled down my cheek. Later, I consoled saying he must be busy with his friends.

That was one such unusual argument we have ever had. It didn't feel right. His odd behavior, careless words didn't let me sleep. It was something which he never did before. I started over-thinking about the reason behind his weird behavior and dozed off when the dawn broke.

***

"Why are you so dull?" Aditya asked me in the canteen during lunch. Vineet, Madhu, and Nisha lifted their heads to look at me.

"Me… dull? No," I said smiling. I smiled overly, trying to make them believe because Aditya wasn't wrong. I couldn't concentrate in the class. I was just thinking about the reason for his behavior and just kept on checking for his message.

"What happened, Ashritha, tell me?" Nisha asked me in the restroom. I broke down narrating the entire conversation.

"Cool down. It's nothing serious," Nisha said calming me down. I sobbed.

"Maybe he was offended when you asked about percentile," she said patting my shoulder.

"I never had any bad intentions, Nisha. Why would I offend *my* Akash?" I stressed on 'my'.

"I understand Ashi. Just tell him sorry when he calls you tonight. These kinds of arguments are common and he might be really busy with his friends," she said brushing my hair. I nodded sobbing. "Arguments and fights are temporary but love is permanent, got it?" Nisha smiled. I smiled back. After all, she is the senior to me in the class of love.

The best thing which I like about Nisha is that the biggest problem on the earth is so minute for her and if it is a minute, it is not at all a problem. She is a positive girl who fills positivity and smiles with the people around her. Some people call her crazy but they don't know that her love is unimaginable. But I'm glad that Sanjay realized that.

***

It was nine when I finished my dinner and was waiting for Akash's call. My phone rang and I picked up it on the first ring. "Hello Ashritha," he sounded normal.

"I'm sorry, Akash." I apologized.

"For what?" he asked me.

"For yesterday, I never thought you would get offended," I explained.

"Oh, forget it. I don't remember all that," he cut me off.

'What don't you remember? That, you did hurt me with your words and you disconnected the call so rudely?' I wanted to ask him but chose to ignore.

He is not angry at me.

"Thank God!" I sighed. "So tell me Akash. When are you getting your locations? When are you coming to Hyderabad?" I asked him excitedly leaning on the pillow.

"Hey, I forgot to tell you".

"Forgot what?" I asked in confusion.

"We got our locations Ashi, yesterday itself," he said chomping his food.

"Oh, really?" I asked him. Though I was angry at him for not telling me about the locations, I didn't want to nag that. "Hyderabad, right?" I asked expecting a yes.

"No Ashi. I didn't opt for Hyderabad. Got Pune itself," he said happily. I couldn't understand three things- first of all, he didn't opt for Hyderabad. And then he got Pune and strangely, he was happy for that. Lastly, he didn't tell me all those things.

"Why Pune, Akash? Hyderabad would be easy for both of us to commute whenever we want to meet, right?" I asked him

"No Ashi. It's good here. I like the culture here. Moreover, I have all my friends here," he said without any hesitation.

Oh. He likes the culture over me.

"But Akash, we thought…" he cut me in between.

"Please, not again Ashritha. I'm tired, I will call you tomorrow," he disconnected the call. I couldn't hold the anger anymore. I dialed his number back.

"I told you that I will be calling you tomorrow, right?" He shouted at me as soon as he picked up the call.

"Do you remember that we are not spending time on calls like we used to? I never forced you to talk or message me but can't I expect at least ten minutes of your time. I am missing you, Akash. You don't know how I am feeling here surrounded by your memories," I was on the brink of tears.

"Ashritha, stop missing me," he answered.

"Missing? You are not missing me?"

"It is not about that Ashritha."

"Akash, what do you think, you don't care about my feelings?" I shouted back.

"Damn feelings Ashritha? Why do you keep aggravating every small thing?" he yelled.

"What did you just say Akash?" I sobbed. "I am aggravating on small things? Here, I am waiting for your calls daily like a mad girl and have been dreaming that you would come to Hyderabad," I said sobbing.

"Please don't cry, it's irritating," he shouted, which made me cry even more.

The person once who couldn't see tears in my eyes is now saying that it's irritating.

I just wailed. He disconnected the call. He left me alone when I was crying. I slammed the phone on my bed and wept. I couldn't grasp the change in his behavior. I felt lonely, I felt empty. Later, I consoled myself saying, maybe he had a bad day at work or maybe he really doesn't like Hyderabad.

Poor me!

***

"What am I doing? Akash is staying away from home and moreover his work pressure, office tensions. I should be the first person to understand his situations and support him, instead I'm fighting with him," I woke up scolding myself. I decided "no arguments or fights with Akash from now on." I pulled out my phone and texted him,

"Good morning baby, sorry for whatever happened last night." No reply. I assumed that he might be sleeping and I went to freshen up. It was 10:30 am, break time, I checked my mobile expecting a text from him. No calls, no messages. I got worried. I thought of calling him, "He must be in office. I can't disturb him." I dropped my idea of calling him. I just waited for the rest of the day. It was eight in the night when I was worried and decided to call him. "Hello, Akash. Is everything alright?" I asked tensely.

"Yeah, Fine," he answered curtly.

"Then why didn't you text me since morning?" I made sure my voice is not sounding rude.

"Listen, Ashritha. I'm in a movie with my team-mates. I will call you later," he cut the call. I stared at my mobile screen. I was scared for a moment.

"Is he really *my* Akash?" I started doubting. I thought of calling back and shout at him but couldn't. I didn't want to hurt him. I leaned on the bed staring at the ceiling. Few tears rolled down my cheeks. I cried, cried and dozed off with blood shot eyes.

26.

There were only five minutes left for me to turn twenty-one. Everyone slept. I sat on my bed holding the phone expecting Akash's call. It was my first birthday away from him since our relationship began. I thought he would come but he said that he spent all his leaves on roaming the city with his friends. I didn't want to bother him either. But somewhere in my heart, I thought he would surprise me. We, humans, tend to have expectations.

I was startled when the doorbell rang suddenly. I walked to open the door. "Is it Akash or did he send his friends to celebrate my birthday?" A thought popped up in my mind.

"Happy Birthday Ashritha," Nisha, Vineet, Madhu and Aditya shouted as soon as I opened the door. Nisha jumped in to hug me. I was totally surprised.

"Everyone must be sleeping. Come out, we will celebrate outside," Vineet said and we walked near their bikes. I checked my phone. It was 12:02 am, no call from Akash.

'Signal must be weak.' I thought. Then I checked it and it showed full signal. 'Maybe his,' I assumed.

"Come, come; cut the cake," Aditya unpacked the cake box. Nisha lit the candles and handed me the knife. I cut it, offered cake to everyone and they chose to slam it on my face rather than eating. Mom and Varun came out hearing the noise. Varun was too sleepy to wish me but he ate a big slice of cake. Nisha clicked few selfies in the deadly darkness.

"What happened? Aren't you happy for this?" Nisha asked me staring my pale face.

"I am so happy," I lied her. Yes, I wasn't happy. The one who has to wish me first didn't even call me. "Nisha, one moment," I stopped Nisha who was about to start her bike. "Whose idea is this?" I asked her wanting to hear Akash's name.

"Aditya's. He insisted that we should make you cut the cake at twelve," she said pointing Aditya.

"Thank you Aditya," my words filled with gratitude.

"What? Only thanks? I want a treat," he protested.

I smiled. "Definitely." It was 12:40 am when they finally decided to leave. They wished me once again and drove off. Dejected, I came into my room. Yet, no call from him. I don't remember when I dozed off crying.

***

"Helloooo" I snoozed without opening my eyes.

"Happy birthday Ashritha," said the person, from the other side. I woke up immediately recognizing the familiar voice, I looked at the screen. It displayed Akash. I sat on the bed pushing the blanket away. "Sleeping?" he asked again.

"No, tell me Akash," I spoke pleasantly expecting him outside my house.

"Happy birthday Ashritha," he wished again.

"Thank you, Akash." I was overwhelmed with his wishes. "Where are you?" I enquired

"Woke up just now," I could hear him yawning.

"Sorry, Ashritha. I couldn't call you at night," he said convincingly.

"At least he didn't forget," I thought. "That's okay Akash. You must be tired." I helped him in convincing me.

"Actually, I had set the alarm, but couldn't wake up," he said and laughed. He couldn't wait till twelve, so he set the alarm and then that failed too.

"Oh." That was my response.

"Okay, then have a nice day, I will call you later," he said and cut the call. I couldn't move. It was my birthday. He didn't wish me first, no proper wishes, no proper apologies. I just couldn't believe that it was Akash who was speaking to me so carelessly.

***

"What happened, Ashritha? Why are you so dull?" Nisha asked me placing her arm around my shoulder. It became a daily task for Nisha 'sensing my gloomy face and enquiring if everything was okay.'

I shook my head. "Nothing," I said without looking at her. We were sitting in the classroom. It was lunch break.

"Don't lie. Even at night you weren't happy. I thought of asking but couldn't as aunty was with us," she said again.

"Nothing, Nisha. I will be back," I said and hurried to the washroom. Standing in front of the mirror, I felt something was missing. I looked at my dress. I wore a light green long cut chiffon chudidhar. It looked perfect. I looked at my gold ear studs which mom bought for me. Even they looked perfect. Lastly, I looked at my face. The charm, the happiness, the smile, were missing. I never wanted my birthday to be special. I just wanted it to be a normal day. It wasn't good, not normal either, worse than normal.

I could no longer hold my tears. I buried my face in my hands and broke down. I didn't know the exact reason for my sadness, but I clearly knew that I was missing something. I let go all the pain and washed my face and returned to my classroom with a smile which wasn't real.

***

Tears gushed from my eyes when I was driving back home. Not because of the dust in my eyes but because of the pain in my heart. When Aditya and Nisha asked that we would go out for dinner to celebrate my birthday, I denied.

Akash would call me, so I didn't want to miss talking with him. The noticeable change in Akash's behavior kept disturbing me.

"You came so early, I thought you would spend time with your friends," Mom said looking at me who was watching TV.

"No Mumma. I'm having little head-ache so I came early," I said removing my sandals.

"Oh, is it? Go and change your dress, granny will give you a head massage," she said standing up. Granny who was sitting next to her, nodded approvingly. My granny gives the best oil massage.

"No Mumma. I will just sleep," I said walking into my room. There were days when I used to run behind my granny with coconut oil pleading her to give a massage. She puts love in it.

"Okay, you sleep. I will wake you up once dinner is ready," she shouted from the drawing room. Waiting, thinking and crying, I dozed off. I woke up with Akash's call around eight.

"Hey Ashritha, how was your day?" he enquired.

"Not bad," I wanted him to ask why it wasn't good.

"Umm… okay. Had dinner?" He asked without worrying why my day wasn't good.

"Not yet," I cut off.

"Okay then. Have dinner and sleep," he tried to end the conversation.

"Akash, it's my birthday!" I shouted

"Yeah, I know," arrogance in his voice.

"Can't you give at least ten minutes of your time on my birthday?" tears flooded out of my eyes.

"Offo! Why do you get emotional for everything Ashritha?" he shouted.

"Do you know that I have been waiting for your call all the day?"

"Did I ask you to wait? No, right?" I couldn't speak. I couldn't answer to his stupid logic. I just sobbed.

"Bye Ashritha!" He cut the call. He couldn't wait for my response, he yelled at me on my birthday, and he didn't even ask me to stop crying. The man once who waited excitedly to propose me on my birthday and once who wanted my birthday to be special, now couldn't give at least 10minutes of his time. I never forced him to talk to me in the entire work phase. But it wasn't like I didn't want to talk to him. I just waited so that he could finish his work and call me. Just five minutes of conversation affectionately was all I wished for.

Humans create their own heartbreaks through expectations. There were times when he cried with me but now he is irritated. This is what people call CHANGE? I know change is inevitable, but not so soon, at least not this way.

"I will not let the little temporary misunderstandings and small fights cease our relationship." I decided.

27.

Slowly, the ratio of calls and messages decreased. He never spoke to me the way he used to speak with me when we were together. Our conversation stopped exceeding five minutes. But I never stopped waiting for his calls.

One night I decided to end the misunderstandings between us. I decided that I would compromise. I didn't want to lose him at the cost of our ego. I finished my dinner early. I was constantly tossing and turning on the bed waiting for his call. "Hey Akash," I tried sounding happy.

"Hello Ashritha," he sounded low.

"So how was your day?" I asked trying to know his mood.

"Ashritha, I have something to tell you," he opened up.

Aw, my baby, I know that even you are feeling bad about our fights.

"Yeah baby, tell me," I sat on the bed.

"Ashritha. I don't think the magic between us still exists. I just want to ask sometime so that I could figure out the reasons behind these and we will resume it again"

"Magic? Time? Is this what you wanted to discuss?" My voice trembled so did I.

"Yes," he shot back.

"You are not joking, right?" I asked him again.

"Why would I joke with you Ashritha? I'm pretty serious," he almost yelled.

"What is the reason behind all these things, Akash?" a tear fell on my hand.

"I feel like I'm restricted in a closed room. For some days I want to be free without any commitments like love," he said.

"You are calling it a commitment, I call it a relationship and I never restricted you," I stammered.

"I know, but please understand, give me some time to think." He appealed.

"Okay, how much time do you need?" I asked wiping my tears.

Please say a day or two.

"Umm… maybe a month," he answered without any guilt.

"A month? Can you stay a month without talking to me?" I started wailing.

"I don't know. Give me some time." He disconnected the call. I dialed back. No response.

"Is he my Akash? Is he the one who once won me with his love? And now, he needs time to think about his decision?" The complete days which I had spent with Akash flashed in front of my eyes.

I wanted to feel the warmth of his hug, smell the odor of his shoulder, run my fingers through his hair, look into his electrifying eyes and confess "No matter what happens in the world I can't lose you." I didn't give up calling his number, and then I got a text from him.

"It's for us Ashritha. Just give me some time, stay strong."

How am I going to stay strong, when he is my weakness? How am I going to smile when the reason behind the smile is abandoning me? How am I going to sleep in peace, when the person in my dreams stops visiting?

I spent a sleepless night, crying and praying that Akash should come back to me. I just wished he would call back which didn't happen. I consoled my heart saying “Everything is going to be fine. He is just disturbed because of the things happening between us. Even he can’t stay away from me. He will call back.” My head started aching and I fell asleep.

***

The morning I woke up with a wet sensation on my fingers’ craning my neck out of the blanket to look at Bruno. He stopped licking and started wagging his tail as soon as he saw me.

“Oh my baby,” I pulled him up and it started rolling on the bed pushing me. I looked for my phone. No messages, no calls. My heart pricked; still I dialed his number- switched off. I didn’t make eye contact with my mom that morning as my eyes were swollen and she could easily figure out. Entire day, I spent dialing his number and wrote numerous texts. Nisha, Aditya, and Vineet everyone tried their best to lighten up my mood but they failed to bring a smile on my face.

“Come Ashi, let’s go for lunch,” Nisha stood up taking her bag.

“You please go. I am not hungry,” I answered without looking at her.

“*Acha*, don’t you remember that Akash handed your responsibility to me, he would kill me if he comes to know that you are starving,” she said, bringing her hands to her hips. I wished he should kill, I just wanted a small sign that he still cares for me. All I was craving for was his call, his care, his attention, his love. I managed to eat four spoons of rice and dal. I wasn’t hungry. You don’t feel hungry for two reasons, when you are happy and when you are not.

Yes, I wasn’t happy, I wasn’t thirsty, and I wasn’t hungry. Actually, my mind wasn’t there. It was busy in searching for possible ways to get my love back.

You know what hurts you the most? The person to whom you once meant the world, who couldn’t imagine their life without you, who couldn’t stay away from you, suddenly acts like they don’t need you anymore. The ‘unwanted’ feeling starts killing you from inside. You still smile because you don’t want people to know since they can only listen, they cannot feel what you are feeling. The pain will be yours. *Only yours*.

***

"Ashritha, can you tell me your phone number?" Rajesh, our class CR asked me. He was collecting everyone's number as he lost his previous mobile.

"Okay," I told my number and he left. "What happened?" I asked Nisha who was glaring at me.

"It isn't your number, Ashritha," she looked straight into my eyes. Yes. It wasn't mine. It was Akash's. That moment I realized how desperately I was waiting for Akash's call. I took out my mobile and dialed his number. Switched off. I took my bag, bike keys and started walking out.

"Where are you going?" Nisha asked from behind.

"I am not feeling well, I will go home," I answered without turning back. I drove off; I couldn't feel anything happening around me, not the horns of the vehicles on the road, not the chaos of the people, not the sun that has been striking directly at my face. I could feel nothing.

I drove until I reached RK beach. I sat there exactly when I saw Akash for the first time.

But today, I feel a void created by his absence.

There were missed calls from Nisha and Aditya, I ignored them and dialed Akash's number- switched off. I kept scrolling the mobile reading our old conversation, at a point of time, I stopped scrolling, I read a message,

"Ashi, I really don't know what I did and what I was like before you came into my life. I mean, I barely remember anything, but when you walked into my life, with that enticing smile, I cherish every moment spent with you. The way your eyes smile, when they find me. The way your lips lit up a smile when they talk to me. I never knew that you would become my lifeline. I smile when I think about you. I laugh when I remember your arguments. Mostly, I am glad that you are in my life. You are like my dream that came true. I don't know whether my words express how I feel about you, but you always hold a special place in my heart and in my life."

I noticed my thumb quivering on the screen. The screen was blurred or maybe my eyes were. I looked at the place where Akash stood staring at me. I still remember his smile. The mobile dropped from my hands lacking strength. I couldn't hold my tears. I buried my face in my hands when tears became unstoppable. I noticed few people staring at me with pity, I wiped my tears.

It was seven; I didn't want to go home. I just wanted to sit there and cry for the whole night. I looked at my phone, forty-seven missed calls- five from mom and the rest from Nisha, Aditya, and Vineet. None from Akash. I didn't want my parents and friends to get worried about me when I was least worried about myself, so I drove home. I called Nisha on my way and informed my whereabouts.

"You weren't picking calls, where were you? And why does your face look so pale?" Mom showered questions at me when I stepped in.

"Yeah Mumma, sorry. I was playing badminton with Nisha and my phone was in the bag," I said removing sandals.

"Oh okay, go and freshen up., I will call you once I finish cooking," she said and walked into the kitchen. I walked in without making any eye contact. In between "Faking illness to grab the attention of our parents" and "faking wellness to avoid tension to our parents" we all grew up.

I sat under the shower letting myself drenched in the cool water running from the shower. I came out rubbing my hair with the towel. I threw the towel aside and jumped on to the bed when my mobile buzzed displaying Akash's name.

"Hello, Ashritha," my name sounded so sweet.

"Hello, Akash. How are you?" my eyes became wet.

"I'm good. How are you?" He asked me softly.

"It was like hell till now. But you are back now, I'm so happy," tears rolled down with happiness and I didn't stop them.

"I am sorry for whatever happened," he apologized.

"Please don't be sorry. Just please don't let the misunderstandings spoil our beautiful moments," I said wiping my tears.

"I missed you so much Akash."

"I missed you too," he confessed. After so many days. He said he missed me, he said he loved me. My happiness knew no bounds. *Finally, My Akash is back. I will never let him go.*

"You are so happy. What happened?" Mom asked me at dinner.

"Because you cooked chicken today," I said pointing to the plate. She laughed.

Finally, I won my love back. *I don't need anything more than this.* I slept happily cuddling Bruno.

28.

"Please Ashritha, just five more minutes," Akash insisted. It was around nine and I was on the call with Akash. Yes, Akash was insisting me to spend time on call. After that fight, though I can't say that we were completely fine, things were definitely far better than worse. There were few misunderstandings and fights; still I chose to put my focus on the best parts of our relationship.

"You there?" Akash inquired. Well! I didn't want to end the call either but my dad asked me to meet him after dinner to discuss something. Well, I knew what he wanted to discuss.

"Akash, please understand, I have work," I tried convincing him.

"What is that work? Tell me," he asked again.

"It's nothing Akash, I will call you back soon," I whispered as I saw Varun coming inside my room.

"Dad is calling you," he said playing with a tennis ball.

"Yeah, coming… two minutes," I answered Varun and he ran out bouncing the ball. "Bye Akash," I disconnected the call without waiting for his response. 'Akash, please don't be angry. I am doing this for us,' I spoke to myself.

"Yes dad," I said and sat on the couch. It was exactly 10:15 am when I came to my room wiping my tears off. I unlocked my phone and read the texts which Akash had sent me. "I never knew there are things that you hide from me, I am alone here and you don't even care to talk to me for few minutes. I am really hurt." I smiled and dialed his number.

"What?" he almost shouted as soon as he picked up the call.

"Aww, my baby is so angry" I changed my tone to babyish. Akash loved it when I did that.

"Please stop it Ashritha," he ranted.

"Don't you like it when I talk like this" I laughed.

"I said stop pretending like you care for me," he shrieked again.

"Why would I have to pretend when I actually do care for you," I smiled.

"My friends are correct, girls are like this only," he murmured.

"What did you say?" I wasn't smiling anymore.

"Yeah, you heard it correct. Now, Akash is far away and he is nothing to you, isn't it?"

"When did I say that Akash and why you are so upset all of a sudden, what did I do?" I was on the verge of my tears.

"You have to know what you did," he mocked.

"Akash, dad wanted to discuss something and I had to go," I shouted as I wailed.

"Who knows? I am not in Vizag. So you can do whatever you want and I would never come to know anything. Even if you lie, I would never come to know the truth, right?"

"What? Do you doubt me? Don't you know anything? I share everything with you. I tell you what I did entire day. And you do know about my friends- Nisha, Adi. There is really nothing to hide from you. Please don't talk like this." He cut me off.

"Stop it, Ashritha. Adi, Vineet, please stop it. Every single time…"

"Akash, they are my friends, please, you know that too," I wept.

"So, I am nothing to you, right?" he scoffed.

"Akash, how relevant is your question? You are the most special person in my life."

"Oh please! Stop saying that," he said contemptibly.

"I mean it."

"Bye Ashritha, I got to go," he disconnected the call.

Please don't do this Akash. Dad is already angry with me. Please talk to me. This is for us.

I dozed off weeping.

29.

My school-mates had planned for a get-together, though I was least interested, I chose to attend it as nobody knows when I could meet them again in life. I slowly started losing interest in things which weren't related to Akash. Every single time, my friends would plan some outing and I would cancel it at the last moment. Though I was guilty of that, I couldn't forcefully push myself into things in which I wasn't happy no matter how much I tried. After our fight that night, he called me in the morning and apologized for his behavior. He never spoke to me like the way he did that night, I could sense carelessness in his words.

Well, to be frank, his words really hurt me deeply, but I couldn't be angry at him for a long time.

Akash is my weakness! I never ever thought that a guy could rule my mood swings.

Well, they planned the get-together in MGM water world. Out of forty-five students, almost forty attended. To be frank, I actually didn't expect such a positive number. I thought only a few extroverts would be coming. Well, I was really happy to meet my childhood friends almost after five years.

"Hey Ashritha, how are you?" Nikhil my classmate since sixth standard came to me during lunch and greeted me. Nikhil, being a poly technic student, he directly joined B.Tech after tenth in the second year in Gayatri College of Engineering. I heard that he started working in some MNC.

"Hey, Nikhil I'm good ...what about you?" I greeted him. For few minutes we spoke about my studies and his job and then he asked me.

"So you are in a relationship with Akash, right?"

I nodded with puzzlement and asked, "How do you know?"

"We work in the same team and we were in same training batch too," was his answer.

"Oh okay," I smiled

"Are you guys really serious about the relationship?" he asked sipping his cool drink. I found his question really weird.

"Of course yes," I shot back. "But why are you asking like this?" I asked him confused.

"No nothing, so how is your aggregate?" he asked trying to switch the topic.

"No, tell me." I insisted.

"*Arey...* Just normally," he said adjusting his rimless spectacles.

Nope, something is wrong.

"Hey Ashritha, come, let's ride the roller coaster," my friend Sravanthi shouted excitedly pulling my hand.

"One-minute, Sravanthi," I said letting go of my hand. Nikhil and I exchanged our numbers. Later in the afternoon, I couldn't enjoy the rides; I was lost in my own thoughts.

"You guys are serious about your relationship?" That was the question which didn't leave my mind. "May be he assumed that we are just dating," I answered myself.

After reaching home, I don't know why that thought came into my mind. I logged into my FB account after many days maybe like four months. After few minutes, I found myself glued to the laptop, scrolling his profile. There were more than thirty new posts on his timeline. There were some photographs too where I couldn't believe my own eyes.

My heart started beating fast as I came across a picture. A girl stood next to him and Akash's hand was on her waist. I checked her profile too. Arpita Singh, a Delhite. She was fair complexioned and had a tattoo on her neck. She wore a bodycon mini dress in that picture. My index finger trembled on the mouse pad. My lips dried. The screen got blurred.

"Is he cheating on me?" - was the first question that came into my mind. "No no, he can't, they might be just friends, even Vineet and Adi touch me, *but they never touched my waist*. He really loves me." The optimistic me defended him again. But I couldn't understand why the optimistic me, couldn't stop the tears from streaming down.

"Hey Nikhil, what was that, you were trying to say?" I texted him that night, out of uneasiness.

"Hey, hii...I will be leaving to Pune tomorrow. I will ask about everything and will let you know," came his reply.

I can't wait for so long. How can I sleep in peace, how can I eat with desire, how can I pass the day, with these thoughts running through my mind?

I was completely stressed out mentally. If it is a physical stress, it has an expiry but if it's a mental one, it will start eating you from inside. Every second seemed like an eternity, there was a continuous battle in my mind with both the defending and accusing thoughts and I couldn't sleep even for an hour. The breakfast and dinner which I had forcefully stuffed into my mouth, I puked. My stomach burned. I couldn't concentrate in any class. I didn't speak to any of my friends though they tried to know the reason behind my silence. I didn't tell any of them not even to Nisha. I just waited for Nikhil's call.

"Am I spying on Akash? He regretted the ignorance, we are happy now. He apologized for his behavior and harsh words. He loves me, he really does." Lot of thoughts popped up.

"Hey Ashritha. How are you?"-came Nikhil's text around nine.

"Hi, you found something?" I replied instantly. I didn't bother to answer his how are you nor did I ask him how was he.

"Mm… yeah. There is a girl named Arpita in our team. She is from Delhi. They say they are just friends but I felt there is something fishy between them. Now I confirmed that I am not the only one who deemed their relationship odd, many of my friends in our team have the same feeling." His reply sent shiver in my body. He sent me a message again "I know you from sixth standard, you are a very nice girl. I'm just concerned that you shouldn't have any false hopes on him. That's it."

I couldn't reply. I dialed Akash number to ask everything straight. I disconnected the call. "Why should you believe Nikhil so easily, Ashritha? Don't you have a conscience? You know what your relationship with him is," my heart questioned. "But what is the need for Nikhil to accuse Akash?" My mind questioned.

"May be because people are so judgmental to misunderstand their friendship?" My heart intervened again. "People are judgmental but how can everybody say one point in common?" my mind spoke with logic. I felt a twinge in my heart. At some point, I blamed myself for not having trust for my love and at some point; I cursed myself to come into reality.

If I ask Akash, he would feel so bad because the one who is ought to believe him, started doubting him.

Akash called me that night. I tried hard not to sound low. I thought I would ask him and clear all the doubts. But I didn't, actually, I couldn't.

"Akash, is everything fine? You want to tell me something?" I asked expecting an explanation.

"No, why?" He asked me back munching his food.

"Nothing," I lied. He spoke about his office and friends but he did not bring up her name. Finally, I said "Okay, Good night," and disconnected the call. This was the first time I disconnected the call without waiting for his response because I couldn't hold my tears anymore. I couldn't sleep in peace. "Whom should I believe? Akash or Nikhil..."

"How stupid are you Ashritha, you are comparing Akash with Nikhil?" I scolded myself. The battle between my mind and heart continued and I couldn't decide whom to believe.

30.

It was fifteenth of November. Akash's birthday was on seventeenth. Nisha, Aditya, Madhu, Vineet and I had always wanted to go to Shirdi but every time we planned, something happened and the plan got canceled. This time I definitely wanted to make it so that we can visit Shirdi and throw a surprise to Akash on his birthday in Pune. My main intention was to meet Akash directly, clear all the misunderstandings and come back happily. Even my mom was so convinced about our Shirdi trip and everything was set.

I warned my gang not to post anything on Facebook about our travel and plan as I wanted to surprise Akash. I was so excited about the thought of meeting my love after almost eight months.

"Careful," Vineet said holding my hand while getting down from the train. We reached Sai Ram station and headed towards the accommodation we had booked. We got freshened up and dressed up in new clothes which we specially bought for the darshan. I wore a white cotton Chinese collared kurta with orange leggings. I couldn't hold my tears when I saw the statue of Sai baba, it felt like Sai baba sitting there alive and looking at us affectionately. It gave me goose bumps. I just wanted to stand there looking at him without blinking but the security didn't let us stay there more than 30 seconds, we came out and got astonished when I saw the dresses of baba preserved in the Sai museum, there were long Kurtis and a pair of sandals. The kurta itself was of six feet length and that made me believe baba had a stout personality.

We had free prasad and free lunch served by the temple committee and headed towards the stalls.

I bought bangles for mom and grandma, Sai Baba crystal idols for dad and grandpa, T-shirts for Varun and a neck chain for Bruno. I bought a pair of ear rings and bangles for myself. We finished our shopping and went back to our rooms and then again visited the temple for evening h*arati*. I was totally mesmerized at the simplicity of Baba. I wondered and appreciated the builder of the statue. It was so graceful; I couldn't blink my eyes staring at it.

After the *harati*, I closed my eyes and prayed for prosperity and healthy life to everybody. We reached our rooms tired and dozed off. We boarded the early morning Srinagar Shirdi train at five. I enjoyed the sunrise sitting near the window. Nisha, Vineet, and Aditya were sleeping in their berths. Though I tried making myself comfortable in the berth, I couldn't sleep. With each passing minute, my excitement increased. I opened my backpack and took out the gift I had bought for Akash. It was a Fossil wrist watch. I took out a blank empty card and started scribbling,

Akash, I know this wouldn't be the best gift on your birthday, but I hope the good news that I am going to tell you would be the best present ever.

You remember the night of our argument. My dad called me to discuss something and you were pretty angry at me for leaving you when you actually wanted to spend some time talking to me. Do you remember? Do you know what he wanted to discuss? It's about my decision to pursue my MBA in Pune, for which he is totally against. Yes, I got an admission in Symbiosis Pune. You know how stubborn I was to join IIM Bangalore. Do you know that it took one month for me to convince my dad? He stopped talking to me for a week. Later, Mom convinced him saying even Symbiosis is a good University.

Do you know why I did that? It's not for me, it's not for you. It's for us.

Because if it is Pune, we can meet whenever we want. I will be just a phone call away, whenever you feel like meeting me. Whenever you are low, I would be there to cheer up or if I fail in cheering you up, at least I will be there to lend my shoulder for you to cry on. It's not the disputes that have been convoluting the things between us, it's the distance. So, I thought why it can't be that I too move to your place. And I also know that you would feel guilty for my decision, my request is please don't, whatever I did, it would give me happiness which IIM couldn't. I have already been missing you from months. The wait is over. I can't wait to experience our old good days again. This is a way to tell you, that you mean more than anything in this world to me.

Happy Birthday Akash. Love you more with each passing day.

"You didn't sleep?" Aditya asked me getting off his berth. I shook my head.

"Excited?" he asked as he sat in front of me.

"Yeah, I am going to see him after a long time," the excitement ousted my face. He nodded soberly.

"You told Akash about your Symbiosis thing?" Aditya enquired.

"No, I will tell him today. I can't wait anymore to see him," I said rubbing my hands.

"Is uncle still angry with you?"

"Pretty much," I sighed.

All of my friends were aware of my MBA program. Nisha scolded me when I admitted my decision to her. "Are you kidding me?" Nisha rebuked me in canteen one day.

"Why would I? I am pretty serious," I answered softly.

"You wanted to go to IIM Bangalore, then why this change, all of a sudden?" she frowned.

"Things are not going well between me and Akash, I can't stay away from him, and he is my weakness," I confessed.

"But aunty and uncle? Are they fine with this?"

"Dad is pretty angry, but I am sure he will be fine," I said without looking her. She nodded steadily.

"Akash is really lucky," Aditya said breaking my thoughts.

"You really mean that?" I asked raising my brows.

"Of course," he shrugged.

"I think we have to wake them up, we have almost reached," Aditya said glancing from the window. It was eleven when we finished breakfast in Pune. I called Akash.

"Happy Birthday Akash!" I shouted as soon as he picked the call

"How many times are you going to repeat the same?" he said hesitantly. I chose to ignore that. I called at twelve and then sent many wishes through texts.

"Okay tell me, where are you?" I asked him.

"I'm in office. I will call you in the evening," he whispered.

"I will meet you in few minutes," I murmured.

"What?" he asked again

"Nothing. Love you." I was so excited. Within an hour, we made all the arrangements, bought a cake, candles, snow spray everything and reached a cafeteria near his office. I called Nikhil to make it a complete surprise to Akash.

"Hi, Ashritha. What's up?" Nikhil said after picking the call.

"Hey listen, can you ask Akash to come down, don't tell him anything. Just ask him to come to the office main gate," I pleaded him.

"What? Are you in Pune? But Akash isn't in office. I didn't see him since morning," he said

"What? He said he is in office," I replied in confusion.

"Wait let me call him and then I will call you," he said and disconnected the call. Aditya, Nisha and Vineet were looking at me in excitement. But I wasn't excited anymore. There was confusion around me. I signaled them to wait.

I got a call, "Ashritha, he is in his flat. It is just a kilometer away from here. Flat no-401," he said. I thanked him. We reached the flat.

"Happy birthday!" we shouted in unison as soon as Akash opened the door.

"How come you are here? And suddenly?" he asked nervously. I couldn't see any kind of excitement or happiness in his face. He was in boxers and shirtless. He was sweating profusely.

"Will you keep asking questions or will you let us come inside?" Nisha asked Akash and he opened the door completely.

"Who is she?" Aditya asked pointing his finger to a girl who came out of the bedroom. I turned my neck side wards to look about whom Aditya was asking.

There was a cigar in her hands and the smoke made tough for me to look at her face. I squinted, "I know this girl, I have seen her somewhere," I murmured trying to remember.

Yes! She is Arpita Singh.

She was in boxers that ended near the butt line.

"She is my friend," Akash stammered.

"What is she doing here, Akash?" I shot a direct question. She walked towards the balcony.

"Nothing, she has just come to wish me," he said in a defensive tone.

"But what is she doing in your bedroom," I walked straight and then Akash tried to stop me. Nisha, Adi, Vineet, and Madhu excused themselves and walked out. I pushed his hand and hurried to the bedroom. The blanket was laid down in a clumsy way, room stunk with the cigar, empty beer bottles rolling on the floor, the whole room was a mess and then I found an awful thing on his bed. It took few moments for me to realize that it was a condom. Akash held his head. My heart skipped a beat. I stood there frozen. There was a dreadful silence.

"Did you sleep with her?" I asked looking straight into his eyes. He looked away.

"Eye contact," I ranted.

"What do you want?" he shouted back.

"Just a yes or no."

Look into my eyes; you will get everything you want. If that doesn't suffice, I will try giving more. Please say no, just a no... My heart pleaded.

"Yes."

His answer whacked me in my heart. I winced. My body trembled on my legs, hands froze in the air. I couldn't look at him, not a tear came out of my eyes. I couldn't see. I couldn't hear. I couldn't cry. Something has clogged my throat. I turned back and ran out of his flat. My head whirled. I hurried down, ran through the steps tentatively helping myself from not to fall, until I reached the cellar. It got tough for my knees to hold my weight, they wobbled and I collapsed on my knees. Nisha came behind and held me by the shoulder. That's it, I broke down. Tears flooded through my eyes.

Nisha held me tight. I was puling with my shoulders flumped.

"Please don't cry, Ashi," Nisha said, indeed she was crying too.

"Such a bastard," Aditya was fuming. Not the bad words Aditya was using to abuse Akash. Not the soft words uttered Nisha to make me stop crying. Nothing worked. I was just lost, completely lost. There can be nothing worse than seeing your love sleeping with someone. It's better to die than to cry in the pain.

"Ashritha listen. I can explain," Akash came there. He held my hand, I pushed him away.

"Don't you dare touch me," I shouted. "Aditya, please ask him to leave," I said sobbing.

"How could you do this to her? Are you a man?" Aditya held Akash by his collar. He pushed him away.

"Ashritha, listen to me once." He spoke again.

"What do you want to say Akash? Do you want to describe me how you had sex with her?" Nisha asked with a repellent expression on her face.

"You lied to me about everything and I trusted you so blindly. You said you were in office; I went there and then you were in your flat romancing with her. You ignored me, you neglected my feelings, took me for granted... Still, I never stopped loving you; I just remained silent so you took advantage of my silence." I cried. Nisha tightened her grip on my shoulder. She didn't leave me even for a moment.

"Please stop vexing Ashritha. Why are you so emotional? You are over protective," he said without a speck of guilt on his face.

"Emotional? Don't you remember that you said you loved me for being emotional? Isn't *love* an emotion? Answer me," I shouted back. He looked sideways.

"Whatever, I don't think I have anything left for you. You and I are completely different Ashritha." He said throwing up his hand. I stood up.

SLAP!!!

Yes. I slapped him for the first time. He hung his face down holding his cheek.

"When you had nothing left for me or if you found me a nerd or if you had assumed that the magical spark between us has vanished, you should have just broken up with me, the day when you said you need time, you should have dispersed that day itself. Though it's tough, I would have let you go for your happiness. But you came back, you created false hopes. Still, I never gave up trusting on you. I put every ounce of my courage in trusting you. What right do you have to play with my feelings? The day you slept with her, I wasn't on your mind, I was dead, right?

The trust, which I had been building from all these days- it just took a second for you to break, isn't it? Do you think you are the one at fault? No, I'm the one at fault. I should have pushed you away when you tried getting closer to me. I should have ignored you when you tried getting my attention. But, I let you walk in my life and cared for you with all my heart. I believed that you were honest as much as I was.

When you were searching for possible lies to comfort me, I was searching for possible ways to love you more. When you lied to me, I remained silent even after knowing the truth. Whenever you were irritated by me, I assumed it as my mistake and scolded myself, whenever you said you were busy, I just waited for your call. Every time when you gave plenty of reasons to hate you, I tried searching for one reason to love you hard. Because I know how it feels to be ignored by our loved ones.

Shame on you for naming the fake thing, which you had on me as LOVE. Shame on you for taking a girl's feelings for granted. Shame on you for promising me things which you couldn't keep. You said my decision was important for us to get into a meaningful relationship, but I wonder how you could forget that my decision is equally important for us to break apart. You just pushed me away, like I am a damn fiddling thing. Right?

You know what, Akash- you did not cheat on me. You cheated on yourself. You gave up on a pure and chaste girl who would never give up on you. You gave upon a girl who put your happiness above her. You gave upon a girl who would choose only you, no matter how many guys she might be surrounded by. Even if my life were to change, you would be the one person whom I wouldn't want to leave. Even after you started ignoring me, I loved you without resentment. I gave you so much love even after you stopped reciprocating it. You loved me for being emotional and now you are leaving me for being emotional. You gave me the pain, which I don't deserve because I gave you the love which you don't deserve.

And let me tell you one more thing, I gave up my IIM plan and applied for MBA in Pune just to be with you. I gave up my career plans. Now, I realize how stupid I was.

How could you do this to me Akash? I blamed the situations for the misunderstandings between us but I never knew that you are the one who was trying to tear this relationship apart. I couldn't realize that your love for me has an expiry date. It's not just about you and me. It's about our feelings, our time, our precious moments, our promises, and our dreams. You shattered everything.

I wiped my tears off, "If you have anything left for me, I beg you only one thing. Don't come back into my life, ever. You should have just broken up with me Akash. What you did is the worst thing that can ever be done."

Please hold my hand, make me believe that everything I had seen is a lie. Hold me tight to your heart. I love you Akash.

He didn't move. Slowly, gathering the left-over courage inside me, I walked away from him and his life. I could see the rash on his cheek, the result of the slap which I delivered and I also know that it can never match the scars he left on my heart.

We reached the airport and landed in Vizag by eight. Dad came to the airport to pick me. Everyone was dull. I felt bad for spoiling everyone's mood and trip. After all, friends are the one who supports you in your tough times.

31.

"Ashi! Akka, what did you get me from Shirdi?" Varun came jumping when the car reached the main gate.

"Wait. First, let her come in," Mom said taking the backpack from me. "You look so tired," Mom said touching my forehead with her hand checking if I had a fever.

Tired? I still wonder how I am still alive.

"Yeah, mumma... No enough sleep," I said and rushed into my room. I locked myself in washroom turned on the shower and sat down. For a moment all the moments I spent with Akash replayed in front of my eyes that gave a pang in my heart.

What did I do? Oh God! It's not easy. Send him back to me. I want him, I really need him. I wept.

I felt betrayed, the worst thing is, I was betrayed by the one whom I trusted the most. I cried under the shower so that no one could hear me sobbing. Not the tears, not the scars on my heart could measure the pain I have been enduring. Death seemed easier.

"Ashi come, it's already late. Have dinner," mom called out for me. She fed me two chapattis which I had to eat forcefully. I thought it is better to eat rather than explaining why I wasn't hungry.

At around twelve, I found myself rolling on the bed. The more I consoled myself, the more I wailed. I unlocked my mobile, which was lying on the bed. There were few messages from Aditya and Nisha. Not a single text or call from Akash. It killed me. He didn't even call me to check how I was doing. I scrolled up to the previous messages and stopped at one.

"Ashi, how lucky I am to have you in my life! I still feel the tenderness of your lips on mine. I can still feel the freshness of the odor of your hair. I can never forget the passion in your eyes which I beheld when we kissed last night. I always wonder how I survived all the days when you weren't there in my life. Now that you are in my life, I want nothing except more and more moments with you.

There are times when I feel low, broken and then your smile flashes in front of my eyes reminding me that I have you in my life and all my woes start to fade away. The way you take care of me with your warm love, no one has ever did that to me and no one ever can. I know that we get into fights, misunderstandings but trust me- those things can never change the way I feel about you. With you around, the world looks so beautiful, I feel myself as the happiest person on the earth, you always show me reasons to smile and make me feel I am worth something and I wish to feel the same for the rest of my life. Just like honeybees collect pollen, you draw away a piece of me each day with your beautiful smile and warm love. I will be so hypnotized that I can never let you go. Love you to the core. I can never do anything that hurts you in any way." He had sent me the text when we returned from Araku. I tried to hold back my tears but failed.

You said you will never leave me, you promised me that you will be with me for the rest of our lives. You said I am the only one in the world for whom you actually care. Every word that came from your mouth, was it fake? The long conversations, endless chats, surprises, caring for each other. Was everything a lie?

I wished it to be the worst nightmare, but it wasn't. I wished Akash should call and say everything was lie except the thing that he loves me. That did not happen. I wished my life should end. It didn't too. I cried and cried till the sun rays pierced into my teary weary eyes.

32.

"Ashi Akka...Grandpa" Varun panted waking me up.

"What grandpa? What happened?" I asked wearing my sandals. "Is he calling me?" I asked back.

"Come," he said and pulled my hand without answering my question. He took me to grandpa's room. It was seven.

"He should be jogging this time." I thought as I walked. I looked at him. He was lying on his bed. Mom held granny by her shoulders who was sitting on the bed, granny was wailing with her pallu near her mouth.

"What happened?" I asked puzzled. I had no idea why they were crying.

"Your grandpa left us all alone," granny said jiggling my grandpa's hand.

I must have heard it wrong.

"What?" I recited.

"He is no more," Granny wailed. I couldn't believe my ears. He was such a healthy person. He never passed a day without walking, meditation. I rushed towards him and touched his hand for the pulse. Forget about the pulse, his body was cool like ice. My fingers twitched on his body. My grandpa, my jogging partner, my savior from dad's anger has left us.

"Daily he used to wake up at six and go for a walk. Today he didn't, so I thought I would wake him up. By then" Granny said weeping heavily. He got a sudden cardiac arrest in sleep. My dad who went to market came back hurriedly when my mom called him to tell this news. Not a tear came out of his eyes. He turned numb.

I had already lost my love and then my grandpa. *No not two losses.*

I ran to my room and locked myself. I had no strength left in me. I stumbled on my knees as I fell on the floor crying. Life is unpredictable. The moment when you are smiling whole heartedly, the very next moment someone snatches your smile and leaves you behind with tears. No matter how wounded you are, life keeps throwing stones at you on the same wound again and again.

Yesterday Akash and I, am not still out of it and today grandpa left us permanently.

Mom called me when they moved the body out. I couldn't bear the fact referring my grandpa to a body. Slowly, my relatives and neighbors started showing up with garlands and decorated the glass coffin. I looked at my grandpa through the glass. It felt like he was just sleeping. My grandma has fainted as she has wailed all day long. My dad was taking care of the funeral formalities. Though, my mom was herself in a mental trauma, she didn't leave my granny even for a second. She forcefully made her drink some juice and made her rest for a while.

Nisha, Madhu, Aditya, and Vineet visited my home in the evening around six when the men took the body for cremation. I got scared when I saw my grandma at that time. She pleaded not to take the body. She insisted that she would go with him. But according to Hindu rituals, women are not allowed to the cremation ground.

"Sorry for the loss," Nisha, Aditya, Madhu and Vineet sat on my bed. I was just looking at the floor. My eyes loaded with tears. No one spoke for few minutes. Nisha, sensing my tears, walked near me and clenched my hand "You have to be strong," she said.

I broke down. "Why Nisha, why me? What did I do? How can life be so unfair to me?" I hugged and cried like a baby. She had no answer, may be no one does.

"Please don't cry," she pleaded rubbing my back. Aditya, Madhu, and Vineet sat silent, helpless. I released myself went to the washroom, washed my face and returned to the room. All the four of them were staring at me with solicitude. It killed me. They left after a couple of hours, offering their condolences. By night, dad returned home after cremation and he broke down holding my grandma.

"It's tough to imagine this house without dad," dad said sobbing. He wasn't wrong. I didn't eat my dinner. Some of our close relatives stayed back in our home. No one slept but everyone acted like they did. I knew everyone was sobbing and trying not to whimper. My position wasn't any different. I unlocked my phone hurriedly when I got a text from Nikhil.

I was anticipating him to say that whatever he told was a lie, Akash still loves you, but it read "Heard about your grandpa's loss, my deepest condolences. I don't know whether it is right to tell you this at this point or not, but I have to tell you because you really should know this. I heard that Arpita Singh and Akash had moved into a separate flat almost a month ago. They are living together." My phone slipped from my hand, my whole body shivered, my face has gone withered. Something stabbed my heart, deep. It ached. I looked at the Sai baba portrait in front of me at night.

"What did I do to deserve this? He cheated on me, yet he is happy there. And here I lost my love, my grandpa, what else do you need? Do you have some compassion for me? For this little girl who is abandoned by the one whom she thought would never. Why are you making me go through all this shit? Do I really deserve all this? Do you know how painful it is for me? I don't ask you for happiness. I just ask you to give me the strength to overcome all these." I wailed like an abandoned child.

Though all my questions remained unanswered, the pain didn't leave me alone. I was petrified for no reason. That moment I realized how deeply I loved Akash. *Nothing in this world can compare to the things I have been experiencing.*

I wanted to end my life, the only way to escape from the pain. But suddenly my mom's face flashed in front of my eyes. I couldn't imagine the pain on her face. The pain of losing her beloved, grown up child.

33.

Living became hell and I turned into a corpse. My friends who once waited for my mouth to shut were craving for me to talk. I stopped talking to my family members because there was no desire left in me to speak to anyone. They assumed the reason as my grandpa's death. However, it was included in the reasons and they never stopped asking me to stop brooding over it.

Once, I thought of keeping Bruno away as it kept reminding me of Akash every moment. But one day when I found myself crying in my room, I felt some touch on my hand, and then I found this wet nose creature staring at me.

"Please don't cry. I'm here with you," that's what he was trying to say. His eyes were filled with concernment. Dogs do speak. But, it takes the right person to understand that.

That moment I realized how cruel I was. "I'm so sorry, Bruno. I'm so sorry for keeping you away. How could I do that?" I cried hugging him. It licked my entire face with affection. From that day, it became a companion for me in my lonely hours of crying. The only thing that I hated about myself was I still loved Akash. I did. Even after knowing that he hooked up with some other girl, even after mistreating me, even after lying to me, even after belittling my feelings, I still loved him. No matter how much I tried hating him, I ended up hating myself for not being able to hate him.

I realized that we can get addicted not only to habits, we get addicted to a person too. You get addicted to some drugs or habits, they eat you physically. Try getting addicted to a person; their absence will start killing you emotionally.

The worst dilemma is when you can't stop missing them and at the same time you can't accept them again. It's the worst battle in life that you fight with yourself. A part of me hated him and the other part of me was craving for him. I wanted him to go through the pain I have been facing but then I realized if I were in his place I would never do the thing which he had done to me.

I missed his warm touch on my hand whenever he held while walking together. I missed the odor of his body whenever I buried my face into his chest. I missed the wet sensation on my forehead whenever he kissed there fervently. I missed the tickling sensation behind my ear whenever he rubbed his nose there impishly; I missed the saggy sensation of my cheeks whenever he pulled them teasingly. I knew that he was not going to come back and I wanted to get over him, but how would I? When everything I did, everything I said, everything I thought kept reminding me of him.

When they are aware that they mean the world to you, that they are the ones who can create happiness or pain in your life by a single gesture, when they possess the option whether to win your trust or lose you for a whole, I still don't understand how a person chooses to betray someone one who has given them nothing except pure love.

I realized how a person can turn your whole life upside down by just being a part of it.

***

When my fourth-year first-semester results were out, I realized how badly my relationship affected my studies too. I had two backlogs, till then I maintained an aggregate of eighty- one of the top five. My attendance has declined. Even then, I couldn't put the blame on Akash. I still hoped he would regret his mistakes. I didn't tell mom about my backlogs, but I was in confusion how to pay the supply fee.

I had no money left with me. The money I had saved till the date, I bought a Fossil watch for Akash which I threw on his face that day. Though my friends could arrange money if I have asked them, I didn't.

"You should get over this and be normal Ashi," Mom said one night at the dining table. It's been almost a month after grandpa's death. Mom was assuming the reason for my delirium. I nodded chomping, without looking at her.

"Is there any other thing that is bothering you?" Mom glowered at me.

"No Mumma... Everything is fine," I faked a smile.

"Mumma I need two thousand rupees," I murmured without looking at her.

"Two thousand? I gave you five thousand last month right before going to Shirdi and dad booked your to and fro tickets, isn't it?" Mom shouted at me.

"Yeah, mom. I really need the money right now." I didn't lift my head up. Because I knewI would start crying if I look at her.

"Tell me why you need. I will give," she said folding her hands. I looked here and there, I was afraid to say that I have backlogs left. But I wasn't left with any other option.

"Results are out Mumma..."

"Oh, you need to treat your friends for that?" My mom chuckled. I lifted my eyes up to look at her happiness. Her smile was genuine, she had wrinkles near eyes.

"No Mumma. I have two backlogs. I'm so sorry," I started crying with my head low.

"I really studied hard but I don't know" I added sobbing.

She held my hand, "Ashi I understand your situation. You were disturbed by the things that had happened around you, I can't blame you for that," she said trying to console me.

'How nice of you, Mumma,' I thought. Since childhood, unlike other parents, my mom never forced me into studies, she knew the fact that stress affects children. I still remember the nights when she used to appeal me to sleep early when I used to do late night studies during exams.

She walked into the kitchen, came out and handed me three thousand rupee notes, “Take it.”

“Fee is only two thousand, mumma,” I said looking at her.

“With the extra thousand get a cleanup for your face. There’s no life in your face,” she said concernedly. *There is no life left in me Mumma.* I thought and stopped the tears by faking a smile.

34.

And my tale of woe continued. Everything in my life was the same other than his presence, but to me, everything seemed different in his absence. The beach which we used to walk at holding each other's hands was still the same, but he wasn't. The canteen which once resonated with our laughs was still the same, but he wasn't there. The girl (me) who loved him truly was still the same, but he wasn't.

The college, canteen, beach, every place reminded me of him. The bitterness is, even my street, my house, my room in which I have been living for twenty years started haunting me with the memories of a person who came into my life a couple of years of back and left. My mom was so worried about my reasonless behavior. It had a reason but she wasn't aware of that. Even dad asked me once while dropping to college.

"Is everything alright? You look so mundane these days?"

I smiled and nodded, "Everything is all right". How would I tell them that your pampered daughter is crying for a guy? I couldn't. I barely came out of my room. I hardly ate my meals. I had no strength left but I wondered how tears streamed during the nights. Everything around me seemed colorless or may be my eyes turned colorless. The things which once made me happy, beach, rain, college, and canteen turned out to be the reasons for my misery. But the irony is, the person responsible for the animosity in my life had no clue what I have been facing here.

The places which once were peaceful and pleasant started threatening me with his memories. I couldn't digest the fact that he is not going to come back in my life. I couldn't withstand the truth, moments turning into memories. Whenever my phone buzzed, I would just grab the phone expecting him, because my poor heart doesn't know that I was no longer a person in his contact list.

Whenever I got to hear a familiar bike horn, turning my head has become a reflex action expecting Akash; my poor heart doesn't know that I was no longer his destination. Whenever I lay crying, I told myself that he will be back, he can't pass days without me, my poor heart doesn't know that I was just a passing cloud in his life. When the dawn broke each day, I thought he would be waking up with guilt, but my poor heart doesn't know that he has been waking up with someone else. When my mind said, *please move on*, my poor heart doesn't know anything except to hold on. It kept on hoping, it kept on waiting, and it kept on crying.

Actually he did not leave me, I found him everywhere, at every place I visited, in everything I did. He was there looking at me, laughing at my pathetic condition. With each passing day, the pain became cumbersome. Nights and feelings are best friends, *sometimes foes too.* Each day, when the sun started setting, the fear slowly crept into my body making every inch of my nerve tremble.

Every night his memories haunted me like the worst nightmare. I just stayed up staring at the ceiling, holding the tear stained pillow and asking myself, *is this why I liked him so much? Is this why I loved him so much? Is this the life which I dreamt? Is this my value? Is he worth? Is my pride so small?* And in case if I had fallen asleep, I would sleep with a weight on my heart knowing that he had hurt me so deeply.

In the middle of the night, I would wake up trembling with sweat all over my body like something terrible is frightening me and then I would realize that it was nothing but his memories that started piercing my heart slowly and then I would sleep crying. And every day I woke up trying to digest the fact that he is no more in my life. My stomach felt empty lacking his presence and my heart ached, leaving me weak and tired, yet I couldn't eat, I couldn't sleep. I felt something in my throat, I just wanted to scream and let the pain all outside, yet I held my breath to keep quiet. I strongly believed nothing lasts forever except love but also learnt that it is not the same with everyone. I gave him everything I could. I did whatever I could do on whole myself. It was he, who pushed me away.

It felt like I was missing an important element of my Life, an element of my happiness, element of my survival. Like, when a writer loses his hand when a runner loses his leg. I found no life around me. I perceived that I was not living days; I was just trying to get to the next day. Vividly, there is a lot of difference between the two. I craved for his love each day and failed. Every day I woke up realizing that I was missing him more than the previous day.

I stopped looking both ways before crossing the road. I stopped wearing the seat belt while driving. I never tried killing myself, I just stopped caring whether I lived or not, because I was already dead inside.

35.

I saw mom waiting near the main gate, one evening. I went to temple with grandma on her request. Though I had lost complete trust in God, I found peace in temples. Just like any other day, I faked a smile to mom and walked ahead of her. Faking a smile, faking hunger became my habits.

"Akash is the reason behind your behavior?" she shouted from behind.

I turned back in astonishment. "How could she know?" I wondered. Looking here and there in embarrassment, I found spectacles on the coffee table. Those were Nisha's.

"Did Nisha come here?" I questioned her back. Mom was suspicious about my behavior from the start, so she sent me to temple with grandma on a purpose and she called Nisha. She first requested her, pleased her, threatened her, finally Nisha blurted out, she had to.

"Did Nisha tell you?" I asked again.

"I knew that you were in a relationship from the start, do you think a mother cannot sense the change in her child's behavior? But I never asked you, I thought you are grown up to be able to differentiate what's right and what's wrong and I assumed that you were happy. I thought you would come and tell me by yourself. But I never knew that you have been facing this from all these days." She spoke without pause.

I hung my head low, I felt ashamed. She knew, yet she didn't ask me. My granny was looking at us having no idea about what was happening around her. "Please don't tell me that my daughter is so weak to brood over a guy," her voice changed. I looked at her. She had tears, so did I.

"Mumma!!" I blurted out holding her.

"I'm so sorry; I never wanted to hide it from you. I just didn't get the right time," I wailed.

"Everything is fine Ashi, don't cry" Mom said caressing my hair. I was lying on my bed with my face in her lap and crying from the past half an hour. Bruno was lying next to me looking at us. I wailed like a hungry child.

"Ashi is a strong girl. Don't cry like a kid," mom said brushing my hair. I knew mom cried inside, there can be nothing worse for parents to see their child crying for something which they can't get.

"Ashi do you remember, when you were in kindergarten, you got missing in an exhibition?" she asked enthusiastically trying to recall an incident that happened one and a half decade ago.

"No Mumma. I don't remember," I sat with legs crossed.

"You were five years old and Varun was just a few months' baby. Your dad wanted to take you to a kid's fair. But you said you didn't want to go alone with dad. You wanted me and Varun to also come along. You urged and I couldn't say no. We four went together. Feeling suffocated in the crowd, Varun started crying and I chose to sit back in a stall and your dad took you inside.

Within few minutes, he came running and said you were lost; my heart sank on hearing that. I immediately handed Varun to your dad and searched for you here and there like a madwoman, it began getting dark and my fear had no bounds. Your dad and grandpa searched every lane and filed a complaint too. With tears in my eyes, I sat helplessly outside a house and then I saw a group of kids playing there. I ran up to them hoping I could find you there. Luckily, I did.

You came running to me happily "Mumma, they are my new friends," you said pointing to the children with you. Then I saw you, your cute little cotton skirt has gone dirty but your smile on the face was still the same. I couldn't see any sort of fear. I embraced you.

"Oh. She is your child?" An old lady who was sitting there came near me.

I nodded wiping my tears.

She spoke then, "She has been playing since evening. When I saw her playing with these kids, I thought she doesn't belong to this area and I asked her about her parents, she said "Mumma and papa has gone somewhere, they will come to pick me."

At the age of five also, even when you were alone, you didn't cry like other kids. You had trust, you were strong and do you know that you offered your shoes to one of the kids who said she likes your shoes and she doesn't have one. You are so generous and beautiful girl," my mom narrated the incident with a spark in her eyes.

I nodded watching her with a smile on my face. "Ashritha, how long have you been in this relationship?" Mom asked straight.

"It's been more than two years, Mumma," I answered in confusion. "But what has this got to do with it?" I added.

"Do you know granny's age?" she questioned again.

"Umm... May be around sixty-seventy," I said looking at the wall thinking about the number.

"Yes, she is sixty-six and do you know that she got married when she was just eighteen? Which means that she shared a bond of forty-eight years with your grandpa." She said widening her eyes.

"Isn't that really huge number?"

I nodded. *Gosh! Forty-eight, yeah.* I was surprised.

"Can you imagine what granny is going through, now?" she shot a question. My head hung low.

"I know, Love isn't about time, it's about the feelings. I'm not belittling your love or your feelings either, I'm just trying to make sense." She continued holding my chin. "Losing a partner with whom she has spent almost half of her age, do you think it's easy? Just look at that old lady." I nodded thoughtfully.

"I know that you loved him like he is the one in this world, started dreaming about your lives together. But, if he had neglected you for his family or career, I wouldn't have blamed him, but he left you for some other girl which depicts his instability. Even if he regrets and comes back to you, will you be able to trust him like you did before?" she said.

I shook my head looking down. My eyes got wet again.

Yes, he left me for a girl.

"Then, why do you want someone, who doesn't want you back? Why are you wasting your tears for someone who didn't shed a single tear at your loss? Why do you keep thinking about a guy who abandoned you so ruthlessly?" I didn't have an answer for any of those questions.

"I know it isn't that easy to overcome this pain, but at least it's not impossible. Ashi, don't repress the pain. Just let it go. Let it flow out in the form of tears because it is not worth holding. Don't get over it just get through it and remember that I will stay beside you when you get through these things." She spoke affectionately after which I couldn't help myself from crying. I cried like a little baby and dozed off in her lap.

36.

I woke up as I was dying of thirst. My throat and mouth had gone dry. I could feel a burning sensation in my stomach, may be because of gastric issues as I have been skipping meals regularly.

It became hard to open my swollen eyes. It was dark, I couldn't see mom around, and I found Bruno sleeping near my legs. I slowly pulled out my phone to check time. It was one. I walked into the kitchen to fetch water, drank more than half of the chilled water bottle. My head was aching badly. I was toddling to my room and then I heard some whispers from dad's room which is adjacent to the kitchen. At first, I ignored and started walking. I stopped when I heard my name. I walked back near their room and stood behind the door which wasn't latched.

"Cool down, Sumati. She will be fine." Mom was whimpering and dad was consoling mom.

"I had never seen her like this. She is such a strong girl, I brought her up like that, now she is crying for a guy. I am not able to see her like that"

"Shall we consult a psychologist?" dad advised.

"What? What do you think? She is a patient?" mom ranted suddenly.

"No Sumati, may be she needs a couple of counseling sessions," dad said again.

"Not required, I can take care of my daughter, I can't send her to a mental doctor," she was weeping. Tears rolled down my cheek. I covered my mouth not to sob. Dad did not speak anything.

She continued, "I brought her up like a little princess. I felt happy whenever I saw her smiling, whenever she laughed over telephone conversations. I believed that she was really happy. I was ready to accept her relationship. But that relationship has screwed my daughter." My mom who consoled me a few hours back, who asked me to stay strong, has herself gone so weak.

In the process of thinking about Akash, I never thought about my parents. I thought I was crying alone, I never realized that I was making them go through the shit just because of my simple mistake. Listening to my mom's sob killed me. I could no longer hold the tears. I pushed the door and stood in front of my mom and dad.

"Ashi, you didn't sleep?" mom stammered. She looked down to hide her tears. I couldn't speak. I just cried. I sat there on the bed opposite to her and just kept staring at her.

"Ashi, it's nothing. I am fine," said mom, trying to smile.

"I am so sorry, Mumma." It became harder for me to frame words. I was fighting for breath. This time I started crying heavily. Varun started rolling on the bed disturbed by our sobs.

"Everything will be alright, Ashi," dad said rubbing my back.

"I'm so selfish, I only thought about myself, I never thought I'm making you people suffer too. I'm so stupid, I'm sorry Mumma," I said and buried my face in her lap.

"It's nothing like that Ashi. Everyone does mistakes and loving isn't a mistake at all. We love you so much, that's why we couldn't see you crying," mom said gesturing her hand at dad and herself. Dad nodded.

"Remember one thing Ashritha. Love should be your strength, not your weakness. God removes people from your life for a reason, don't run behind them who don't even deserve a single step," my dad said. I nodded approvingly. I hugged him and he caressed my hair.

"Do you still want to go to Symbiosis Pune?" my mom asked. I shook my head without looking at her.

"I will attempt CAT," I spoke slowly.

"As you wish," dad smiled.

"I love you, dad" I conceded looking into his eyes.

"Then what about me?" mom made a face trying to lighten up the mood.

"I love you too," I smiled. "You are the best parents ever," I spoke to myself.

"You want to sleep here?" my mom asked when I stood up to leave.

"No Mumma, I will sleep in my room. Bruno is with me, Varun is already disturbed, make him sleep," I stood up to leave.

"Ashritha," mom called me from behind.

"Yes Mumma."

"In life, before you cry for anything, let it be anything, a thing, a person or anything. Take a breath and question yourself "is it really worth?", If it is a yes, do not hold the tears but if it is a no, you know what to do." I nodded as I smiled. My heart felt light, the weight which I had been carrying for all those days was gone. I took my phone and started typing,

"Hi, Akash! I guess you must be having really fun right now with your new girlfriend. Well, I'm writing this just to inform you that I'm not going to give a damn about you from now on. You know what Akash. You messaged me first, I replied. You said that you can't live without me, I believed. You fell for me and eventually, you made me fall for you. Then the chats, conversations, cuddles went on to such an extent that I couldn't imagine my life without you. You made everything happen so easily and quickly that I couldn't realize that I turned blind in your love. You just walked in my life creating false hopes. I had gone so deep in the relationship with you assuming that you will remain same for the rest of our lives. When I was committed to you, I was honest, I was loyal, I was caring, and I was faithful. But you choose someone else over me. For everything you did, I continued defending you. Every false hope, every broken promise is the reason for tearing my heart into pieces. When you had no intentions of staying in my life forever, you shouldn't have awakened my feelings. I thought you were my everything and finally, you left me with nothing.

I comforted myself every time you mistreated me. Even though, you treated me in a way which you weren't supposed to, I still wanted you with the same passion and love. No words can describe the pain I am facing right now. I forgive you, not for you but for me because not being able to forgive is like really holding up again. I never wanted this to end but you made me do that. You ended it so ruthlessly. This day, I realize one thing, YOU'RE NOT MY WORTH." I clicked on the send button, unlike the rest of the days I didn't wait for his reply. With a heavy heart, I deleted his number; I didn't block him as I didn't want to see his number even in my blocked contacts. I let the tears, the final tears away. I took a deep breath.

"Stay strong, everything is going to be fine," I told to myself.

I typed a message for Nikhil, "Hey Nikhil, I really owe you a lot, you made me realize what was going on in my life behind my back, thanks is really a small word. Whatever he does from now, you need not inform me, because I'm no longer holding him. I'm moving on." That night, I slept. I had no melancholy in my mind except serenity.

37.

"Ashi results are out," Aditya came running to the canteen where we were chatting with a round of snacks.

"Cool down, you will clear all subjects," I said offering him Pepsi.

"You know what, you are the topper," he said and lifted his hand expecting a high five.

"Wait? You can't be serious; you are kidding, right?" I asked raising my brows. If he was really kidding, that would be the last day of his life on this planet.

"Absolutely not, you are the topper," he shouted and I hugged him.

Nisha came behind, "Happy for you, babe." She held me tight. Everyone over there congratulated me. Everyone was happy for me. In fact, I was happy for myself. Every day I woke up so different. I invested every minute of my time on myself, to make myself better. I started getting engaged into many things to keep myself busy and to distract myself from his thoughts. Hopefully, they worked, *sometimes*. I started spending time with my grandma, joined swimming classes; moreover, I started studying hard to cover my percentile. Whenever I felt low, I started spending time with my friends and family who were happy to see the new me but not the old me before Akash's episode.

Yes, I deleted his number, but I still remember his number. Yes, I erased all the texts but I still remember the content in those texts. Yes, I erased every trace of him in my life but I couldn't erase him from my mind. Love may not last forever, but the memories do and eventually, the pain does. His name still gave me heartache. I knew that in the midst of all the people around me and all the laughter I still missed him. I just learnt to live with memories which I knew that I can never get moments back. I smiled with the pain not to fool people but for myself, to make myself believe that everything falls in place.

Love can take you to the world where you have never been. Love can make you experience things which you have never seen. It can elate you and deflate you. I learnt that time rules everything. The bad times, the pain, the wounded heart, the loneliness was the thing that made me strong, reminded me that I can still fight in life.

I let the pain flinch my heart to remind me that I was still alive. When the memories make you stuck in the past, the pain helps you in moving on. I never knew how strong a woman I actually was until I chose to be one.

"I think we should celebrate," Aditya said gulping his juice and halting my thoughts.

"Yeah we should, our batch has finally cleared all the backlogs." Vineet gobbled his sandwich. These guys always find a reason to celebrate.

"And treat will be from my side for my friend's achievement," Aditya said pointing me. I felt lucky to have such selfless friends.

"What should I wear for the evening?" Nisha started thinking about the dress.

"Umm, I will wear the one piece which I bought recently on Myntra," she said making her eyes bigger.

According to her, happiness is wearing new clothes. That pertains for every girl, though.

38.

My college life ended leaving loads of memories. Nisha got placed in Infosys and left for training in Mysore. Vineet got placed in HCL and he left for Delhi. Aditya flew to the US for MS. As I had plans for MBA, I didn't attend any campus interviews.

In the midst of my CAT classes, I had to go to Hyderabad for a week to attend Pooja's marriage. Pooja's mom and my mother are cousins. Pooja is elder to me by two years. As granny was in depression she chose to stay back at home. Mom requested our maid to take care of my grandma which she accepted generously and for the generosity we had to pay her thousand bucks extra.

A wonderful city to live in, I always loved Hyderabad. The last time I visited Hyderabad for Prakash Uncle's housewarming function of their newly bought Villa in Jubilee Hills. Pooja's dad Prakash uncle has lots of business. Cashew business is his main. I always wonder, despite consuming tons of cashews themselves and gaining pounds of weight, how they still managed to be rich. Their complete family was stout in personality.

At each function, everybody maintained a dress code- green colour on Mehandi function, and yellow colour on Haldi function except on Sangeet. At Sangeet function, it was completely the guest's wish. Myself, being a fan of Mehandi, I applied Mehandi on both my hands till the elbow line. Aunties pushed their hands in front of the Mehandi designer asking to apply the best designs and finally, they cursed them for applying the designs which couldn't meet their expectations. The irony is, they are the best Mehandi designers in Hyderabad. Another example of how a woman never gets satisfied.

On the marriage night, I sat on the sofa in the second row staring at the bride and bridegroom; actually I was espying their forced smile towards every guest who came to wish them. The bride wore a green and pink colored heavy silk sari. The diamonds sets around her neck illuminated more than the lights decorated in the wedding hall. Arjun *jiju* wore a black Armani suit and looked like a decent techie guy. He was a software engineer in the UK.

I was so bored there, and then dad called me near the group of relatives. They were chit-chatting as in some round table conference. He introduced me to many uncles who were dressed in white and white Khadi.

"I think they were representing *Ujala* indigo," I laughed at myself. Then I greeted them with Namaste. They offered me to sit and very soon, I became a member of their round table conference. In no time, I realized that my boredom was far better than their useless conference. They were shouting, laughing, and whooping. I took a leave and then mom called me near her group of friends.

Dad did, so mom has to do. *Why should boys have all the fun?* The thing is, I became a prey for them.

"Mumma. I'm hungry, I will change into a *salwar* and go for dinner," I pouted.

"Why do you want to change, you look gorgeous dear," an aunty whom I had never met before, said to me pinching my cheeks. I wore a plain red georgette sari with a black blouse that had stonework. The red colour in the lighting was a head turner. Even the videographer focused on me for almost ten minutes that made my face burn with the heat of the light. I smiled a little.

"Ashi, she is Arjun jiju's aunt," Mom introduced her.

"Namaste aunty," I greeted her.

"And she is jiju's masi, she is jiju's aunty," she introduced me to her gang too.

"It's okay if you are feeling uncomfortable you can go and change," the same aunty said when she noticed my pale face. I took keys from mom and dispersed. I changed into a white salwar suit and convinced Varun to have dinner with me. I couldn't wait till the completion of marriage, so I went to the room that had been allocated for us and I dozed off.

39.

It was eleven in the morning when I woke up with a throbbing headache. I found no one in the room. I shouted for my mom, no response. Irritated, I decided to step out of the bed to find my mom. I went down to the dining hall, where a group of jobless aunties were gossiping about the dowry, jewellery and some other nonsense stuff.

"Look at this girl, isn't she Vizag Suresh's daughter, she woke up now?" an oversized aunty who styled her hair with jasmine flowers was whispering to another aunty who was sitting next to her. I was in my nightdress, track pants and a tee shirt. I looked at her annoyingly. I wanted to pull the flowers from her hair and mess her over face full of make-up. However, I chose to ignore, the thought that we were leaving for home tonight made me little peaceful.

After a lot of research and investigation, I found mom and dad in a room on the ground floor. Other than mom and dad, Prakash uncle and his wife Sarala aunty were inside the room along with some other couple too. "I have seen her somewhere." I spoke to myself. "Yes, the previous night." Yeah, she was the lady who complimented me the previous night.

"But what were they discussing about? Must be related to Pooja's dowry." I questioned and answered myself. In India, no matter how rich the groom's family may be, they never stop expecting dowry from girl's side. Sometimes they demand too. "I'm sorry, I was looking for mom," I apologized and eyed mom to come out.

"No, no, Ashi. It's okay, you can come in," Sarala aunty invited and signaled me to sit. I sneaked inside and occupied a seat between mom and dad.

"So the thing is, my son will be leaving for Canada in a couple of months." Padma aunty said and paused. My dad nodded.

"So you want my dad to come and bid a bye?" I couldn't understand her point. I raised my eyebrows at mom in confusion, she didn't respond.

"Sure Padma. We will discuss this for a minute and we will let you know our decision," Prakash uncle intervened and Padma aunty and her husband stepped out.

"Listen, Suresh, we will not be getting a better match than this." Prakash uncle said placing his hand on my dad's shoulder who was busy thinking, staring at the carpet under his legs.

"Match? What are you talking about?" I screamed throwing my hands in the air.

"You got a match, Ashi. Padma aunt's son, he is a computer engineer in Canada. Wow Ashi, you are so lucky," Sarala aunty was almost dancing on her legs. My pulse started pumping faster, not letting me respond. I just looked at my mom with questioning eyes.

"Leave us three alone for a moment, we need Ashi's decision personally," dad said to Prakash uncle.

"Okay but think well, you can't miss such a good match," he reminded again and both left. I was staring at the carpet beneath my legs.

"Ashi," dad said and put his hand on my shoulder and I broke down.

"Mumma. I don't want to marry him, I don't want to marry anybody, please Mumma, tell them," I cried like a five-year-old baby who would be sent to school for the first time, forcefully.

"Please don't cry Ashi. We will never go against your wish," mom assured me.

"But think about us too, Ashi. I spoke to him last night, he is a nice guy, one and only son, well settled, you will be happy with him, talk to him once and then we will do according to your decision," dad stated.

"No, I'm not going to meet anyone, I will not," I said holding my head. Mom joined me in crying.

"Please don't cry mumma. I can't do this. I just can't," I said breathing heavily. I wanted to run from there, from the so-called 'emotional drama'.

"Ashi, listen, do you trust mumma?" Mom asked me holding my right hand with her both hands and looking into my eyes.

"I do, but…" she cut me off in the middle.

"Do you think we always choose the best for you?" I nodded without looking at her.

"And now, it's your marriage, your life matter and moreover it's our life matter too," mom said gesturing her hand at herself and dad. I started sobbing again.

"Listen, Ashi. You are precious to us. He is really a nice guy, I'm sure he will take care of you more than I do," dad spoke softly. I hugged him and wept.

"He is here, just talk to him once, but the final decision is yours," he said convincingly. Mom nodded her head pathetically. I agreed for their sake.

"Okay, but don't force me if I don't like him," I stated a condition.

"Sure. We will not," he said looking at mom. Both nodded, happily....

40.

"Hi Ashritha! I'm Karthik" I turned my head back on hearing the low pitch voice from behind, then I lifted my head to look at the six feet frame. He extended his hand expecting a shake-hand.

"Hello," I replied and shook gently without making an eye contact. He was in a grey colored shirt and black denim, rimless spectacles with a lean body and thick hair. He wasn't bad-looking at all. I found him handsome and decent. For the next ten minutes, no one spoke. I sat there glaring at the same carpet and noticed him stealing glances from the corner of my eyes. I wore a black kurta, black leggings and a pink mirror-worked dupatta.

"So what are your hobbies?" he asked me breaking the deadly silence. "Swimming, badminton" I answered with half smile. For the next fifteen minutes, he spoke about many things, his job, his life, salary and everything. I just sat, nodding and smiling.

"Last night, you were wearing a red saree, right?" he asked me. "Yeah," I nodded.

"You looked extremely gorgeous, I did observe you," he said playing with his gold ring on his finger. He had a smiling face.

"Thanks," I smiled. I wanted to tell him about my past, but couldn't. My mom had warned me not to talk anything about Akash. She took a promise too. We, humans, don't believe people, we only bind to promises. So I remained silent.

"You are not saying anything?" he asked sipping his coffee. I smiled nervously.

"I know that you have a really wonderful smile, but you can't answer every question with that," he winked at me.

"Yeah I understand, it's little crazy fixing our marriage, in someone else's marriage, but believe me I am as surprised as much as you are," he paused to sip his coffee and continued "Marriage isn't a little thing especially for girls," he said looking into my eyes.

"And yeah, I heard that you want to do MBA. Right?" he said placing the empty cup on the table.

"Yeah, I have been attending CAT classes too." This time I responded with descending excitement. He listened to me carefully paying complete attention.

"That's good, I really like ambitious girls like you. If you want, I can help you in finding good universities in Canada too, but only if it is a yes from you." He air quoted the last sentence. I nodded.

"Oh my God, you just nodded, that means it's a yes!" he sounded excited.

"I mean," I stammered figuring for an answer.

"Chill! Just kidding. You can discuss with your parents and decide. From my side it's a yes, definitely yes," he smiled and stood up.

In the entire conversation, in that room, I discovered two things. There was a lizard in the room and Karthik's left cheek gets a dimple whenever he smiles. The first thing freaked me out, but I liked the second thing.

***

"How is he? He is cute no?" Sarala aunty questioned and answered herself. Everyone fired a thunder of questions at me. But mom and dad sat silently anticipating yes from me.

"He liked Ashi a lot, Ashi is really lucky," Sarala aunty was blushing. *Wait. I'm the one who is supposed to blush right?* Mom squeezed my hand gently.

"Mumma...Will you be happy if I say yes?" I asked her.

"Yes, because you will be happy with him..." she smiled. I nodded my head approvingly and smiled. I already took a decision which proved me that I was wrong. This time I let my parents decide about my life because parents are the one who know about you more than you know about yourself. The one wrong person in my life changed my perspective of taking a decision to such extent that I literally stopped taking decisions. Not because I wasn't clear but because I was scared.

Mom started crying again, this time in happiness. "Mumma not again, you cry over everything," I frowned. Mom smiled and wiped her tears and kissed my forehead. Dad hugged me. I looked at their faces which beamed with utmost happiness. They started calling our relatives. At last, they are happy, that's all matter to me, I thought.

Life is so unpredictable. When you think of living your dreams and start dreaming about your framed future. Everything shatters and takes you to a destination which you never expect.

41.

"Aaaareeee youuuu serious?" Nisha was screaming over the phone when I told her about my engagement that happened two days back. Vivek gave me a weird look hearing the noise coming out of the phone. I was in my CAT coaching class; I called her when our trainer gave us a break.

"Yeah sorry Nisha, I couldn't tell you earlier, everything happened so suddenly," I said looking at the diamond ring on my ring finger.

"Karthik specially selected it for you," Karthik's mom whispered in my ear on the engagement day. I smiled looking at her.

"Did you like it?" Karthik asked me. I nodded as I glanced at him.

"It's beautiful," I answered.

"Well, I'm happy then," he winked at me, his dimple drew my attention.

"I just can't believe this!" Nisha shouted breaking my thoughts. I imagined her dancing.

"Yes, even I can't. Listen, marriage is in June. I will kill you if you don't come at least before a week," I warned her.

"Sure baby, you think I am that type of person who would wait for invitation. I will start packing," she said grinning. She is such a shameless and a darling, both at the same time. I missed her company.

"I should start my shopping," she said excitedly. When I was about to disconnect the call, she asked "Ashi, are you sure about this?"

"My parents are sure and they are really happy and you know that I have no hopes left in my life, I'm just going with the flow," I said softly.

"But I wish, all the best in the world happens to you, babe," she said and gave me a telephonic kiss. Vivek looked at me doubtfully, maybe he assumed me to be a lesbian.

"Okay, I have a session now, don't forget to share engagement pictures," she said hanging up.

"Yeah okay, I will WhatsApp them," I answered and hung up. For the rest of the class, I couldn't focus on the questions. Vivek solved every question in less than a minute. I started imagining him on the front page of the newspaper as CAT topper. He is capable enough. I took out my phone and scrolled the FB news feed. A lot of things were changed on my FB profile.

I was not single anymore; I was officially engaged to Karthik. Every night when he called me, I gave him some stupid fake reason to end the conversation. I really don't know whether he believed those reasons or not, but he never forced me to talk. Dad started making accounts, making a list of relatives' names regarding reception, wedding cards everything.

"Marriage is not a small thing Ashritha, we have only one month left," Mom used to say whenever I asked the reason for her nervousness. She used to call all of our relatives and would spend hours on call boasting about Karthik's family. I once heard mom conversing with her sister over the phone "Ashritha is really very lucky, Swapna. Karthik's mom treats Ashi like her own daughter. All the prayers I have done till date are showing their worth," she said and wiped her tears.

After hearing to that, I found myself in tears. Every parent, no matter how well educated or how rich they might be, they get scared when it comes to their daughter's marriage, they get anxious, they spend sleepless nights thinking about their child's future. My parents, they were no different, they were equally nervous.

Rather than the thought of leaving my home, leaving Bruno made me insane. And I knew that Bruno will not miss me as he had himself found a Pomeranian girlfriend in our colony.

***

After one week of our engagement, Karthik visited my home as he had to attend a friend's marriage in Vizag. He brought video games and chocolates for Varun, for which Varun got elated and gave him the title- "Best jiju in the world". Mom got so tensed and I noticed her fumbling with the utensils in the Kitchen.

"Mom, chill. Why are you so tensed?" I asked placing my hand on her shoulder.

"My son-in-law is here and you ask me why?" she answered without staring at me. I sighed shaking my head.

"You are still in track pants. Go! change and come," she taunted suddenly.

I denied saying, "No, I am not going to change, he has to accept me like this after marriage, right?" She gave me a weird look and started loading sweets in our fancy guest plates.

"Try these Karthik, Ashritha prepared them," Mom said pushing a plate with motichur laddu towards him. I looked at mom in puzzlement. *When did I really make them, Mumma?* Indian Mothers! She must have forgotten about the coffee which I had burnt two days back. I thought and smiled at my mom's trail of creating a good impression of her daughter in front of her to-be son-in-law.

"Aunty, I want to take Ashritha with me to this marriage so that I can introduce her to my friends," he asked mom taking a bite of the laddu.

"No no, I'm not going anywhere," I muttered to myself and eyed mom to say no.

"Sure Karthik. Ashi, go and fresh up," she said pushing my hand. Left with no choice, I walked into my room. "Shall we go?" I said after coming out of my room almost an hour later. He didn't speak, he just stared at me.

"Karthik," I waved my hand.

"You look ravishing," he said and smiled. I wore a simple full sleeve orange color salwar suit with gold studs. I smiled in response.

On our way to the venue in the car, I acted like I was sleeping as I didn't want Karthik to start a conversation with me. Luckily, he didn't disturb me and drove silently. I also noticed him reducing the volume of the music system and adjusting the AC temperature when I tried covering myself with the dupatta. Though I found it caring, I didn't bother to break my acting.

" I always wanted to see the lucky girl who is going to marry you. So, she is the one?" Karthik's friend, Rekha said staring at me as he introduced me to his friends in the wedding. I smiled.

"Actually, now I change my words, you are lucky to get her, she is really beautiful," Rekha said holding my hand.

"I agree, I'm really lucky," Karthik smiled holding my hand. I blushed or at least I tried. He didn't leave my hand there even for a moment. He was with me the entire time and checking whether I was comfortable or not. He was really protective. We had dinner there.

"Are you okay?" he asked me sensing my discomfort.

"Yeah," I smiled. I didn't want to spoil his mood.

"Okay. Come let's go home," he said holding my hand.

"No, no, it's okay, I'm seriously alright," I smiled more trying to make him believe.

"Oh, really? Then when is your hand sweating?" he asked lifting my hand up. I did not answer. We took leave from there. On our way back, I didn't sleep. I just sat peeping out of the window, lost in my own thoughts.

"So, aren't you excited about marriage?" he asked me.

"To be frank, I'm scared," I answered vapidly. He laughed.

"I understand. But I'm really so excited. I can't wait anymore to see you as my beautiful bride," he said looking at me. I dropped a light smile. He stopped the car on an empty road.

"What happened?" I asked looking around. He did not answer instead he took my hand into his. A feeling of warmth ran inside my lungs.

I experienced this before. I did. I really did. Yes, Akash did hold me like this.

I gulped in tension. My breathing paced up with the nervousness.

"Ashritha, people say there isn't love in arranged marriages, today I strongly believe that they all are wrong. The moment when you put the ring on my finger, I was on cloud nine. You have no idea how many dreams I started dreaming about us together. You really don't know how crazy I had gone in choosing our honeymoon destination, later I came to know that you love Paris, and I have planned everything. We will directly fly to Paris after our marriage and then to Canada from there. And I know that you are worried about leaving your family and live with a new person in a different country. You don't have to worry about all those; we have a maid to run errands in our house. You will go to college, you will do MBA, and everything will remain the same for you. And trust me; I will do my best to keep you happy." He spoke looking into my eyes. I looked into his.

"Words can be deceiving Ashritha," my wounded heart reminded me. My hand started sweating. I pulled back my hand gently. I fell short of words. I looked into his eyes again. "Does he really mean that?" I asked myself.

"People change with time." My heart spoke again. "Or maybe he is not like others" another logic popped up in my mind. An air of bleakness surrounded me. I felt uncomfortable, guilty, but I wasn't sure of the reason.

Am I cheating on him by not telling my past? I think I should tell him everything.

"Karthik. I want to tell you something," my heart started beating fast.

What if he gets serious? What if his parents blame my parents for this issue? What if my parents get ashamed in front of my relatives?

I ended up all those 'what if's' and chose to switch the topic.

"Actually, those sweets, Mom prepared them, she lied," I confessed.

"Haha, I know" he chuckled pinching my cheek. Yes, he did. He pinched my cheek. I smiled, seeing him smiling. He had a nice smile. I smiled nervously. Mom's call broke the silence there. He turned on the ignition.

"Yeah, mumma. On the way," I replied and disconnected the call. It was eleven when he dropped me at my home. He declined politely when my mom asked him to sleep in our home.

"No aunty, it's fine, they have already booked rooms at Novotel. I will drive there," he said and drove back to the hotel. I could not sleep that night. I was tossing on the bed continuously.

Am I cheating on him, or is he cheating on me? Does he really love me? Hell lot of useless questions kept poking me. When I tried to remember the way he treated me, I smiled. He had a smile on his face the entire time he was with me, he didn't let go of my hand, he didn't stop stealing glances, though his friends kept teasing him. Moreover, he said he was lucky to have me. He deemed me precious. I kept reading the message again and again. The one he had sent me after dropping me.

"Ashritha, you have no idea how many times I thanked my mom for choosing you for me. Mom has seen many girls for me, but the feeling which I got when I saw you? I didn't get that for all the previous girls. That moment I understood why I let all the other girls go. You deserve my heart. But I don't think you are as happy as I am. I feel that you scared of something and I also feel that your eyes are searching for something; I wish I could get that thing for you. And then, when I started figuring out the reasons, I realized that it's not easy for a girl to leave her family behind and move out with a stranger, but trust me, I will not make you regret your decision of marrying me. To be honest, I'm dying to start a new life with you."

I wish I could tell you what my eyes are searching for, but I don't know what they actually need. Maybe they need a person into whose eyes they look, that can give rebirth to the dead trust inside me.

I didn't reply. I didn't understand what to answer him. Before answering him, I wanted to find an answer to the question which my heart fired at me. "Do you love Karthik?"

"I like him" I answered myself and dozed off.

42.

"Ashi. I am gonna take a nap, you wake me up once you finish blinking your eyes, then I will apply kajal." Nisha scolded me sarcastically. She has been trying to put kajal from the past half an hour to and as I wasn't used to it, I was continuously blinking. It was my marriage night.

Marriage. The one lifetime event which would make Karthik and me, a husband and wife.

"Sorry, Nisha. This time I will not blink. Sure," I assured her.

"Okay," she sighed and came to me. Madhu was helping in plaiting my hair.

"I just put it right here," she said looking for it here and there. Then she found her expensive Lakme colossal kajal in one of our relatives' hand. Nisha snatched it from her who was busy drawing numerous lines around her eyes.

"How rude? How arrogant she is!" the aunty said and started cursing her.

"Yeah, she is from North. Fair people are always arrogant," another aunty joined her. She ignored that and was about to apply Kajal.

"Akka, Karthik Jiju arrived in a white Audi A4," Varun came jumping into our room. He is always so obsessed with cars. He looked cute in his kurta pyjama.

"Yes, it has an open top too." Kaushik, my brother's friend said making his eyes bigger. I nodded and smiled.

"This is ladies room, first you guys get out," Nisha said pushing them out.

"Then you should also come out with us," Kaushik uttered and they both ran away. I don't know what was running in Kaushik's head, he just said that. Everyone laughed out there. Madhu fell on the couch laughing. Nisha was fuming. I tried hard not to laugh but burst into laughter. She moped sitting on the sofa.

"Sorry, Nisha. He is a kid," I tried convincing her. She walked to me silently and this time the task was successfully done.

"You look elegant," Nisha said putting a kajal dot behind my ear. I was dressed in a dark red vintage silk saree with gold jewels studded with gems around my neck and ears. Two dozens of bangles on each hand made a sound whenever I moved my hands. A Telugu bride is incomplete without a broad gold waistband. It served me like a belt whenever I thought the saree would slip from my flat stomach. Everything was done. I looked myself as a bride. Every girl's dream was to see herself as a bride. But I think that is not applicable for me.

"Nisha please make it fast. Everyone has arrived," mom came there hurriedly. She stopped speaking when she looked at me. She scanned me from top to bottom and bottom to top.

"You look beautiful," she said kissing my cheek affectionately.

***

"You look stunning my love" Karthik said as I was made to sit beside him in the beautifully decorated *mandapam* with colourful flowers. I looked at him. He wore a navy blue suit with brown leather shoes. He looked perfect with the suit on his 6-feet frame. He replaced his glasses with lens. I smiled nervously.

As I glanced around, I found people looking at us admiringly and whispering how adorable we were looking together. I couldn't understand what was happening around me. I just sat beside him and tried sorting out the reason, *why everyone is happy excluding me?* I tried hard not to cry whenever the cameraman instructed me to smile. My eyes started burning, everything seemed blurry and clumsy, and my legs were trembling inside the sari- thousands of faces and eyes on me. I wanted to scream and run away from there. I looked at my mom who was standing down in front of me. She was already staring at me.

"Everything will be fine, trust me." That's what her look meant. I wanted to trust her. I looked at Karthik. His face was glowing in the lights; he was happily receiving the guests those who came up to wish us.

"Why am I not able to smile like him? Why am I not able to enjoy the most precious moment of my life like him? Are we really meant to be together?" I kept asking myself posing for the photos. I still remember how I dreamt about my marriage, but the person whom I had dreamt wasn't Karthik. Akash's place was replaced by Karthik. We never know what life has for us in its nest.

Nothing made sense to me, not the seven sacred steps we walked around the fire promising each other, no matter what happens in life, we will stay together till our last breaths. Nisha held my plaited hair, when Karthik bend to tie the three sacred knots which would make us one, he looked into my eyes.

I closed my eyes. *This is what I can do to make my parents happy.* A tear rolled down my cheek. Karthik held me by my cheeks and kissed on my forehead. I looked at my mom who had tears of happiness in her eyes. Everyone clapped happily. Mom included.

43.

"Are you cooking well?" mom started questioning me over the phone. It had been three months since I got married. And it's been a month I started pursuing my MBA. I got admission in University of Alberta, which was just thirty minutes away from our home in Edmonton. We live at Roper road. We went to Paris immediately after marriage.

The first day, we visited Saint Chappelle which is absolutely breathtaking. No picture can do justice to the view which you witness it with your eyes rather than a camera lens. We climbed up through the narrow steps to take a view of the glass surrounding the cathedral, holding hands. *I am still a virgin.*

Second night, we climbed up the Eifel tower which was completely packed up with couples holding each other in arms and kissing passionately. Maybe that is why they call it "the most romantic place on the earth" (I did not find the romance in myself though). The 324-meter long tower looked adorable with the blinking lights. I grabbed Karthik's shirt tightly when I bent down to see the ground from the top and he held me back gropingly with an intense eye contact. *I am still a virgin.*

The third day, we walked inside the Rodin museum admiring the works of the artist Auguste Rodin. Each sculpture is a masterpiece holding a hidden significance and history. Post lunch, we laid next to each other in the garden of freshly cut perky grass, staring the blue sky above us and the little drops of rain hitting our faces. *I am still a virgin.*

The fourth day, when we were sitting on a plane to skydive in Tandem, he sensed my nervousness and clenched my hand, encouraged me and then I experienced the most wonderful adventure, the ability to fly like a bird in the air, fifteen thousand feet above the ground. *I am still a virgin.*

The fifth day, being completely tired, we decided to stay back in hotel room. We were lying on the bed wrapped in a single blanket and then he tried to kiss me holding my face, I pushed him embarrassingly and I ran into the washroom which he believed was because of my shyness. *I am still a virgin.*

After a five days' vacation (the so-called honeymoon) in Paris, we flew to Canada. We both were welcomed with a surprise party thrown by Karthik's close friends. I was amazed when I got to see Karthik's house. It was a two-storied building, definitely spacious for a couple. Unlike other guys, Karthik maintained it really hygienically. The cooking vessels, clothes, beds, everything was in place. I came to know how organized Karthik was, when I saw his room and wardrobe. His clothes were perfectly ironed and hanged in his wardrobe. I loved the way he arranged the indoor plants near his bed and on his laptop table.

Like Karthik said, there was a middle aged Srilankan maid who would come in the late evening to clean vessels, but I made her quit forcefully when she demanded for extra five hundred dollars a month. Though Karthik urged me, I couldn't agree with him to pay her thousand dollars a month. But, I promised Karthik that I would definitely tell him if I find difficulty in handling those things. It took one month for me to convert the bachelor building into a home. We had to shop furniture, extra vessels, cooking ingredients, bed sheets, cushion covers.

I remember that after two weeks of our marriage, one night we were in the bedroom. "Karthik, I want to tell you something," I said as I walked near the window.

"Yeah Ashritha, tell me" He sat on the bed.

"I am not ready for any physical contact until I finish my studies," I said without looking at him. A moment later, I found his hand on my shoulder. I thought he would scold me or suspect me but he said,

"I understand, I will never do anything that hurts your personal space," his eyes full of solicitude.

"Thanks," I smiled.

"Hello! Ashi are you listening?" mom's question halted my thoughts.

"Yeah, Mumma. I'm cooking well" I said to make my mom believe. Every weekend I would try something new, watching different cookery shows and asked Karthik to taste it. No matter how bad it might taste, he would just simply smile and say "It's yummy."

44.

It was a Sunday night. Karthik took me to a Chinese restaurant, The Lingnan. "Thanks," I said sitting on the chair when he pulled it for me. We occupied a corner table. "This place is really good," I admired, staring at the ceiling.

Well! It did feel like I was sitting in an authentic royal Chinese house. There were different framed portraits on the walls. The red curtains and the dim hanging lights were the eye catchers. "I love Chinese food," I said making my eyes five times bigger than the Chinese waiter who stood in front of me.

"I know." He smiled. "So, choose what do you want to eat?" Karthik asked me pushing the menu towards me. I looked into his eyes. His eyebrows rose questioningly. I smiled and shook my head. Whenever Akash and I went out for any place to eat, he never asked me to order, it never felt bad then, but now when Karthik put my choice first, it felt so good. I dived into the menu flipping pages with my mouth watering.

"Chicken Westlake soup, ginger chicken and soft noodles." I finally blurted out my order to the waiter who had been waiting for ten minutes with an artificial smile (a part of his job) on his face.

"And, you sir?" he inquired about Karthik's order.

"Same here," Karthik said and the waiter dispersed. "You look so good in this dress," Karthik said admiringly. I wore a peach-coloured sleeveless one piece with textured multi-strap stilettos.

"Thank you," I smiled adjusting my hair.

"So how are your classes going? You like it?" Karthik inquired adjusting the napkin on my lap.

'He is so caring.' I thought. "Yeah, everything is good. I got two new friends too. Vikram and Jyotsna whom we call Jyo. Vikram is from Kerala and Jyo is from Bangalore." I grinned.

"That's nice!" he nodded with a smile. The waiter came back with our food. Karthik watched me avidly when I was having the food. "You want to order anything else?" he asked again.

"No, I'm full," I said lifting my hands.

"Are you sure?" he asked again.

"Yep," I confirmed.

"You liked the food here?" He questioned looking into my eyes. "What's that?" he said bending forward, looking at my face.

"What?" I asked.

"It's the ketchup," he said pulling out the dining cloth. "It's gone," he smiled wiping my mouth.

"I love this." I chuckled. "I mean the food" I stammered. Well! I loved the way he wiped my mouth.

"Well, I am happy then," he said putting his card on the table.

"Thank you so much," I smiled. "Where now?" I inquired.

"Shopping?" he giggled. We drove off to Kingsway Mall. He bought shirts for himself, a pair of shoes for me, bakery confectioneries and groceries.

"One moment, Ashritha," he said and paused his walk when he got a call from his colleague. I nodded leaning to the rail opposite to the Forever 21 store. My eyeballs rolled all over the store and suddenly they glued to a dress. It was a black one piece, thigh length with a see-through boat neck.

“This is beautiful! I will buy that,” I told myself walking near the glass. My eyeballs grew its size again when I saw the price tag.

“Ninety-eight Canadian dollars!” I unlocked my mobile to check the available balance in my bank account.

“Eighty-five dollars.” I moped. “Should I ask Karthik?” I asked myself.

“No, he already bought me shoes worth one twenty dollars, I can’t ask him,” I answered myself again.

“Done Ashritha, shall we go?” Karthik asked breaking my thoughts.

“Yeah Karthik, let’s go,” I answered and followed him. Though I convinced my heart that the dress is not for me. I could not stop myself from turning back and admiring that beautiful one-piece.

45.

"Good morning," I shouted yawning. No response. I checked for the time. The clock showed eleven o'clock. Karthik had left for work by then. He usually leaves for office at ten and he never disturbs me when I am sleeping.

Well! I was in no hurry, as I took an off from college that day. Jyo is a huge fan of Shahrukh Khan and didn't want to miss the film Happy New Year. So, Vikram, Jyo and I planned to bunk college and go watch the movie. Sluggishly, I walked to the kitchen to prepare a coffee for myself and then I found a note stuck to the fridge.

"Hey, Ashritha. From the first day of your college you never asked me money for your expenses. I really feel bad about this. Every single time I ask you, you say you have money. But I don't think you do. And today you are going out with your friends and I want you to be the one who would take out money to pay the bills, because they are your friends and they are still students. Anyways, I'm putting the card on the fridge, it doesn't have any pin or limit. Do not curb yourself if you want to buy something. I actually wanted to give this directly but, I thought you would get offended." This was written on it.

He was right. It had been almost six months. The money which I brought from India was already spent. I never asked for money. So I started working part-time in my college canteen. I never told that to Karthik as he would feel bad if he comes to know that his beloved wife is working part-time as she is embarrassed to take money from her husband. Whenever he asked me, "Ashi, do you need any money?" I would lie saying, "I still have the money which mom and dad gave me before coming to Canada."

Things were fine between me and Karthik, but definitely, we weren't sharing a husband-wife atmosphere. I treated him as a nice friend with whom I was sharing a roof. I was taken aback by his gesture. I could have declined but I chose not to. I didn't want him to get hurt when all he cared about is my happiness. I decided to quit the work. "Thank you so much." I texted Karthik.

A smile crept over my face when I read the reply "Anything for you, my love :-)

46.

"Happy birthday, Ashritha," Mom wished me over video call. A married woman, yet a virgin. "How are the celebrations going?" Mom asked excitedly.

"Umm, cake cutting at twelve and now getting ready to college," I said applying lipstick. Karthik woke me up at twelve. I was really surprised when he took me to the drawing room. The room was beautifully decorated. Colorful balloons with ribbons hung from the roof, ribbons with my pictures and some pictures with Karthik. A beautiful cake and a four feet teddy and a gift. Guess what's the gift?

Yes, the black one-piece. I didn't know that he noticed me staring at that dress. He bought that for me. I was totally surprised when I unpacked the gift with the dress.

"College? Don't go to college," mom frowned. "Go out with Karthik" she demanded. I myself wanted to go out and spend some time but how do I tell her son-in-law hadn't invited me to any treat.

"Umm okay, how's dad? Isn't he around?" I inquired.

"He is sleeping, I forgot to tell you, Bruno has won a competition recently. I will ask Varun to share the pictures with you." She shouted

"Wow really? I love him," I tried exceeding her tone.

"But tell me seriously, Karthik hasn't planned a date? I am sure, he must have planned some romantic date," my mom questioned and answered herself.

"Romantic? Are you seriously my mom?" I wondered at my mom's buoyancy.

"What's wrong?" she argued. I was already feeling bad as Karthik hadn't planned anything and then my mom's words added fuel to the fire.

"Okay, Mumma. I will call you in the evening," I disconnected the call and stood up to leave. Karthik was standing right behind me.

"Ashi, if you don't mind, can you take a leave today?" he asked softly. *Oh, finally!* "Even I have called off work today," he said waiting for my answer.

"Of course Karthik. I was waiting for your invite" I murmured. I smiled and nodded.

"Wow, thank you, Ashi but please can you wear a saree?" he pleaded.

"But I am already dressed," I said looking at myself, from top to bottom. I wore a sky blue sweatshirt and dark blue jeans.

"Please Ashritha," he appealed joining his hands.

"Okay, but it takes time," I accepted on the condition.

"Wow, thanks" he jumped in excitement. After forty minutes of struggle with draping, I finally saw myself in a dark green saree with a simple chain around my neck and two-inch gold *Jhumkas*. Karthik was watching TV when I came out of the room. "You look gorgeous." He stammered as he looked at me. I smiled.

"So, shall we go?" I asked him.

"Yeah, sure. Come," he turned off the TV and walked ahead of me. He wore a red and black check shirt with black denims. He held the car door for me and gestured me to sit when he noticed me fumbling with the pallu. A gentleman knows how to treat her lady. I looked at him sitting, his eyes smiled.

"This is why you asked me to wear a saree?" I asked getting down from the car. We came to Iskcon temple, Sri Radha Govindhaji Temple. He smiled and nodded. We walked through the cemented path and reached the entrance. It was my first time visiting that temple. It wasn't a huge temple. It was just a single big hall with a wooden mandir in the centre in which small marble statues of Lord Radha and Krishna beautifully draped in multiple colored clothes which were immensely attractive.

When I closed my eyes as I inhaled the aroma of the incense sticks and camphor in the temple, it felt like, I was at my home. It was something really close to my heart which made me forget that I was in a different continent. "This temple is really beautiful," I said as we sat on the floor. He smiled.

"Actually, I wanted to visit a temple from so long," I said staring at him.

"I know, that's why I brought you here," he smiled back.

"How did you know? I never told you"

"Just an intelligent guess," he chuckled.

"Tell me Karthik," I insisted.

"I heard your conversation with your mom once, you said that you are missing going to temple with your granny," he smiled. He added "Moreover, whenever I come to temple, I find something here that connects to the soul and I feel like I'm at home.," His answer left me speechless. He spoke again "When I came to Canada for the first time, do you know what I asked Sandeep? I asked him to take me to a temple. Then he brought me here. Isn't it peaceful here?" I nodded with a smile.

"Whenever I feel low or when I miss home, I just come here," he spoke examining his fingers.

"Happy Birthday, Ashritha!" He wished me again. I looked into his eyes.

"Thanks" I smiled.

***

"Please Karthik. Where are we going?" It was my fourth time repeating the question. After spending some peaceful time in the temple, I thought we would be returning home. But he drove on a completely different direction. I sat glaring at the car window as we crossed the lanes which I had never seen before. He just smiled ignoring my question.

"Come, get down," he said opening the door. I dozed off in the car, tired as he did not bother to answer my question. It took us fifty minutes to reach the place.

"Where are we?" I asked him rubbing my eyes.

"You get down first," he said giving his hand. I stepped down gazing the place around me. There was a wooden gate which took us to a lawn with green grass. We walked and reached a building which was a few feet away from the road. I couldn't figure out the place. Confused, I walked into the building and a lady in her forties invited us.

"Ashi, you sit here, I'll just come," Karthik said standing from the chair.

"But, why are we here?" I was about to ask and then he walked out of the room. The lady smiled and I smiled in response. I started examining the room where I found some photographs of children in the group. Different drawings and quotations were pinned to the walls. I just sat reading all the quotations and thinking what we were doing there. Karthik appeared in front of me after few minutes with few plastic bags in his hands.

I eyed questioning him, "What are those?" He did not answer. My excitement as well as anger grew. He did not answer even to a single question.

"Please come in," the lady led us to a hall.

I was totally surprised when I entered the room. There were so many children, some Americans and some Nigerians. Only we have differences, children do not- they were happily playing with each other.

"Wish Aunty a happy birthday," the lady instructed the children who were playing on the floor. If I were normal, I would have shouted at the lady for addressing me as aunty. That day, I didn't. I was lost in the children's eyes.

"Happy birthday," the children started singing the birthday song, clapping and whistling. Then, Karthik unwrapped one of the bags, opened a cake and signaled me to cut it. I stood there in front of the cake, all the cute ones looking at me and the cake desperately. I looked into his eyes, a tear rolled down from the corner of my eye. Karthik saw that. He held my hand and he cut the cake with me. He fed me the cake and I fed him, too. He put cream on my nose teasingly.

Then, he opened the other covers and took out few sweet boxes. I wondered when he managed to buy all those- maybe, when I slept in the car. He asked me to distribute those among the children. They happily grabbed them, comparing the size of their sweet with others. Words would be less to explain how happy I was at that moment, the smile on the innocent faces that happened by our deeds. You never know how much it satisfies you, making others happy satisfies your own soul.

I sat there playing with those children. I don't know when Karthik ordered food, the catering boys brought food exactly at twelve, they served the children and everyone ate happily, Karthik and I were included. He cleared the bills off and they left after wishing me. I watched Karthik playing with the kids when the lady was explaining about the organization.

Nothing fell into my ears except Karthik's laugh. Nothing fell into my eyes except Karthik's smile. He caught me staring at him twice and raised his eyebrows questioningly. I blushed and shook my head.

That day, before leaving for home, when Karthik asked me to distribute the books and stationery goodies to the children, when he gave me a cheque worth thousand dollars and asked me to give it to the lady who was running the organization, my perspective on love has changed.

Love is abstract. Love isn't a thing between two opposite genders. Love is a passion, in the child's eyes when you give him, his favorite chocolate and he kisses you gratefully. Love is the care when your mom wakes up in the middle of a winter night to check whether you are covered with the quilt or not even when she forgot to cover herself. Love is the responsibility when your dad scolds you when you score low grades in the exam. Love is the concern when your loved ones say "Drive safe". Love is the joy when you secretly steal your sibling's clothes. Love is a deal between two siblings when they fight for a single chocolate and finally settle on the deal of "50-50". Love is a pun when you tease your brother with their crush's name. Love is the aegis when your grandparents defend you from your parent's anger. Love is the fidelity when your pet waits up for you, for the whole day and runs up to you wagging its tail when you return home after a hectic day at work.

Love doesn't mean a candle light dinner or a diamond ring. It is always in the small things like an ice cream in the rain, like an early morning text, like a forehead kiss. Karthik made me experience each of those things. That moment, I realized Karthik loved me truly but the question was "Do I love him?" The worst thing is when you can't differentiate between like and love. We sat in the car, driving back to home.

"So, how was your day?" Karthik asked turning on the ignition.

"It was amazing," I answered without looking at him.

"Sorry, I couldn't plan any romantic date," he apologized.

"I am sure that I wouldn't be happier if you had chosen a romantic date for us instead of this." A tear escaped my eye. He noticed that. "You made my day, I mean it" I conceded and tears streamed.

"Arey, Ashi. I thought you would feel happy," he said looking at me with his hands on the steering wheel. I had heard the same words from Akash on previous birthday.

"I'm happy. Can't you differentiate between happy tears and sad tears?" I mocked him wiping my tears. He laughed.

"You haven't put on your seatbelt?" he stopped the car on left. "Every time I need to remind you, huh?" Karthik said shaking his head and putting on the seat belt for me.

"Thanks," I smiled.

"For?" he asked.

"For everything." I meant what I said. I sat in the car, lost in my thoughts and wondering how two people can be so different.

"Ashritha," he called out my name from behind when I walked ahead of him after reaching home. I turned back. He was holding a pot with a cactus plant in it.

"What?" I raised my eyebrows.

"Come here," he called me and I walked near him

"This is your special birthday gift," he said handing me the pot.

"Okay!" I thanked him in confusion.

"Confused?" He asked sensing the puzzlement on my face.

"This is just Cactus, right? What is so special about this?" I asked curiously.

"Well! There is a reason." he said folding his hands.

"Okay tell me," I asked him.

"Not now, I will tell you later"

"No, tell me now." I insisted.

"Ashi. It's late, let's go inside," he said pushing me forward.

"Please Karthik," I beseeched.

"I will definitely tell you, but not now," he said and walked inside.

"Ashritha," he called softly when we were lying on the bed.

"Ha Karthik," I responded in a sleepy tone.

"Do you trust me?" He shot a question. I didn't respond.

"Slept?" He asked again.

"Karthik. Trust is really a big word. I believe you," I stated.

"Good night," he said and dozed off. *I know how badly my words had hurt you but you can never imagine what made me say those.*

I wanted to say "My trust has been ditched, played, ruined. Just prove me, that not all the men are same." I wanted to confess everything, every minute thing that happened in my life. But the doubt "will he accept me after knowing the truth?" didn't let me confess. I slept crying.

A silent cry...

47.

"Shit, it's ten," I woke up cursing myself, for not able to wake up even when the alarm tried waking me up thrice. I had set three alarms, one at 9:00, 9:15 and 9:30.

"Hey Karthik, I'm so sorry, just give me ten minutes, just ten minutes." I ran into the drawing room tying my loose hair into a bun.

"Chill, Ashi. Everything is done." I saw him arranging the dining table. "Tada, look here," he said opening the lid of a hot box. He made poha, bread cutlets, cardamom tea and orange juice.

"Wow, Karthik!" I was really surprised. "But, you shouldn't have done this," I said sitting on the chair.

"I woke up early, so I thought I would I prepare breakfast for us," he said and took his seat. "Hey, Ashi. First go and brush, I'm running late," he said looking at his watch.

"Okay," I ran into the washroom. I remember how rudely I had answered him the previous night and now, he wasn't even angry. *How can one person be so cool all the time?* I wondered.

"Fast!" he shouted breaking my thoughts.

"You should have started eating," I advised him wiping my face with a towel when I saw him waiting for me.

"We will eat together," he said serving the poha on my plate. He poured chai into the mug. I ate happily admiring the taste and his hard work. He cooks better than me. "Ashritha, I'm already late, so there is no point in rushing. I will drop you first and then I will leave for work," he said chewing his food.

Aww... how sweet of you!

"Ten minutes," I demanded and ran into the bathroom and returned in a red tee and black denims after twenty minutes. He didn't yell at me though for being late.

"Have a nice day," he waved me when I got down from his car and he drove off.

48.

It was the end of my first year and I topped. My happiness was too extreme. First of all, I wanted to share this good news with Karthik and thank him as he was the one who helped me in teaching accounts and marketing, he helped me in clearing my assignments and presentations as well. He also prepared the best chai for me which helped me in waking up late nights to study. We were more than best friends and definitely less than husband and wife. Still, I started loving the way, he cared for me.

I dialed his number excitedly, but no response. Dejected I walked to the canteen. I couldn't find Vikram and Jyotsna. Being fed up with boredom, I took a bus to home.

"Congratulations!" A mixed sound of multiple voices broke out when I opened the main door. Karthik stood in the front with a bouquet and Vikram was shaking the champagne bottle and Jyotsna was standing beside him. I thought Jyotsna would break my head with the bottle for scoring better percentile than her, but she didn't do those sorts of evil things. Instead, she came to me, congratulated and hugged me. There were few neighbors with whom I barely speak and a couple of Karthik's friends, Vandana and Sandeep.

"Come, cut the cake," Karthik held by my waist, pointing at the cake on the table. It was a Raspberry cake. "For your success and a lot to go" was scribbled on it. Don't you love it when someone recognizes your hard work and appreciates your success? I do. My face was literally beaming even brighter than the syska LED lights.

"Wait, wait, I have another surprise for you." Karthik said when I was about to jab the knife into the cake.

"What?" I asked raising my brows.

"Look, who is here?" he said pointing his index finger into the crowd. As my gaze followed his finger, my mouth fell open.

"Oh my God! I can't believe this." Aditya was standing there with his hands folded smiling at me.

"Adi, is this real? I can't believe my eyes," I ran near him. He extended his arms and I gave him a gentle and affectionate hug. It felt so good. "Meeting my best friend after years," I was least expecting it. "How come you are here? I still can't believe this." I wasn't out of the excitement yet. I forgot that there were people waiting for me or maybe for the cake.

"It's all Karthik's plan. Recently we got connected on messenger and then he saw my FB posts when I visited Canada with my classmates, two days back. He wanted to surprise you and that's why I'm here right in front of you," he narrated the whole story. I looked at Karthik, he stood there with the never fading smile on his face.

"Thank you," I mouthed. He understood that. He smiled.

"Go, cut the cake, people are waiting," Aditya said pushing me forward. I cut the cake and Karthik fed me affectionately and applied cake on my face cruelly. The guests congratulated me, had snacks and dispersed leaving us lot of utensils to be washed.

"So, how is your MS thing going on?" Karthik asked Aditya at the dining table. Karthik, I and Aditya were having dinner. Everyone left. When I asked Vikram and Jyotsna to stay back and have dinner, they declined as they had to travel long.

"I don't know, maybe good," his answer made me laugh.

"And Adi please don't tell me that you are still single?" I asked staring him from the corner of my eyes.

"Unfortunately, yes," he said throwing up his hands.

"What? Seriously? You are not dating anyone?" I asked confused.

"No Ashritha. I would never get into a relationship with a girl just for sex or something, you know, right?" he said looking at me. Adi is a pampered kid in his family yet that never spoiled him. He is such a broad-minded guy with mature thoughts. I noticed Karthik nodded his head approvingly.

"Yeah, I know," I said looking into my plate.

"Ashritha, you are happy, right?" Aditya asked me when we were walking in the lawn post-dinner. Karthik had some office stuff, so he remained inside the room stuck to his laptop.

"Yes, I am," I smiled rubbing my hands for warmth. Fairly strong winds were blowing making us tremble inside the track pants.

"Don't make the poor guy wait for so long, Karthik is a really nice guy," he advised.

"No Adi, everything is alright," I answered without making an eye contact.

"If it is so, I am glad but I think you are still not out of your past," he paused on tracks.

"I'm really out of that Adi. The problem is- I am scared to trust someone again. I really like Karthik but that's not the matter. You can understand, right?" I stammered.

"Remember one thing, Akash is the one who cheated you but instead, you are punishing Karthik," he said patting my shoulder. I looked at him. "Making sense?" he asked staring at me. Yes, he doesn't deserve the punishment. He deserves love, care, respect, and pampering. Aditya left that night though I asked him to stay-back since his friends were waiting for him as they had planned trekking near Great Canyon, the next morning.

When I stood in the kitchen, sweating profusely, biting nails and thinking whether to thank him or not, Karthik came to the kitchen to fetch a water bottle. Suddenly, he hugged me from behind and said, "I'm so happy for you Ashritha." He turned me facing towards him, planted a kiss on my forehead and wiped off the sweat on my forehead. I didn't respond.

I looked into his eyes. I wanted to hug him back, I wanted to experience the love wholeheartedly which he has been trying to shower on me, I wanted to give the same in return but before all those, I wanted to put my past in front of him. But I couldn't dare to trust another person in my life, not because he is not trustworthy, but because I have no trust on myself.

Though, I was aware that we were already married and intend to love each other for the rest of our lives. I just couldn't put my broken pieces of heart on someone again. I couldn't go with the flow. There was something that stopped me from getting closer to him, that's the guilt, guilt of not confessing my past to him. "Thank you," I looked into his eyes.

His eyes seemed so pure and genuine. He smiled and left.

49.

"Karthik, can you pass me the chopped coriander?" I asked Karthik.

"Here," he passed me the bowl and wiped the sweat on my face with a hanky.

"Thanks," I smiled. I had invited Jyotsna and Vikram for lunch one Sunday. Though Karthik said he would order food online. I insisted that I would cook myself. He helped me though. When I was arranging the food on the dining table, the calling bell rang. Karthik unlocked the door and invited them pleasantly.

"Here, we bought these for you," Vikram said sitting on the sofa.

"Wow Bengali sweets, I just love them!" I exclaimed unpacking the sweet box. Jyotsna smiled.

"My mouth already started watering," Jyotsna said inhaling the aroma.

"Come let's eat, food is ready," I invited them pointing to the dining table.

"You cooked all these by yourself?" Vikram asked in shock glaring at the dining table. I had prepared Veg Pulao, Chicken fry, Shrimp masala gravy, Tomato rasam and Kheer for dessert.

"Yeah," I grinned. "Umm, Karthik helped me as well," I said giving him ten percent share of the credit.

"Ah, baby, everything looks so delicious," Vikram said serving pulao in the plate for himself.

"How is it?" I asked enthusiastically.

"Awesome" Vikram said showing a thumbs up.

"It's been ages since I ate Indian home cooked food," Jyotsna said without looking at me. I felt pity for her. She lives in a hostel on a rental basis and I could imagine her situation.

"Keep visiting whenever you want," Karthik invited warmly.

"She will pack her stuff and shift to your house immediately, careful huh!" Vikram said trying to tease her. Everyone laughed excluding Jyotsna. She moped and punched Vikram.

Post lunch, we watched the evergreen 'Dilwale Dulhaniya Le Jayenge' having kheer. "Look at him. He is so handsome," Jyotsna said licking the spoon.

"Either stop licking or stop watching, the timing is too weird," Vikram tried pulling her leg. Vikram would never lose a chance when it comes to teasing Jyotsna. They always remind me of Nisha and Sanjay. I missed her. It was around six when Karthik and I dropped them at the metro station.

"Call me once you reach," I told Jyotsna offering her a box which I had packed with pulao and Chicken Fry. She got highly elated and thanked me.

Spending the entire day on cooking and with friends, I had very less time to finish the presentations which were to be submitted on the next day. I sat on the couch in the drawing room my eyes glued to the laptop.

"Come Ashritha. Let's sleep, it's already late," Karthik said drowsily and turned off the light.

"Can't you see that I'm working?" I shouted at him.

"Sorry," he apologized turning on the light and left to sleep.

"Shit, why did I just do that?" I scolded myself for shouting at Karthik. I felt bad for being rude to such a nice person. I dozed off on the couch itself preparing the slides and scolding myself.

"Good morning," Karthik greeted me pushing the coffee mug towards me.

'I shouted at him last night, right? Was it a dream? Or does he have short time memory loss?' I asked myself when I didn't notice any sort of change in Karthik's behavior. I pinched myself too.

"You should have slept inside," he said breaking my fetch.

"I don't remember when I dozed off," I answered bending forward to reach the coffee. He sighed and stood to leave. "Karthik, I am sorry," I said softly without looking at him.

"For what?" he asked turning back.

"For shouting at you," I stated the reason.

"C'mon., I'm your husband, you have that right," he said simply and walked into the kitchen to dump the mug, leaving me behind surprised. I have seen people who break up just because of some ego problems. But coming to Karthik, I have never seen any sort of attitude or ego in him.

50.

"How can a person be so selfless and caring all the time, Vikram?" I asked him when we were sitting in the canteen.

"You are talking about me? I know I'm born like that," he stated sarcastically.

"Oh please!" I grimaced.

"Haha, jokes apart. Who are you talking about?" he asked taking a large bite from his burger.

"Who else can it be? Obviously Karthik," I said with my hands under my chin and staring my feet.

I should change the nail paint.

"He really loves you, Ashritha," he struggled to speak with food in his mouth. I nodded thoughtfully. Vikram and Jyotsna were aware of my past relationship and present. Vikram asked me the next day after his first visit to our home.

"Things are fine between you and Karthik?" he asked.

"Umm yeah, why?" I questioned back.

"Nothing, I couldn't find the husband-wife atmosphere between you and him, so I just asked. Hope you are not offended," he put his opinion.

"There's nothing like that, I just want to finish my MBA first, later we will think about having kids," I lied looking away. As time passed, I couldn't hide the truth from my friends. At last, your friends are the one who finds the reason for your insecurity before you find it yourself.

"Listening?" Vikram asked breaking my thoughts.

"Yeah," I replied sipping my black coffee.

"You can't judge everyone, Ashi. You can't assume that Akash and Karthik are same. Not every guy is same, but I know it's hard to trust someone again, but it's been more than a year you started living with Karthik. Please don't tell me that you didn't find a single reason to trust him." He stopped to catch a breath and continued. "You said you both never met physically. If there was any other person in Karthik's place he would have left you by now." I looked at him in anguish.

"What? That's the fact," he shrugged.

"The only reason behind his silence is his love towards you. You are really lucky," he said munching.

"I don't want to lose him," my voice trembled. *Yes. I don't want to lose Karthik.* He has always been a best friend to me. Needless to say, I had fallen for his selfless deeds- the way he helped me in completing my assignments, the way he explained me accounts without any hesitation, the way he helped me in the kitchen, the way he hugged and kissed my cheek every morning before leaving to work, the way he treated my friends, the way he celebrates my success, the way he treats me like a child. Everything. Each small deed of his, succored in forging love in my heart, day by day.

"Then what are you waiting for baby? Just confess," Vikram suggested having the last bite of his burger.

Trust! To win me, he has to win my trust first.

'Just one strong reason, Karthik. Prove me that I'm wrong in doubting you,' I spoke to myself.

"Come, it's late. You don't know how much I struggled to get the tickets," he said patting his trousers to remove the breadcrumbs. He had booked two tickets for Pawan Kalyan's movie. He calls himself as a devotee of Pawan Kalyan. I couldn't understand how a Malayali guy could have such fondling on a Telugu star.

"Okay *chalo*," I stood up. We hired a taxi and left. I couldn't concentrate on the movie, I was lost in my thoughts whereas the whole crowd inside the theatre was busy in whistling and clapping. I took out my phone and found that it was dead because of low battery. I looked at my watch; it was nine, still one more hour left.

"You slept?" Vikram woke me up as the movie finished.

"Yeah," I said rubbing my eyes.

"How could you sleep without watching the movie?" he yelled as if I had committed a crime. I thought he would dump the leftover popcorn on my head as a punishment.

"Sorry, Vikram. I was very sleepy," I apologized to him.

"It's okay," we hailed a taxi, he dropped me first and then he left for his place.

***

I noticed Karthik walking to and fro frantically when I opened the door. "Hai Karthik," I greeted him pleasantly.

"Where the hell were you, Ashritha?" Karthik shouted at me. In the entire married phase, it was the first time when I saw Karthik getting angry at me.

"Vikram and I," I spluttered. I was literally shivering on my legs.

"What? Do you know how many times I have called you?" he shouted showing his mobile.

"At least when you know that it's going to be late, you should have at least informed me, right? You don't know how dangerous the burglars are," he raised his concern. I hung my head low.

"I'm sorry Karthik. My phone was dead," I expressed my regret. He didn't speak anything; instead, he walked into the room and slammed the door on my face. Wretched, I tiptoed to the kitchen and drank two glasses of water. I sat on the sofa pondering. I felt bad, the man who used to treat me like his child, now shouted at me.

"It wasn't his mistake; I should have informed him earlier. At least I should have called him from Vikram's mobile. He was tensed.

How bad of myself, I didn't inform my husband." I scolded myself. Scolding myself and defending Karthik, I dozed off in the sofa.

I woke up twisting my body. I couldn't comfortably sleep on the sofa. I found none around me. When I bent down to wear my sandals, I found a folded paper on the table.

"I'm so sorry Ashritha. I shouldn't have shouted at you last night, I was just tensed. I have been hearing a lot about burglary attacks in this area. That is my only concern. I just want you to be safe all the time. Please don't be angry at me. I can't bear that. You can go wherever you want but please do inform me. I'm sorry baby, forgive me." Without my knowledge, my lips turned into a curve. There were times when I shouted at him even for my mistakes and to my surprise, he used to apologize. He doesn't have an ego.

Is it that easy for a man to be so humble with his wife in this male-dominated world?

I never expressed my feelings to Karthik. I never treated him special; I never used terms of endearment like he did. First of all, I never wanted to believe him, but he never stopped building reasons to get my trust. I decided to put my ego and anger aside for a moment and texted him.

"Hey, Karthik. Have a nice day and please bring me *rasmalai* while returning." My phone beeped with his reply in a moment.

"Sure baby, Love you." First I chose to ignore that but couldn't. Though I couldn't send 'Love you too', I sent a smiley. A reply with a smiley is definitely far better than no reply at all. Though that means nothing to me, it means a lot to the person at the other end.

Thus, my day started with smiles.

51.

"Ashi, Can you manage your college schedule and take leave for one month?" Karthik asked me one night ogling his laptop screen.

"One month? It's tough, maybe I can speak to my HOD about this, but why?" I shouted from the kitchen. I was in my regular session of experimenting something in the kitchen. That day, it was banana-cinnamon cake.

"Then I will book tickets for the next month end?" he shouted back.

"Okay, which movie?" I asked him. "But why one month for a movie, Karthik?" I missed the logic. I knew, I sounded so stupid. He would never miss any Indian movie when they release it in Canada. He laughed.

"Not movie baby, we are going India," he shouted.

"Wow, Seriously? I am dying to see mom," I came running from the kitchen and stood in front of him with the egg batter in my hand.

"Yeah, there's a wedding of a close cousin and it's been more than a year, you haven't seen your parents," he said shifting his gaze from laptop to me.

"Thank you so much, Karthik."

"But the thing is, I will return in ten days, you can stay there for a month and once you confirm date I will book your return ticket as well," he said shutting down his laptop.

"Why only ten days? You stay with me, we both will return together," I pouted.

"A month? No way, my manager will kill me," he said shaking his head.

"Please Karthik, for my sake, please," I pleaded and sat next to him.

"Okay, let me check with my manager whether I can work from India," he said looking away thoughtfully.

"Aww thank you," I pinched his cheeks in excitement. I don't know why I did that. I looked down removing my hands. All of a sudden, the air around us turned peaceful. He took my face in his hands. His hands were cold. My heart started pumping fast, he ran his thumb over my lips, and they trembled. He slowly bent down bringing his face closer to mine. I shut my eyes hard and gulped. His nose touched my lips, body started sweating.

"Do you smell something?" he said inhaling the air. I opened my eyes. My face was still in his hands.

"Oh no! My cake," I ran into the kitchen. I forgot to set the time. The cake was burnt like charcoal. I cursed the cake for spoiling the first romantic scene between me and Karthik.

52.

"Hi" I greeted Karthik who returned home from office with a sullen face. It was around nine. I was sitting on the floor working on the laptop. "How was your day?" I asked him to find the reason behind his smile less face. He did not answer. He wiped his face removing his glasses. I walked to the kitchen and came back with a glass of water to offer him. He drank silently.

"Is everything alright?" I asked placing my hand on his shoulder. He didn't respond. He just sat staring the floor. My intuition was right. Something was wrong. I tightened the grip of my hand on his shoulder when I noticed a tear on his cheek. That's it. He broke down. I panicked for his sudden odd behavior. I couldn't see him crying. It killed me.

"What happened, Karthik? Please tell me," I urged. My eyes were wet. He wiped his tears when he noticed mine, because he was aware that the only way to stop my tears was to stop his first. I didn't let go of my hand.

"Tell me what happened?" I asked again. He then opened up.

"You know my friend Sandeep, right?" he said wiping his face with a tissue.

"Umm, yeah, your best friend here?" I replied trying to remember.

"Yeah, even in India we were in same college," he continued.

"So what happened suddenly? You both fought?" I demanded.

"He expired this morning." A tear came out of his eye again.

"Oh no! I'm so sorry for the loss. But how did that happen?" I asked shaking my head.

"Suicide," he blurted out.

"What? How could he do that?" I was appalled. He nodded and continued.

"He is such a strong and cool person. I am not able to believe that he really killed himself." He shed few tears.

"Please cool down Karthik. Do you know the reason?" I bent down to look into his face. He nodded.

"What is it?"

"He was married recently, love marriage, for the first few months everything was fine. His wife had a breakup with another guy before marriage and Sandeep was aware of that too." He paused to breathe. My heart started beating fast for no reason or maybe I was afraid to admit the reason.

"She started seeing her ex again. When Sandeep asked her about that, she said that they cleared their issues and were just friends, he believed her, but one day he came to know that she is cheating on him. He was so deeply in love with her that he couldn't hurt her, instead he killed himself." I removed my trembling hand from Karthik's shoulder. I excused myself and rushed to the washroom. I sat down leaning against the wall.

"What am I doing? Am I cheating on Karthik? I just didn't tell my past to Karthik? Right? It's been 2 years and I am still hiding the biggest truth of my life? What do I do now? I have to tell him right now. What if he gets humiliated and leaves me or else kills himself for ruining his trust and belief?" My head turned numb with these questions. I closed my mouth hard to stop myself from crying, still that didn't help. I wailed. "I really like Karthik, I can't lose him, should I tell him or not" my mind battled with its own thoughts. The melancholy was back into my life.

"Ashritha, you are fine?" Karthik banged the door.

"Yes," I spoke from inside wiping the tears off. I washed my face and came out.

"Are you alright?" Karthik asked me who was waiting outside.

"Yeah," I nodded without making an eye contact.

He embraced me tight. "I'm so sorry Ashritha," he said softly.

"For what?" I asked. I didn't hold him back.

"I drank today, I am sorry. I tried but couldn't resist myself," he confessed not letting me go of his arms. I knew that he boozed the moment he stepped inside but I didn't ask him, I knew he would admit himself. And he did.

"It's okay, Karthik. Come have dinner. It's late," I said trying to release myself.

"Sorry," he apologized again.

"Karthik," I said hesitatingly.

"I don't know if I ever hurt you anytime without my knowledge," he didn't leave.

"You are not the one who hurt me, I hurt you and I'm still hurting you," I mumbled.

"What?" he asked.

"Nothing, go and freshen up, I will serve you dinner," I said trying to release myself from his hug.

"I am not hungry, I will sleep," he said and released me. I walked into the kitchen with frightening thoughts which I had never experienced till the date.

"Why are you punishing him for your mistakes? Why are you keeping him away from his beloved wife? Does he really deserve that? What if he does the same thing like Sandeep did to himself?" My heart questioned me. I couldn't answer even a single question, but one thing I was sure that *I can't let a simple mistake of mine to ruin the most beautiful soul alive.*

53.

Things got worse. I stopped talking to Karthik. Every time, whenever he asked me what's wrong I would either ignore or just lie to him. I literally stopped making eye contact with him. I didn't dare to look into his eyes. The guilt started pushing me away from him. I missed the magical spark in his eyes whenever he smiled looking at me. I missed the mellow tone of his laugh. I missed the dimples of his smile. I missed his caring for me, I missed him pampering me.

"All the best, Ashritha! Do not worry, everything will go fine," Vikram tried lightening up my mood. He wasn't wishing me for my academic exams. He wished for the exam which I had to give in my real life. I decided to tell my past to Karthik and seek his forgiveness. I nodded thoughtfully.

"When is your flight?" Vikram asked me.

"Tomorrow at nine," I said without looking at him. The only two good things that happened were- my Dean accepted for my long leave considering the first year's percentile, asking me to attend classes online and Karthik's manager approved Karthik's request to work from India. "I will miss you guys," I pouted looking at both Vikram and Jyotsna.

"We will miss you too," Jyotsna responded.

"Hello babe, it's only for a month," Vikram scoffed. Vikram is that kind of guy who really cares a lot. But he never expresses in words, his deeds depict. My face sulked (a fake expression, though).

"Jyo, we will just come. You sit here," Vikram said and gestured me to come with him. He put his hand around my shoulder and we started walking on the cricket ground.

"You are going to talk to Karthik about your past, right?" he enquired. I nodded without looking at him.

"Aren't you nervous? Don't lie," he asked me sensing my dull face.

"Very much," I replied making my eyes bigger.

"Hmm, but you have to do this, do not let him go," he warned me. I looked at him and nodded. Vikram is single but he gives the best relationship advice. He is the person whom I would contact when something goes wrong between me and Karthik.

"What if he leaves me after knowing the truth?" I raised my concern.

"A real man will not let go a person like you. Whatever you did, you had reasons, there is no point in blaming you and I know about Karthik, he is super cool, no matter what happens, don't be afraid to face the consequences," he said releasing his hand.

"Everything will go fine, right?" I asked him again. I thought he would bang me on my head for repeating the same question innumerous times.

"Definitely dude," he smiled rubbing my hair. I smiled... nervously.

"Get me lots of sweets while returning," Jyotsna ordered me at the airport.

"Sure" I smiled.

"Why? You want to put some more pounds of weight?" Vikram teased her. Vikram and Jyotsna had come to the airport to give me sendoff. She pouted.

"Why do you always tease her, Vikram?" I asked him.

"C'mon Ashi, a true friend never lets you live in peace." He smirked. Jyotsna nudged him with her elbow.

"You don't worry Jyo. I will definitely get you sweets," I assured, patting her shoulder. She grinned.

"And you Vikram, what do you want from India?" I asked looking at him.

"Nothing babe, just come back with the good news," he said staring at a white girl in a miniskirt who was passing by.

"What good news?" Karthik asked in confusion.

"Umm… nothing. Vikram can you please stop drooling, your collar is wet with your saliva," I tried switching the topic. Well! It worked, Karthik did not ask again.

"She is damn hot!" Vikram muffled pointing to the same girl. I punched him. We ate the dinner in the airport itself, they wished me happy journey and left. We flew together with a lot of excitement and nervousness as well.

54.

"You are not eating? Look how much weight you have lost," mom started wailing when we entered the house after two long years. Actually, I had put on five kilos. But moms are like this, they just need a reason to cry.

"Mumma, I'm not thin, actually I have put on so much weight." I argued.

"Shut up, don't tell me," she defended. Yeah, you should never argue with your mom because you will never win. After all, you are derived from her. She is the root. Bruno came wagging his tail.

"Aww baby, you remember me?" I sat on my knees. I couldn't take him into my hands because he turned into a huge dog. For the next ten minutes, he played hide and seek with me and finally came running to me and gave me a lot of cuddles and kisses.

"How are you, Karthik?" she asked pleasantly.

"I'm fine aunty," he bent down to touch mom's feet. She kissed him on his forehead. Varun has left to college.

"Will you please let us come in?" I asked her.

"Please come in," she held Karthik's hand and we walked in. Dad welcomed us happily.

"Where is granny?" I asked mom.

"She is in her room, she has been waiting since morning, both of you go and greet her," Mom said walking into the kitchen.

"Amma, how are you?" I sat on my knees to reach the bed level. She slowly woke up and leaned against the wall. I put a pillow behind her to make her comfortable.

"Namaste," Karthik touched her feet.

"My son!" She bent forward and took Karthik's hand in hers, kissed it and fondled. She pointed a chair to Karthik and gestured him to sit. Just two years had passed, but granny has turned so senile after grandpa's death. She removed her spectacles to wipe her moist eyes.

"How are you Ashi?" she whispered rubbing my cheek tenderly.

"I'm fine Amma. But why are you so dull, sleeping like this?" I asked her not being able to see her in such a weak state.

"I have no strength Ashi. My days are so close," she said wiping her tears. My eyes were already wet.

"Please do not talk like this," I urged.

"Okay tell me this, when are you giving me a great-grandson to play," she tried cheering up. I looked at Karthik. He was already staring at me. There was a captivating intensity in his eyes. I looked away in embarrassment. I laughed at myself. *I am still a virgin and she is expecting a child.* I bluffed like I was blushing. We spoke about many things skipping the main topic, later we excused ourselves and left her room.

***

"Karthik is such a nice guy, are you taking care of him well?" mom asked me when she was oiling my hair. I missed her badly.

"Yeah mom, but I'm not the one who takes care, he is the one who never made me feel homesick," I replied.

"You are very lucky" she stated.

"Why did you cut your hair? Look how short it looks," she complained.

"Mom, it's not short at all and I am not a kid anymore," I argued. No matter how old you are, you are always a kid to your mother.

“Aah,” I screamed when she pulled few strands of hair tightly.

“Careful Mumma,” I warned. She didn’t bother.

“So, have you planned anything?” she said massaging my head with her fingertips.

“Regarding what?” I asked her without turning back.

“Kids,” she shot back.

“Ma, don’t you think I am too young to have kids?” I asked her changing my tone.

“Oh! You are a grown-up woman to have a haircut as you wish and too young to have kids?” she shot back. I couldn’t understand how she related the two different things that spontaneously. I remained calm. I didn’t want to get into an argument when I clearly knew that I would definitely not win against her.

“Karthik’s mom called me last week, she said that she is desperately waiting to hear good news, what should I answer her?” She cross-questioned me.

Oh no! These people will definitely kill me if I say that nothing has happened between me and Karthik which would in turn produce a good news!

“First I have to find a job, mumma. Later we will think about it,” I stated. “Even Karthik never spoke anything to me regarding kids, I don’t understand why you people are so desperate,” I said shaking my head.

“Don’t move,” she said holding my head.

“Because Karthik doesn’t want to give you stress. Show me a married man who doesn’t like to have kids,” she raised a point releasing her hands. She was right. Being a couple, we never spoke about future planning. Maybe I didn’t give him that zone of comfort to discuss all those things.

“Karthik is a really nice guy, Ashritha,” she reminded me again. I nodded approvingly.

“Okay go and rest for some time. Evening you will have to look good. All of Karthik’s relatives will be attending the wedding,” She said tying my hair into a bun.

"Yeah, I will sleep," I said standing up.

"What will you wear in the evening?" she asked me from behind.

"Uff mumma. There is a lot of time, I will think and decide on my own" I replied without looking at her and walked into my room.

***

"Mumma. What should I wear?" I asked mom standing near the wardrobe.

"You said you will decide yourself, don't you remember?" Mom said making a sarcastic comment. It was 6:30 pm. Karthik was already ready in his black soft suit with black trousers. He was waiting in the living room.

"Please mom, not now. Karthik is already waiting," I said and she seemed convinced.

"Just because Karthik is waiting." She made a note, taking Karthik's side. Indian moms are like this. Once their daughter gets married, son-in-law occupies the daughter's place. I nodded. Just in a moment, she solved my substantial issue by pulling a saree from the rack.

"Wear this, I will get the jewellery from the locker," she said.

"Even I was thinking to wear this," I said trying to push her away from the credit.

"Oh please!" she scoffed and walked into her room to get the jewellery.

***

"Ashritha, she is Karthik's aunt," my mother in law was introducing me to their relatives. I touched everyone's feet in a row.

"So when are you giving a grandson to Padma?" said an aunty from the group.

"This is why I hate coming to marriages." I mumbled to myself.

How can they ask such an embarrassing question in front of everyone?

I smiled nervously. "Look at my daughter in law, it's her third year of marriage, she already has a seven months' son and she is three months pregnant again," she boasted as if her daughter-in-law was nominated for a Noble Prize.

"These people are least concerned about Indian population. Two children in three years?"

Desperate people!

I laughed in my head. "Hello Aunty, that's really great!!" Karthik said touching her feet. I looked at him, baffled.

"But aunty, let me tell you, the minimum gap between two children should be three years. I wonder how you are not aware of this!" Karthik said, his words full of sarcasm. I looked at him thankfully for defending me. The group of aunties looked at us mystifiedly.

"Come Mom, let's have dinner. C'mon Ashritha," he said putting his hand on my shoulder.

"You shouldn't have said that Karthik," his mom said while walking.

"These people always try to point out people, it's definitely fine. At least next time when they meet new people, they will keep this in mind," Karthik winked at me.

55.

I was waiting for Karthik who was busy on a call. "Ashritha," said a familiar voice from behind. My heart started beating fast. *Easy... It can't be him.* I turned back to see the person praying it shouldn't be him. But, it was him, yes, it was Akash. It didn't take even few seconds for me to recognize his voice, though we stopped talking years back. And then I wondered *how can someone really forget their first love?*

I never forgot him; after all, he is the person to whom I can relate my complete life. But I never wanted to see him again in my life. *Never.* However, it's not called Life if everything happens according to your wish. That moment, he stood in front of me. I just stood staring into his eyes. The eyes which showed me what is it to love and to be loved. The irony is, those were the eyes which made me experience the misery which I never thought exists. My heart started pounding wildly. I found my fingers trembling when I was adjusting my hair.

"Chill Ashritha," I told myself.

"How are you?" he asked looking into my eyes. The spark which I used to find previously in his eyes was nowhere. His dark lips indicated that he hadn't give up smoking yet. His thick beard and moustache seemed like he hadn't shaved in weeks. He had lost weight considerably but he wasn't fit. His muscles loosened. He was smiling but that smile seemed lifeless.

I gathered all the strength and answered. "I'm good." I did not care to ask him back.

"If you don't mind, let's sit and talk," he said pointing to the chairs. I agreed and we sat.

"It's been so long, so how's life?" he asked raising his brows.

"Yeah good," I replied confidently.

"You did not change even a little, you look the same but even more beautiful," he complimented staring at me. I wore a peacock blue saree with a plain gold necklace. I smiled.

"But you have changed a lot," I said, in turn, wishing that he could understand the real context.

"Haha… yeah," he said running his hand through his beard assuming that I meant physical appearance.

"I heard that you got married," he raised the question without looking at me.

"Yeah, he is somewhere around here," I said and looked around to spot Karthik, but couldn't.

"Okay, what does he do?"

"He is a Software Engineer in Canada," I tried bragging. He just nodded.

"And what about you?" I asked in a casual tone.

"Yes, I'm married," he answered staring the grass under his legs. There was a pang in my heart.

"Oh okay. She is here?" I responded trying not to show the eagerness.

"No," he sounded low.

"She did not come?"

"Actually, we got divorced," he said looking away.

I was like- "What!" *Maybe this is called Karma.*

"Maybe this is called karma," he said looking at me. I was surprised for a jiffy; the words running in my mind came from his mouth.

"Ashritha, I know my sorry means nothing for what I have done to you. When I came to know that you were getting married that moment I understood what it is like getting heartbroken. I tried contacting you many times but couldn't." He said looking into my eyes.

"Oh! You are finally sorry," I thought. I looked away breaking the eye contact.

"Akash, I always wanted to ask you one thing, may I?" I asked him.

"Yeah, sure," he nodded.

"Do you remember that you said you need a month's time and then again you came back saying that you love me? Why did you do that?" I mocked. He sighed.

"Ashritha, whatever has happened between me and Arpita was never intentional. One night after boozing, we were so high and then she told me about her breakup and wailed. In the process of making her calm down, we kissed and one thing led to another. But I swear that was not intentional. The morning I realized what really happened the previous night and I was embarrassed with guilt. I couldn't talk to you, I know I did a mistake, I couldn't admit that in front you and at the same time I couldn't break up with you so I asked for time but I couldn't stay away from you because I really loved you. When I admitted my guilt in front of her she said she wasn't feeling guilty about that. She said she was even ready to move with me. I don't know why that evil thought came into my mind. I thought I would continue to stay in physical relationship with her. I swear I never loved her; it was just a physical relationship. I really loved you but I don't know..." he paused. I looked at him when he spoke again, "I know that is the worst thing I had ever did in my life. That moment when you walked out of my life, I realized how much I have changed in life as a person which made me lose you forever. But I didn't want to disturb you. I had hurt you so badly and maybe God has given me the life which I deserve." He had tears in his eyes.

"When people hurt you, do not blame them. Just smile and walk away. There comes a time in life when they actually repent for their deeds. Then your face flashes in front of their eyes. Your name echoes in their ears. No matter how much they try, the guilt can never let them escape." I remembered my grandpa's words.

"Do you still hate me?" he asked giving a halt to my thoughts. I chose not to answer. My answer was neither yes nor no. "I think you do and I deserve all of it," he said without looking at me. I couldn't understand whether to believe his regret or not. I remained silent. I wanted to know the reason behind his divorce.

"Hello, Ashritha. My manager is a heck," Karthik came there cursing his manager.

"Karthik, this is Akash, my friend" I introduced referring Akash to a friend.

"Akash, my husband," I introduced.

"Hello, it's a pleasure meeting you," Karthik shook his hand pleasantly.

"Uff see, he's calling again," Karthik said showing his mobile that displayed his manager's name. "You guys, please carry on, I have to take this call," Karthik said and walked away.

"He is really cool!" Akash exclaimed.

"Yep, he is," I nodded.

"But Akash, if you don't mind can I know the reason behind your divorce?" I raised my doubt. He laughed.

"It's nothing, Ashritha. Minor misunderstandings led to divorce," he said looking away. Though I could sense there was some other reason beyond that, I didn't dare to ask him.

What if he says that is none of your business?

I remained silent looking here and there. "I'm really happy to meet you after a long time," he said breaking the silence. I smiled.

"So, kids?" he enquired.

"Nope, Karthik wants me to finish my studies first; I am into the second year of my MBA now, the University of Alberta," I bragged again.

"Oh wow, sounds really great!" he exclaimed.

"Yeah, Karthik helped me a lot," I said looking at Karthik who was busy on a call.

"Umm," that was his response. Karthik came there ending his call.

"Okay Ashritha, shall we leave, I think it's already late," Karthik said checking his watch. I stood up and Akash as well.

"It was really nice meeting you," Akash said shaking his hand with Karthik.

"My pleasure too," Karthik smiled.

"Bye Akash," I bid bye to Akash. When I turned back to look at him, he stood there already glancing at me, the look in his eyes was exactly the same which I saw when we returned from Araku, the needy eyes. But that time the need wasn't me.

***

That night, I found myself lying next to my husband Karthik and thinking about my ex-lover Akash. I couldn't sleep. I was just relentlessly tossing on the bed in my room. I looked at Karthik who was sleeping beside me. The innocence on his face with hands in between his thighs made him look like a child.

"What is the reason behind his divorce?"- that was the only thing running in my head. I felt there was definitely some other reason for his divorce which he has been trying to hide from me. "How do I find that?" I started biting my nails.

When I started my journey from Canada, the only thought in my mind was to confess everything to Karthik. Confess my feelings for him. But back in India, everything has changed, nothing made sense. "What should I do?" I started thinking.

By the break of dawn, I made a clear decision. That was to find out the reason behind his divorce and make them together if possible. Yes, I loved Akash. Once he meant everything to me. Seeing him with another girl would burn me from inside. But now, I realized true love is just giving and not to expect anything in return.

For a few minutes, my brain displayed all the happy moments I spent with Akash. Not the worst ones, only the best ones. I still remember the times, when I cursed Akash for making me go through all the pain. But I never wanted to see him in such a worst situation. I could sense the pain behind his smile, his fake smile. "Should I tell Karthik about this?"

I didn't. I couldn't.

56.

"Hey Sanjay, how are you?" I called up Sanjay.

"Hello, Ashritha. I'm good; finally, you found time to call me, uh?" He teased me. After my breakup, I had stopped talking to all of his friends.

"Haha, yeah," I laughed.

"Okay tell me, how are you? How's Karthik?" he inquired.

"Yeah, he is good and first of all, Congratulations!" I wished him. Nisha and Sanjay were engaged officially just a couple of weeks ago, after lots of disputes between both their families. They both were strongly determined about their decision and finally their parents agreed. After all, Love wins it all.

"Thank you, tell me how's life?"

"Hey Sanjay, listen, I heard that Akash was recently divorced, is that true?" I questioned him.

"Yeah, it is," he concluded.

"Do you know who she is?" I questioned.

"No, but I heard that she lives in Vizag," he narrated.

"Okay, do you know the reason behind his divorce?" I asked him

"No Ashritha. We weren't in contact from so long, but why do need all the information? Is everything fine?" he asked me.

"Nothing, just casually," I lied. "Can you please ask your friends and find out the reason?" I pleaded to him.

"Yeah, I can try," he said.

"Please, let me know whenever you find something," I stated.

"Sure," he smiled and we disconnected the call.

***

"Whoa! What a pleasant surprise," I welcomed Vineet who came to my home to see me.

"Yeah, I heard that you are in India so I thought I would come and meet you," he said sitting on the sofa.

"Wow. That's really sweet of you," I was elated and occupied the seat opposite to him.

"Look mom, who has come!" I called out for mom.

"Hello Vineet, how are you? You haven't visited our home after Ashritha left. How is your job?" mom asked him in one go without waiting for his answer.

"Everything is fine aunty; I came home two days back," he answered softly.

"You both carry on; I will prepare something for you. Don't leave without having dinner," mom warned him and walked to the kitchen.

"How is life, how is your cutie pie?" I teased him. He laughed.

"Yeah she is good; she is working in Accenture, Bangalore". I nodded smilingly.

"Hey, Karthik. He is Vineet, my B.tech friend," I introduced Vineet to Karthik.

"Yeah bro, Ashritha mentioned you many times," Karthik said shaking his hand with Vineet. One of the best things I like about Karthik is, he always treated my friends as his. When I talk about my friends, he pays attention; he doesn't pretend, he really listens to me.

"Ashritha, Rajesh is waiting, I will leave," Karthik said looking at his watch.

"It was really nice meeting you," Vineet hugged Karthik and Karthik left.

"Ashritha. We will go out, it's been many days, after college, we never met," he said. I liked his idea too.

"Okay, I will change and come," I said and walked to my room. I was in my pyjamas and kurta. In ten minutes, I came back in a cotton chudidhar.

"Mumma. We are going out, we will have dinner outside," I called out for mom.

"Why outside? I will start cooking." She retorted.

"No Aunty, next time please" Vineet appealed.

"Okay, next time I will not let you go unless you have dinner." She demanded. He smiled.

"Keep visiting whenever you come to Vizag," she said rubbing his shoulder. He nodded smilingly and we left.

57.

"So what are you planning to do about this now?" he asked me as we walked into the CCD. I narrated him about Akash's matter on our way.

"I don't know, my mind stopped functioning from then," I said holding my forehead. He sighed.

"I want to meet his wife, there is definitely something that he is trying to hide," I made a point.

"Do you know his wife?" Vineet asked raising his brows.

"No Vineet, I need to find out, I called Sanjay yesterday," I answered sipping my coffee.

"What did he say?"

"He said he will call me if he comes to know anything about this," I said looking away.

"Karthik," he muttered.

"What Karthik? He doesn't know anything," I said without looking at him.

"Isn't he Karthik?" he murmured staring at a person whose back was facing us.

"Where?" I asked following his gaze.

"Yeah, he is Karthik," I was sort of excited and stood up. I stopped myself from going near him when I saw a woman sitting opposite to him.

"But he said he was going to meet Rajesh," I murmured. "Is Karthik cheating on me?" my heart started pumping fast, very fast. "Karthik is cheating on me," I whispered.

"How do you decide that without knowing what is going on there?" Vineet questioned me.

"He said he was going to meet Rajesh. He is in a coffee shop with a girl, what else reason do you need?" my voice trembled. I stood up to leave.

"Ashritha, do not assume things, come with me," he said and caught my hand. By then, I was on the verge of my tears. He took me to a table behind him and we sat there.

58.

"Why don't you just break up with her and apply for a divorce?" the girl with Karthik said sipping her coffee. My heart sank.

"Please, no Karthik. Not again," I pleaded

"Breaking up with Ashritha? I can't stay away from her.The thought itself frightens me. I can't imagine my life without her." he shot back.

"She introduced her ex to you as a friend and you still believe her," she demanded. I lifted my head up in shock at Vineet who was already staring at me with the same expression as mine.

"What else can she do?" he questioned back. He continued.

"She doesn't know that I know her past. Maybe she tried telling me, maybe she hasn't found an appropriate time to tell me." His voice was low.

"You mean, in the two years of your married life, she didn't find a perfect time to confess her past?" she demanded.

"She might be afraid, Keerthi," he said looking away.

"You always keep on defending her," she argued.

"How could he know? Vikram? No, he won't." My hands trembled on the coffee mug's handle.

"I am sure she must be cheating on you," she said looking him.

"Enough Keerthi. She will never do such a thing. I trust her. I just came to meet you so that you can help me in getting Akash wife's address. I heard that you both were schoolmates," Karthik shrieked.

"She is upset from the moment when she got to know that Akash has been divorced. She couldn't bear if she gets to know that he has very few days left. She just can't take that," he stammered.

"What?" she asked. He nodded and continued.

"Yes, Akash is diagnosed with COPD, 4th stage. His lungs are damaged to the worst. His survival is impossible. I got to know about this a few days back. My cousin whose marriage we attended, is a close friend of Akash, he told me everything. The drugs and smoking screwed him. He intentionally broke up with his wife so that she couldn't bear the truth. But at least his last days should be peaceful. I'm planning to meet her. This is the reason why I wanted to visit India. I am glad that Ashritha met Akash."

My whole body stuttered. Blood surged through my body relentlessly. A sweat bead formed on my forehead and fell on my hand. "He has just a few days left" that was the thing that kept bouncing in my mind.

"I know how much she loved him. I still remember the look in her eyes at the moment when she came to know that Akash was cheating on her." My whole body went numb.

"How does he know?" Vineet whispered. I shook my head.

"I don't know." It became difficult to frame words.

"The pain which I had seen on her face, trust me! I just wish it to be the worst nightmare." He said looking away.

"Which incident you are talking about?" she asked. Though I was pretty angry at her, I thanked her for asking that question.

"Do you know when I saw her for the first time?" he asked her. I craned my ear near to listen carefully. She shook her head.

"Pune," he blurted out. "We went to Pune to visit my cousin who gave birth to a baby boy. My mom forced me so I had no other option but to go. Who would have thought that I would find my love there!

It was around two o'clock when I decided to buy a gold chain for the baby and I went to the cellar where our car was parked. I found a group of people arguing there, I decided to ignore and turned on the ignition, that moment in the brightness of my car lights, I found two pure and innocent eyes crying in pain. I couldn't move. I sat still just staring at them.

People say that you get attracted to someone when you see them smiling, but in my case, it was totally different, I fell in love with her when she was in pain, I fell in love with those teary eyes, with that broken heart. The love, trust behind the tears. That moved me. I opened the car door to hear the conversation. She caved on the floor. The words, which she spoke that day, still echo in my ears. There was no hatred on her face except pain. She wanted Akash to realize the love but he wasn't in a position to realize. Instead, I did there. I saw many of my friends getting into love so easily and breaking up even more easily. But it wasn't easy for her. That moment, I realized how deep a girl can love someone. I fell for her purity. She was beautiful not physically. The purity behind the tears that have been streaming down, the loyalty behind her words that she uttered, that's where I noticed her beauty.

I felt bad for her, though my heart said go and talk to her, console her, hold her tight. I didn't deem that as a right situation. I just sat staring at her and then followed her till the Airport. I thought I missed her. The second time, when I saw her in my cousin's marriage, my cells danced. I couldn't believe my eyes and my luck. I thought there was really some connectivity between us. I sat behind her in the marriage observing her, but she didn't notice me.

Honestly, I never had any wife-to-be-list but when I saw her, I wished my wife to be her. I spoke to my mom, who was fed up looking for matches for me. I told that I want to marry her. She was too impressed by her to deny. Not only she, everyone would definitely like her. She gave up her MBA, to prove her love to Akash. I wanted to give her the best education not to prove anything to anyone, just to see her pursuing her dream. When she topped in the first year, I came to know such an ambitious woman she is. I decided I would not bother her with my feelings until she completes her education.

With each passing day, I discovered a new thing about her, about the beauty of her soul. I am not boasting or flaunting just because she is my wife, anyone who spend time with her has to accept it. The way she talks to plants and animals, the way she treats people around her, the way she does things with a zest, she cries when she watches an emotional movie, she shrieks when she sees a cockroach but wouldn't let me kill, she still plays rock paper scissors with the children. Every petty thing about her is adorable.

As time passed, I thought she would confess her past but she didn't or maybe she couldn't. But she always carried that guilt and you say she is going to cheat on me? I thought time would heal her pain and realize my love towards her and I'm still waiting. I know she loves hard, to experience that I wouldn't mind waiting for a lifetime. Her heart is deep as an ocean and I want to be that one person who would dive the depth." He said looking away.

I couldn't believe my ears. *He knew everything?*

"Why do you like her so much?" she asked, impressed. He laughed.

"Reason for liking? Okay I will put it this way, there isn't a single reason not to like her, she is just perfect," he answered softly.

"Ashritha is lucky to have you," Keerthi said softly. He smiled looking away. A tear fell on my hand. Vineet placed his hand on my hand, I looked at him.

"You are really lucky," he didn't just say that. He meant that. As I fumbled with the coffee mug, it slipped from my hand, touched the ground and broke into pieces creating the havoc in the customers that eventually made their necks crane towards me. I stood up. I looked at him.

"Ashi Ashi," Karthik stammered. I moved out, actually, I ran out.

"Akash is dying? And Karthik knew my past!" I couldn't hold my tears. I took an auto and reached home. I bolted myself in the room. A combined feeling of guilt and pain threw me into dismal.

"He knew everything but never asked me. And Akash, he is dying, what should I do now?" I collapsed on the floor. I could not imagine Akash leaving his last breath nor could I imagine facing Karthik. I might be angry with Akash but once my love was genuine forhim. I was afraid to confess my past to Karthik because now my love is true.

***

"Why didn't you tell me, Karthik?" I asked wailing. It was one. We just lay next to each other facing each other's back and faking sleep but both of us knew that we were not sleeping. No response. "Please tell me," I wept. He did not answer.

After a little while, he turned facing me. "Ashritha, please listen to me, please don't cry and there is nothing for you to feel guilty," he said rubbing my hair.

I cried some more and dozed off.

59.

"Ashritha, can you get ready in fifteen minutes, we are going out," Karthik asked me at the dining table the next morning.

"Where?" I asked looking at him.

"Do you need all the details? Just go," mom taunted me. I nodded my head.

"Where are we going, Karthik?" I asked him in the car.

"I will tell you," he said nodding his head.

In the next fifteen minutes, we reached the Ahuja apartments in Gajuwaka.

"Your relatives?" I asked him in the lift. He smiled.

"Hello. You are Mrs Sruthi, Right?!" Karthik asked a lady of around my age when she opened the door.

"Yeah, who are you?" she gave a perplexed look.

"I'm Akash's friend," Karthik answered and I looked at him in shock.

"Please come in," she welcomed us in. Till then I paid zero attention to her. But when Karthik said that she was Akash's wife, I didn't take my eyes off her. She was shorter to me by two inch and little fair in complexion. We were asked to sit on the sofa and she offered us water.

“I think you are not aware of the truth that I and Akash were divorced a few months back,” she stammered without looking at us.

“We know,” Karthik answered looking at me. She lifted her head in shock and asked.

“You know? Then what made you meet me?” she asked with little hesitation.

“Do you know the reason why Akash wanted a divorce from you?” Karthik asked softly.

“I don’t know,” she mocked looking away.

“I know, I know how much he loves you and I know the reason why he has put you away.” She looked at Karthik in surprise. Her eyes were already filled with tears.

“Why?” she wailed.

“He is diagnosed with COPD, doctors concluded that they can’t help him. His situation is critical. He has very few days left. He doesn’t want you to get hurt because of him,” Karthik confessed. She wailed holding her head.

“No, this can’t be true,” she stood up and shouted.

“Please console yourself. I know that it’s hard to accept but this is the truth,” Karthik stood up trying to console her.

“No, this can’t be true,” she recited and ran into kitchen wailing. I hurried behind her.

“Please Sruthi, be strong, console yourself,” I said rubbing her shoulder sitting beside her on the kitchen floor. By then, tears invaded me as well. “There is nothing which we can do, just be strong,” I just said that to console.

I know that it isn’t easy at all.

She wept. “Please stay strong and make him confident that you are not going to leave him until the end,” I was crying too.

She finally spoke, “Ours is an arranged marriage but I fell in love with him instantly after marriage, we were really happy but then he started hurting me badly in many ways, I thought he didn’t love me like I did. I misunderstood him. I never knew that he has been facing all these things. If I had known all these things, I wouldn’t have divorced with him," she wailed again.

"Just go to him and tell him that you are not going to leave him whatever happens," I said caressing her hair. She wailed but nodded. My hands trembled on her shoulder when I got to remember my dad's words, God removes people from your life for a reason, never chase them.

If everything had gone right between me and Akash, I would be at Sruthi's position, helpless.

I learnt everything happens for a reason.

***

That night I received a message from Akash.

"Ashritha, letting you go is the stupidest thing, I've ever done. If I am answerable to anyone in this world, that is you. I betrayed your trust. I heart fully repent for my deeds but I know that is not going to get our days back, nor can we change our fate. I never thought that I would see you again in my life. But I am really glad that I met you. When you asked the reason behind my divorce, I wanted to tell you everything, I wanted to hold your hand and cry but something stopped me, maybe the fact that you are not mine anymore. You really have no idea what kind of pain I was enduring. I am scared Ashritha. Yes, I am scared, but not about the nights which tried signaling me that 'It is the last day on your earth' but about the mornings when I would wake up in the bed with traces of my own blood which told me that 'you have got to survive another painful day'. I am scared to live and I am scared to die. I really wanted someone who can stay with me in my worst last days, who can embrace me and pat my back and tell me "Everything is fine". Now, Sruthi is with me, and I am ready to leave my last breath in her lap. Ashritha, till now I was searching for words to apologize to you but now, I am falling short of words to thank you. You gave me everything, Ashritha. You gave me a chance to cherish your love, you took care of me like no one ever did, you switched your MBA plan for me and now you gave me my wife. In the world of selfish people, you chose to help someone who cheated on you. I realize how stupid I was for giving up on a girl who gave me everything. Karthik is the coolest person I have ever met. I was totally taken aback when I got to know that he is the person behind all the happiness in my life right now. One thing that I can assure is if I were in Karthik's place, I might not be as good as him. To be honest, I would never consider helping my wife's ex-boyfriend on her wish. Today, I am really glad that you are in the hands of the best person. Love each other. Sorry for everything I did to you and Thanks for everything you did for me."

I was walking hesitantly in the drawing room thinking how to start a conversation with Karthik. It was the third time Karthik noticed me peeking through the slightly open door of my room where he was working on his laptop. The whole house was deserted. Mom, dad and Varun went to some function. Granny was sleeping in her room. "Yes, I will write him an email," I told myself as I jumped on the couch and started typing.

"The man who once pushed me away now wrote a text that I am the reason for the happiness in his life. Isn't it because of you?

Karthik, I am writing this because you deserve to know how much my life has changed because of you. You said my eyes were searching for something. You were right. I was searching for myself. The old me, who would always wear a smile no matter how bad my days are, who would always find the good in people no matter how cunning they are, but now the fear of getting cheated or feeling unwanted has changed me into a completely different person. Actually, I didn't lose Akash. I lost myself holding him.

I stood strong when there was no strength left in me; I smiled when there were reasons for me to break down. I believed in miracles when there was no hope left. I remained quiet when I felt like shouting. I chose to live when life offered me death. But now, whenever you hold my hand. I want to reinvent my life. I want you to prove that not all the people are same. You didn't love me when I was happy; you loved me when I was in pain. You were with me not only in the times of joy; you stood with me in my misery. You loved me when I was lost, when I was broken, and when I was weak. You stood with me in the most challenging situations of my life. Now I have everything in my life, most importantly I have you in my life.

People say true love is when the person who saw you at your worst but still wants to talk only the best about you. You accepted my flaws, you corrected my mistakes. I know, I am never perfect but every time when you stand by my side, it makes me feel so.

I am who I am, because of you. The people who, once looked at me in misery are now surprised to see my courage. You gave me everything-love, care, support, strength. You taught that love isn't taking, but giving, you were tolerant to my reasonless stupid behavior.

Karthik, you are the perfect person I've ever met.

You are handsome, smart, caring, and lovable. It was I, who couldn't realize that you are the best husband any girl would ever wish for. I couldn't realize that you are the best because you are the one who brought the best out of me. I am now a woman, which I always aspired to be. This moment, I feel I don't have to explain anything to anyone and nobody's opinion matters except yours and I also know, that I never wanted anything so much in life as much as I want you right now. Don't promise me that you will never leave me just remain with me forever and make me realize such a fool I was to ignore you all these days.

I love you Karthik. I really do, not because you helped Akash for helping me but for making me understand what it is like really loving someone unconditionally and for giving the true definition of love. Can you become the man in my heart? Can you become my soul mate? Can you be that one person who could dive into my deepest heart?"

A tear escaped from my eye and fell on my hand as I finished typing. I prayed before clicking on the send button. In the next few minutes, I found Karthik standing in front of me. I stood up. He did not speak anything. Not even a word. There was a deep silence around us but not a dumb one, it held an intense meaning. I wailed "Why did you do this?"

He just looked at me. After a long silence, he said, "Because I love you".

With teary eyes, I looked at him. And then, I found everything in his eyes that I ever been looking for my whole life. He held my hand and pulled me closer. Our eyes met and then our lips, our eyes locked so as were our lips. The next moment, I felt like I was fluttering in the air.

I opened my eyes. Yes, I was in Karthik's arms. He carried me all the way from drawing room to my room. "Don't you want to know why I gifted you a cactus plant?" he asked me lying next to me on the bed. I nodded with a smile.

"Well, that is the one thing which I can relate to both of us. Thorns are symbol of strength and independence. They don't need anyone to protect them. They are self-protective. You are the strongest woman I have met till now, strong enough to let go a person whom you never wanted to lose in your life. And your self-esteem is till one such level that you didn't mind to work in the cafeteria to earn your expenses." He locked the eye contact. "I could have given you flowers which shrivel with days, but my love for you is like cactus, it just grows with each passing day." He added.

He grabbed me closer when he noticed my eyes streaming. That night, we had sex, not the one with lust but the one with love. Indeed. We made love. That was divine.

I wasn't virgin anymore; I lost my virginity to the man who gained my trust.

60.

"Invite Mrs Ashritha Karthik to come up onto the dias and receive her medal." It was the most important day of my career. The Convocation day.

With nervousness and happiness, I walked towards the dais, thanking the audience for their applause.

"Congratulations," the senior most Professor said giving me a handshake. I shook my trembling hand pleasantly.

"Would you like to address the crowd?" The host asked me who was expecting a no.

"Yes," I answered firmly as I walked near her. Making a place for me at the podium, she moved aside. I began trembling when I saw the crowd. I scolded myself for saying yes. I closed my eyes and inhaled deeply. "Easy, chill," I told myself.

I opened my eyes, I saw Karthik sitting in his chair and looking at me eagerly. He gestured me to speak. I smiled with confidence. "Honorable chief guest Mr. François Desjardins, respected Professors and everyone who has assembled here on this day, I wish a very good morning to every one of you"

"She is the topper," I heard our Professor whispering in the chief guest's ear.

"Well! It is not surprising that I have gone speechless on this day, for which I have waited the most. But more than me, there is another person who has been waiting for this day. Before I speak about anything, I would like to talk about that person, who is the reason behind my success. I am right here in front of you, because of the one special person in my life." I smiled looking at Karthik. He smiled back.

"Yes! He is my husband but I have never behaved like his wife all these days. Yes, he loves me but I never valued his feelings. Yes, he always treated me special with his little gestures but I never at least used terms of endearment to address him. I didn't respect his feelings. I hurt him in each and every way but he never stopped loving me. He loved me unconditionally. It took many days for me to realize what it is like to respect other's feelings, appreciate people's hard work and encourage people. He is the one who has seen my true potential and has always been treasuring my soul. He discovered my hidden passion and talent. He is the one who believed in my hard work and guided me in each step. He is the person who supported me, who helped me, who defended me, who cared for me. He is the one who always wanted to see me independent and successful. Amidst the insecurities and the chaos in my life, he is the one who made my life smoother.

When people believed the fake smile on my face, he is the one who noticed the scars on my heart. When people judged me pointing their fingers at me, he is the one who accepted my flaws and treated me like a perfect person. When a person made excuses to leave my life, he is the one who made efforts to enter and stay in my life.

Usually, people say, to gain something, we have to lose many things. But to gain this, I didn't lose anything; in fact, I gained a trustworthy person in my life. I am incomplete without him. He made a big difference in my life by making me his life. Whatever I am now, it's because of him. Before I wind up, I just want to confess one thing to him.

Karthik, I don't say 'Sorry, for being so annoying' because I am like this and you accepted me the way I am, instead I would say 'Thanks, for bearing me.' I would like Karthik to come and collect the medal on my behalf." I said wiping the tears off. I eyed Karthik to come and then he stood. A huge applause broke in the crowd. I noticed Vikram whistling. “Sir, if you don’t mind, I want my husband to receive the medal.” The guest approved.

“Congratulations!” the chief guest shook hand with him and put the medal in Karthik’s neck. I caught a glimpse of tears in Karthik’s eyes. He held my hand tightly and I held his hand in turn, very tight.

EPILOGUE

"Karthik is such a nice person," Kate said pleasingly. I found tears in her eyes.

"These white people cry too?" I wondered. I smiled with a proud feeling.

"But Akash?" she asked. Tears started flooding without my knowledge.

"He is no more. He expired last year." Kate shook her head in grief.

"The best thing is that Sruthi is pregnant. Maybe she can see Akash in their child," I said wiping my tears. She nodded thoughtfully. I looked at Karthik, the man behind all my happiness. People say you are lucky when you get a good life partner. But I can bet that even the word good wouldn't suffice to explain how selfless Karthik is. Every minute, he craved for my happiness.

I looked at the sky; the Sun rays came out piercing the clouds, fading out the dullness and filling energy in everyone. "Wow, it's sunny now, I can tan my body. I will change and come," Kate said running towards the cottage to change. I turned my head to see Karthik who was playing on the shore. His face was glowing in the shimmering rays of the sunset with *undefined* happiness.

They say after every devastating storm, there comes the cheerful sunshine. Well! I can't say no. Days wouldn't have been the same if you hadn't seen me on that day when I was crying like a child. Though you could have gotten any girl of your choice, you still chose me and have given me the best version of love. What can I give you Karthik? To you, to the man who defined love, how would I repay you?

"Ashi, look at him," Karthik was jumping in happiness. My thirteen-month old son Akira has started toddling. It was the *fatherhood* happiness. Yeah, I already repaid him. I can't give anything other than this and I also know that nothing can match with the happiness which I have seen on his face, a few minutes ago...

Root of my blood, fruit of his love.

I walked near Karthik. I held his hand and looked into his eyes.

"You are my sunshine after all the storms," I whispered in his ear. He looked into my eyes back.

"You are the reason why I shine," he said rubbing his nose with mine. There came Akira toddling near us and pulled my hand. I took him in my hands, Karthik hugged me. Three of us united.

Oops! Sorry, it's four.

Jimmy, Bruno's son (We had to get him from India on special permission!). Four of us united.

My world.

***

"Aww, my Shona woke up," I said tweaking Akira's nose, lying next to me. Karthik had already left to work by then. He smiled looking at me. His smile resembled Karthik's. I loved his dimples, whereas his eyes resembled mine.

After my Post Graduation, I started working as Associate Manager in Walmart. But after Akira's birth I quit my job. Though Karthik said we would arrange a baby sitter for him, I didn't want to.

"How can I miss his childhood? I can't get it back." This is what I said and Karthik kissed me affectionately.

"What is this?" I murmured when I saw a paper in Akira's hand. I sat on the bed opening the folded paper.

"The first time when I saw you,
The world said I can do anything for you,
The time decides to stop for a while,
When your lips turn into a smile,
No matter, how much my day might be hazy,
Just the spark of your eyes can drive me crazy,
You are beside me as my wife,
Nothing more I want in this life,
Forever you will remain mine,
Just like the sun never forgets to shine..."

After reading that, I couldn't stop myself from smiling. He wrote something by himself, which made me feel special. Five years down and still a lot to go. Karthik neither stopped amazing me with his love nor did he stop surprising me with his rhyming poetry. We are deeply in love with each other. In the entire journey, he taught me many things.

The first thing- how to love ourselves, that's all that really matters. How to reciprocate love but not the anger or the things which others did to hurt you. I also learnt, no matter what happens never have regrets in life for the things which you did in past. If you hold the regrets, you cannot move on and whatever has happened is destined to happen. If you have the guilt of your mistakes, confess, apologize that moment itself.

Karthik would always say, "Life is too short. Never let the shadow of yesterday spoil the sunshine of tomorrow." He came into my life as a blessing, helped me in searching myself and shaped me into a wonderful and strong woman which I am proud to admit right now.

Our story may end here but our love won't.